She had made her promise to Matthew. They had planned a good and happy life. And yet . . .

Her eyes closed as Aaron's mouth, warm, moist, urgent, and alive, came softly down on hers, holding her in an embrace that encompassed all she had ever imagined such a kiss of love might be, free of all restraint, released from all confines of convention, given up to the joy of conquest and surrender.

Neither heard the clop of hooves on the drive. It was the sharp tap of a servant's heels going past the drawing room down the hall to open the front door that brought her back to reality and she thrust herself from him. She stood breathing deeply and he half-lifted his arms to her in a gesture of appeal, knowing that momentarily he had lost her.

"No!" she said, agitatedly, making a little movement of her hands as if to keep him from her. "It can't be!"

ঙ্গ

"A GIFTED WRITER WITH A SPECIAL TALENT."

—*Library Journal*

Devil's Fire, Love's Revenge

*Also by Barbara Paul
now available from Ballantine Books:*

THE SEVENTEENTH STAIR

Devil's Fire, Love's Revenge

Barbara Paul

BALLANTINE BOOKS · NEW YORK

Library of Congress Catalog Card Number: 76-13048

ISBN 0-345-25950-5

This edition published by arrangement with St. Martin's Press, Inc.

Manufactured in the United States of America

First Ballantine Books Edition: November 1977

1

ALONG the narrow country lane fringed by acid-pink willowherb and bordered by low dry-stone walls went the horse and wagonette driven by a girl with whip and reins in her slim, capable hands, her velvet bonnet ribbons dancing madly over one shoulder, her full, striped skirt a flurry of wind-ruffled frills. It was a blustery morning after the previous night's rain, but shining, bright, and clear, the sky full of swallows and martins, a few sea gulls careening on lazy wings. Racing clouds, riding high and billowy, dappled with a moving pattern of sunlight and shade the broad flanks of Howling Hill, which dominated the undulating landscape. The wind, blowing in vigorously across the Lancashire fells from the Irish Sea, created the particularly drafty current that had given the hill its bleak name long since and brought with it the blended scents of watermint and wet earth, meadowsweet and crushed wild thyme.

With a little upward tilt of her chin Delia Gilmore blissfully inhaled the potpourri. A signpost went by when she turned the horse at the crossroad, but she gave it no glance, being more than familiar with the route she was following. She was on the last lap to the house known as Halewood Hall, which graced dramatically the summit of the great hill. Twice a week for over a year she had made the short journey from the market town of Penghyll where she lived, and the little tasks she did at Halewood gave her an exhilarating sense of independence at a time when no young woman in her station of life was expected to do more than decoratively await the day when she would marry. But it was a state of affairs not without its disadvantages, too. First of all there was the strange empathy she had with the house itself, which tore at her heart with its mellow stone beauty and sometimes exerted on her a pressure of unknown secrets that caused her a disquiet she felt unable to discuss with anyone. Then there was the curiosity she encountered whenever people heard that she had *entrée* to a place that had kept its gates locked against the world for a number of years. They tried to question her in devious ways, and even her closest friends were not above trying to trick information out of her, but she knew how to keep her own counsel and would no more have revealed the happenings at Halewood than her father, Dr. Charles Gilmore, would have betrayed his patients' confidences. Last, but by no means least, was Matthew Shaw's disapproval of her visits to the house. He hated Halewood. If he could possibly help it he would not mention it by name, and the only time he ever referred to it of his own free will was to ask her if she had decided to give up going there yet. She guessed he considered it an affront to his male dignity that his betrothed should even partly earn a living as a scribe and general factotum, no matter that it was in the capacity of friend to a titled personage, Lady Hart, who was virtually a recluse, but this show of antagonism toward the house was his only real fault and she loved him deeply, the man who had been her childhood sweetheart, and she knew how greatly he loved her.

With a slight frown she glanced down at her gloved left hand that was gripping the reins and tightened it into a fist, making the fine kid stretch over the pearl and ruby ring. Why, then, when she had cared for Matthew for as long as she could remember and had no

2

doubts that he would be all she wanted in a husband, did she avoid setting a date for their marriage? Could the reason be that which he had once shouted at her in sudden exasperation? Had Halewood set up a barrier between them? Was it true that it had laid some kind of spell on her? She did not entirely disbelieve it. There were many kinds of enchantment. All she knew was that she wasn't ready to break her ties with it yet. Not until the last possible moment, which would come sooner than she wished, for Halewood was shortly to be sold.

The horse, its satin rump dancing in the shafts, took the last bend in the lane. Ahead, set between dragon-headed pillars in a high stone wall, were the tall gates of Halewood. As usual she experienced that odd, ambivalent pang of the heart at the sight of the house beyond them. Giving the reins a tug, she slackened the horse's pace. The lodgekeeper had spotted her, but he was old and it took him a long time to move his arthritic joints to the gates, which he would unlock with a key fit for a castle fortress.

The horse, familiar with the routine, came to a placid halt facing the gates, and Delia sat looking directly through the veil of intricate ironwork to the beech-lined drive, which curved no less than half a dozen times before it opened out into the forecourt of the house that crested the hill. Out of the glory of the Elizabethan Renaissance had been created that edifice of great bay windows, elaborate carving, and giant pilasters. An archway in its glorious, symmetrical south front led to a vast inner courtyard around which the house formed a perfect quadrangle, and therein lay the grand porch entrance with an impressive flight of twenty wide stone steps. On her work-a-day visits Delia used the less imposing but no less splendidly built doorway in the rear of the building, which faced a spread of lawn and gave convenient access from the house to the stables and coach-houses.

Long ago in childhood she had woven tales about

Halewood, for she had been able to see it from her attic bedroom window in the living quarters above the surgery in Penghyll's market square, and if her parents had not decided to move into a larger, grander house when the practice had expanded, she would have been able to see it still. It was years before she discovered it had its own stories to tell, more dramatic and tragic than anything she had ever invented. By that time she was growing up and her mother was dead. And far away in a foreign country Edward Hart, the estranged only son of Sir Harry of Halewood, had died, too, and for the first time in three hundred years there was no heir that anyone had heard of to inherit the great house on the hill whenever the time should come.

Local people thought that was why Sir Harry had married again so late in life, bringing home from one of his occasional visits to London a wife much younger than himself, a woman whom nobody had heard of or could discover anything about, except that undeniably she came from a lower social stratum, but if he had hoped for a child it was not to be. He had gone to his grave a year ago, leaving everything to his beloved wife, Berenice, who had made one of her rare public appearances at the funeral, but the heavy black veil she wore gave no curious person a better chance to see her face than on any other occasion when she ventured out of the grounds in a closed carriage. Delia's friendship with her had come about by chance several months before Sir Harry's death, and the fact that Berenice was one of her father's patients had strengthened the bond between them.

" 'Mornin' to thee, lass." The lodgekeeper had come shuffling into sight, swaying with every difficult step, the key in his knotted hand.

"Good morning, Mr. Newby," Delia replied. "What a lovely day."

"E-ah, it is tha'." The key screeched. The gates began to open.

The horse went trotting through. The lodgekeeper's wife gave the girl a wave from an upper window, which was returned generously. At nineteen Delia, friendly and outgoing, possessed appealing looks, an intelligent mind, and a slim-waisted figure. Her face was finely molded with a neat, straight nose and firm chin, her skin creamy, and her eyes, which were a clear, light gray, direct and straightforward in their looking, were shadowed to a deeper shade by the sweep of dark lashes under arched brows. There was an unconscious sensuality about her mouth, which was full-lipped and red, for she was capable of enormous passion, but the knowledge of it was not yet hers, the rigid conventions governing a betrothal having kept her wholly chaste, and it would not have occurred to her that it might have been otherwise.

Although the beech trees bordering the drive created a wind-break to a certain degree, nothing ever kept at bay the gusts that swirled about the hill, causing branches, bushes, flowers, and grass to sway and dance in rhythm under its spasmodic onslaught. Only when thick mist came rolling in did the endless friction of the wind die into silence, and then the whole countryside would lie oppressed by a gray canopy, leaving Halewood enclosed in stillness and shut away from the rest of the world.

Throughout its history the house had known many dark times. Delia herself had had an intimate glimpse into one of its emotional tragedies when Berenice, then recently widowed, had discovered among Sir Harry's papers in his desk a sealed and unread letter, a quarter of a century old, written by a long-dead Edward Hart far away across the ocean in the New World. In Delia's presence Berenice had opened it, and they discovered it had been sent to inform Sir Harry that he had a grandson, born of Edward's American wife at their Boston home, who had been baptized with the name of Aaron. It was obviously the only communication that had ever been dispatched by

Edward to Sir Harry, who had gone to his grave still nursing his grudge and ill will over the bitter quarrel that had severed them, never knowing that the last in the line of the Hart family was not his own son, whom he had banished from Halewood forever. Delia, at Berenice's request, had written to the Boston address, informing the young man of his English grandfather's demise, and in return had come his polite condolences to Berenice, and that had been that. Until recently. When Berenice had announced her intention of selling Halewood, which under a stipulation laid down in Sir Harry's will had to be sold by public auction, Delia had suggested to her that it was only right that Aaron Hart be informed that the home of his forefathers was going up for sale, and Berenice had acquiesced.

Pressing her bonnet a little more firmly onto her head, the wind having tugged sharply at it all the way, Delia drove around another graceful curve of the drive and saw ahead of her a brougham coming from the direction of the house. When it drew near she recognized the passenger inside as Mr. Radleigh, a local lawyer who attended to all Berenice's legal affairs. He was sitting with a leather briefcase on his knees and lifted his hat as he passed. No matter how important his business had been with his client on that particular morning it could not possibly compare with the news that she herself had brought on this momentous day, which was contained in the letter folded into her reticule. It had come to her home with the early post. It was from America! It was from Aaron Hart!

In the east wing room which had been allotted to her as her own study from the first day she had started work at the house, she hung away her bonnet and jacket in a cupboard, and then with the aid of a pocket-glass she tidied her windblown light brown hair. She wore it parted in the middle, drawn smooth over the temples, which emphasized her high forehead, and dressed in long ringlets over her ears. Satisfied

6

with her appearance, and carrying the letter from across the ocean in her hand, she set off for Berenice's apartments, which by tradition had been occupied by the mistress of Halewood ever since the house was first built. The suite was on the same upper floor as the office, but in the parallel west wing, which gave Delia a daily choice of route to take to get there. She could either walk the corridor that spanned the arch-way in the south front, or she could traverse the por-trait gallery, which stretched the length of the north wing and was still used by Berenice, who was follow-ing in the footsteps of generations of Halewood ladies before her, as a place to stroll for gentle exercise when the weather was bad and it was impossible to venture into the grounds. Usually Delia chose the corridor, for the gallery was a gloomy place on dark days, having no windows and being illuminated by a vaulted roof of glass, which was entirely original. Unfortunately the charming distortions of the old glass were masked by a film of greenish dirt outside, for due to the in-accessibility of the roof for cleaning, a mammoth and hazardous task, it was left untouched from one year's end to another, and the strange underwater light that resulted gradually deepened in hue and made the gallery a place of mystery and shadows.

But today being bright and sunny Delia went to the west wing by way of the gallery and ran the gauntlet of those rows of Halewood eyes, which ar-rogantly returned the gaze of anyone studying the portraits. More than once she had experienced a sense of unease when, lost in thought or contemplation of some task in hand, she had happened to glance idly to the left or right and found herself enmeshed in a cold Halewood stare that followed her relentlessly until the doors at the end of the gallery swung closed be-hind her.

Whenever Delia entered the small yellow drawing room she never failed to appreciate its charm and lightness. Today with the sun streaming in through the windows it was like a golden bowl filled with light, a buttercup sheen to the silk-panelled walls, a reflecting glitter in the crystal droplets of wall sconce and chandelier, and in the woven carpet a pattern of tiger lilies and mimosa made a circular spread of matching brilliance.

Berenice could not be said to have any liking for the room, for she liked no part of Halewood, but she disliked it less than the rest of the house and used it often. She was lying against cushions on a sofa, wearing a gray taffeta morning gown with sloped shoulders and fashionably full sleeves that came in tight at the wrist. Although a widow and a matron she did not wear a cap, but preferred always to drape a mantilla of filmy, scallop-edged lace over her head, crossing it under her chin to fall behind her over both shoulders. It gave her protection should she come across some person whom she had no wish to acknowledge or address, the merest incline of her head bringing the lace drifting forward to shadow her features; in addition it helped keep in place her burnished, red-gold hair, which she wore looped over her ears up into a topknot, for being gossamer-fine it would tumble at the slightest disorder of pins into a flaming cascade down her extraordinarily beautiful face, the bones of which stood out a little harder and more brilliantly than they should have done, due to her thinness, for she ailed in the north country dampness and often declared she had never felt well since coming to Halewood. Well matched to the magnificence of her hair and enhancing beyond measure the perfection of her features was her flawless complexion, pale indeed to be almost transparent, although the faintest hint of applied rose color gave a glow to the wide cheekbones. Most striking of all were her eyes, velvet-dark as purple pansies, but so lustrous that the light seemed to go from her whole countenance whenever she closed her lids.

When Delia crossed the room to her, Berenice

smiled in greeting and gestured languidly toward the small table covered with a lace cloth on which stood a silver chocolate jug, shell-thin cups, and a gilded dish of ratafias. "Pour the chocolate, Miss Gilmore. It's just been brought in and it's fresh and hot. Mr. Radleigh was here, but he wouldn't take any refreshment. He came to inform me that he has received from Italy the deeds of the residence in Florence that has been purchased there on my behalf. My new home! Think of that! I shall depart from this place even as it goes up for auction at the Assembly Rooms in Penghyll." A curiously bitter-tragic look was held in the depths of her eyes and her mouth twisted wryly. "A fitting time to turn my back on it, don't you think?" She did not pause for an answer. "Mr. Radleigh suggested this morning that the contents of the house be auctioned under this roof where they stand, but that I'll not allow. Hordes of people are not coming to poke and pry in idle curiosity. Viewing the house is to be by appointment only, and I'll leave it looking exactly as it did when I first walked into it eight years ago. Only then will the removal men take over and all the furniture, the pictures, and everything else will be boxed and crated and dispatched to the best London saleroom. I want the contents of Halewood dispersed far and wide. Only thus do I see a lessening of its power to hurt and to destroy. A superstitious whim, perhaps, but one that I intend to follow through."

Delia, although impatient to impart her own news, did not wish to stem the impassioned flow of words, knowing that it was only to her that Berenice was able to talk without restraint, having no other confidante. "I know you have never been happy in this house," she said quietly, putting aside the letter temporarily to pour the steaming chocolate into the two cups.

Berenice gave a harsh, little croak of laugh, lifting her chin in self-mockery as she took the cup handed to her. "I've loathed every minute I've had to spend in it. Do you know, I married Sir Harry for this house.

Not for his money or his title, but for Halewood. I thought to escape from a life that had brought me much misery and heartache. In my folly I saw Halewood as a refuge, a retreat, a place of peace. How wrong I was! It's a watching, hostile house, its walls permeated with old sorrows, old tears, old hates. If I hadn't had to wait for the complicated affairs of Sir Harry's estate to be settled I would have gone from Halewood the day he died. I'm taking nothing from it to remind me of my days here."

Delia, sipping the hot chocolate in the chair where she had seated herself, the letter on her lap, raised her eyebrows in surprise. "Nothing at all? But there are so many beautiful things in the house!"

"Every single item is to be sold. I want none of them." Berenice put aside her cup, which she had barely touched with her lips, and leaned her head back against the cushions, the mantilla wafting down into folds, an expression of blissful anticipation on her face. "At last! At last! I feel like a caged linnet watching the unlocking of its prison."

It was on the tip of Delia's tongue to blurt out a warning not to tempt Halewood with such innocent and defiant optimism, but she refrained, reminding herself that this was the nineteenth century, the year of 1848, a time of enlightenment and great industrial progress. Not the Dark Ages. Yet the old belief that Halewood enveloped in an ancient curse all those bearing the name of Hart was impossible to dismiss, for the family had been dogged by misfortune and tragedy throughout the centuries. Although she loved the house, her eye delighting in its beauty, at times the sudden upsurge in the turbulence of its atmosphere, particularly when the wind hammered against the windows, could be terrifying, although always to her it seemed as if the house sought to break free of the evil bonds that held it. Berenice's reminder of the family curse dulled her earlier excitement over the letter she had received, making her wonder if she had done right a few weeks ago to remind Berenice that there was still another who bore the family name. She placed the remainder of her hot chocolate on a small table by her chair and took up the letter in both hands, noticing that they were trembling slightly.

"I've had a reply from Aaron Hart! He's coming to England to make a bid for Halewood!"

"Without having ever seen the place! Mercy me!" Berenice threw up her thin and lovely hands. "A reckless young man and a true Hart by the sound of it! But he was born in the New World and his roots are there. England is a foreign country to him. How can he expect to settle in Lancashire? I'd not be surprised if he didn't know where it was on a map! Has he a wife? How will she take to being uprooted?"

"He's not married."

"That's just as well in the circumstances. Nevertheless he must be a gentleman of some means to be able to afford such a venture."

"Not at all. The tone of his letter suggests he is all but scraping the barrel."

"Then his action is even more foolhardy than I at first supposed. What will he do if some rich cotton-mill owner is set on purchasing Halewood and living in it? The price could soar beyond Aaron Hart's pocket."

"Don't say that!" Delia exclaimed with a frantic intensity. "I don't even want to think such a thing could happen! He has more right to Halewood than anyone!"

Berenice sucked in her cheeks slightly, her eyes narrowing suddenly at Delia. "Are you trying to say that his claim to it is greater than mine?"

It was dangerous ground, but Delia spoke frankly. "The fact that his father quarreled with Sir Harry and was disinherited is no fault of his. Halewood is his natural birthright. Had Sir Harry ever opened that letter and learned that he had a grandson, his last will

11

and testament might have been penned very differently."

"You are impertinent, Miss Gilmore!" Berenice swung her feet to the floor and rose to her full height with an angry rustle of stiff petticoats. Her skirt swayed like a bell as she took a few paces one way and then the other, the ends of her mantilla floating out behind her. But after a minute or two she came to a halt, her indignation gone from her, and looking sideways at Delia she gave a sigh. "You've pointed out a true fact to me and it's not to be denied. With his name and lineage he should be accommodated at Halewood until the day of the auction, but I neither want him here during my last days, nor do I wish to meet him. It could be both humiliating and embarrassing for him to stay in a common hostelry with everybody soon knowing who he was and that he had come to bid against all comers for a house that he should by rights have inherited. Have you an solution to offer?"

Delia rose and went to her with a smile. "Don't worry. That has been taken care of. It was my father's suggestion that I invite him to stay with us. He has accepted gratefully."

"I am grateful too. How typical of Dr. Gilmore to consider my feelings at such a time. Not only is your father a clever physician, but he is a most understanding man."

Delia gave a quick little nod of agreement. "I have always found him so."

"I shall miss his care and sympathetic ear when I am far from Halewood—and I shall miss you, too, child. It is eighteen months now since you were first carried into Halewood with those terrible injuries to your leg, and we have been good friends ever since. Yes, parting from you and your dear father will be my only regret in leaving this abode." She returned to her reclining position on the sofa, her thoughts diverted to the long journey she was soon to make. "I have been mulling over all that I need in the way of new

12

garments and other items. Sit down at the escritoire and make a list of everything I want you to get for me. Now, gloves—a dozen pairs, I think. And petticoats—four times that amount."

The business of the day had begun. With list in her hand and notes about other matters she had to attend to, Delia returned to her study. Before starting work she looked again at Aaron Hart's letter before returning it to her reticule. What a strong and positive hand he had, the writing of a man who knew what he wanted out of life. Still holding the letter, she moved over to the terrestrial globe and stood in a corner of the room and sent it spinning slowly on its axis. Ah! There was Aaron Hart's city! Boston. Rich in its own newly molded history, where on a fateful day British soldiers had fired at unarmed citizens in its streets and brought the American Revolution that much nearer. Her finger, pinpointing it, rested on the wavy blue rim of the sea into which the famous cargo of tea had been dumped with such angry defiance and with such shattering results. All that had been over long, long before, when Edward Hart had turned his back on his home among the gray, rainswept fells of Lancashire and set his face toward a new life in a new land, knowing the past was behind him forever. Yet, in spite of bitterness and anger and filial enmity, he must have managed to instill in his son something of his inherent devotion for an ancestral home that had been old when the Pilgrim Fathers had first set foot on American soil.

Suddenly she shivered, seeing herself and the letter she had written as being instrumental in bringing Aaron Hart back to Halewood. Had the house used her? Was it through her that the Halewood curse had reached out to bring the last of the line home to his doom? No, no! She mustn't think that! He was young and strong and alien-born, and perhaps he alone had the power to defy the curse and put an end to it for all time. That was what she must hope for. That was what she must keep uppermost in her thoughts.

A sense of foreboding stayed with her when she sat down at the desk to start work, and would not be dismissed. It was as if in the innermost recesses of her mind she retained the knowledge that no Hart had the power to lift the curse. Those who had tried had been crushed down by tragedy. How could she expect anything to be different for the young man from over the ocean?

It was late afternoon when she arrived home at Sycamore House on Victoria Avenue, which was situated in a quiet, residential area of Penghyll. Ellen, the parlormaid, opened the door to her and informed her that Mr. Shaw had called to see her and was waiting in the drawing room.

Hastily she shed bonnet, coat, and gloves. Never had she been more pleased to know that Matthew had come to see her. Never had she needed him more. With as much speed as she could muster she hurried to the drawing room door, which stood ajar, and she paused on the threshold, savoring the sight of him, happy to remain unnoticed by him for a few moments until she chose to make her presence known.

He was leaning over a dissected puzzle which lay spread out on an unfolded card table, the light of the window behind him making a fair halo of his smooth, well-brushed hair, and he was trying to fit in one of the dozens of intricately cut wooden pieces that would eventually make up a picture of a pastoral scene. Even as she watched he clicked the pieces down and, still unaware that she was there, he reached for another and tried again.

She took in every detail of his appearance. He was wearing a gray frock coat that she had not seen before, its elegant style suiting his lean, long-limbed frame, the paisley silk handkerchief which flowed from a tail pocket toned tastefully with his cravat; his profile was turned toward her, clear-cut as a monarch's

14

head on a golden sovereign, his forehead broad, his prominent nose balanced by a strong chin, his mouth narrow-lipped and full of energy. Seeing how deeply he frowned over the puzzle, all her feelings for him swept over her in a warm and loving wave. A month since she had last seen him. Far, far too long!

She moved forward with a little swaying swoop of her skirt. "You look extremely busy!" she exclaimed teasingly, holding out her hands to him.

He raised his head with a start, broken out of his concentration, and his whole face lighted up at the sight of her. "Delia! I didn't know you had returned!"

He came swiftly to her, taking her outstretched hands in his, and he drew her to him, kissing her lovingly on the mouth. There was a faint, familiar aroma about him of Macassar oil and starched linen and clean, young maleness, and she swayed against him, her eyes closed. His arms went about her and he kissed her more ardently, holding her close to him. When they drew apart, smiling at each other, she gave him a little reproachful tap on his chest with her forefinger.

"Why didn't you let me know you were coming? Not a word in your last letter! I would have left Halewood an hour ago if I'd known. Have you been waiting long?"

They had moved to the sofa while she had been speaking and they sat down beside each other.

"Not more than twenty minutes at the most, I suppose. I'd have driven to meet you if the parlormaid hadn't reminded me that you sometimes leave Lady Hart early and do shopping for her in town."

"Ellen was right to stop you. You could have missed me quite easily if that had been the case. I want to know why and how you managed to spring this surprise visit on me! The last I heard you were practically working around the clock to get the eastern end of the Manchester and Huddleston railway line finished ahead of time."

He laughed, sitting back and crossing one leg over the other, his hand resting against her wrist. "So I have been—and the work went through faster than we dared hope. I've already been transferred to a new assignment—not a minor assistant engineer any longer, but promotion! I'm to be in charge of the construction of a new branch line that is to have its terminus at Penghyll!"

"Matthew! How wonderful!" She flung her arms about his neck and hugged him. "Congratulations. It's what you've been hoping for! And to be at Penghyll itself!"

"I'll simply be visiting the district now and again while surveyors investigate suitable sites for the tracks, but after that I'll be permanently in this area until the line is finished."

"Does that mean we'll be able to see each other really often?"

He clasped her hard to him, his face close to hers, his expression very serious and intense. "Why not every day and every night, Delia? Let's get married. There's no need to wait any longer. We've been betrothed a long time—and before my ring was ever on your finger we both knew that one day you'd be my wife. I love you! If only you knew how much I love you!"

He bent his head and put his lips yearningly against her throat, sending a delicious shiver through her, and tenderly she smoothed her fingertips from his temple down to the line of his jaw. There was nothing to keep them from marrying. When Halewood was sold her extremely pleasant little tasks there would come to an end and she would find time on her hands again. Why not use that time looking after Matthew?

"Where would we live," she whispered.

He knew it was the answer he had longed to hear. He raised his head, his expression adoring and jubilant. "Dearest! You shall have any house that pleases you!"

The thought came unbidden to her mind. If only it

16

could have been Halewood! Then she thrust it from her and let him sweep her into a joyful discussion of wedding plans. They talked of the church and the guests and the wedding breakfast, where they should live, and whether the village of Miryclough would be more convenient to his new assignment than the town of Pendlewick, both of which lay within a seven-mile radius of Penghyll, but when they came to settle on the actual date for the ceremony she surprised him by saying she could not decide until she had seen Lady Hart again.

"Why ever not?" he asked, grinning in puzzlement. "She'd never come to our wedding! Not unless it were held at Halewood itself with no other guests but her!"

She did not smile and he regretted his poor joke. That damnable house had been a bone of contention between them ever since she recovered from her accident and started to go to work there, for paid employment was what it was, no matter how genteel the tasks she carried out. He hadn't been able to understand how her father could have allowed it. When he had tackled Dr. Gilmore about it the reply had been that it did Delia no harm to be useful and in his opinion his patient, Lady Hart, benefited greatly from having young company to cheer her isolation. So that had been that. But, Matthew thought grimly, as his wife Delia would have enough to do running their home and entertaining their friends and sharing with him countless delights that would drive that place forever from her heart.

Then he knew. It came to him why he loathed Halewood. In some extraordinary, indefinable way it had taken some part of her affections from him, and instinctively he had been jealous of it without understanding why.

"Lady Hart told me today that she will be leaving Halewood on the eve of the auction, but I'm not sure whether she meant that quite literally or if there is to be a leeway of a day or two. Anyway, I want to stay with her until she departs, because I know there'll be many ways in which I'll be able to assist her. There's also another matter I haven't disclosed yet. Aaron Hart, whom I told you about, has written that he is coming to bid for the property and he will be staying at Sycamore House with father and me until he can move into Halewood. I think it's best if we make up our minds that the wedding will be after the Penghyll Annual Ball. By that time Halewood will be sold, Lady Hart will be on her way to Italy, and the new owner will be settled in. My responsibilities toward everyone else but you, dear Matthew, will have been discharged."

"That means it will be late autumn when we marry," he said, somewhat disgruntled. Now that he had pinned her down to a definite decision the burden of waiting even a short while longer seemed quite unendurable.

"What could be better?" Smiling, she leaned forward and put her cheek briefly against his in a velvet touch. "It's such a wonderful time of year. There are still rowanberries on the trees and old man's beard on the hedges. If there's hard frost or early snow we'll draw the curtains tight against the night and sit together by the hearth with a cozy fire leaping up the chimney. There'll be time to talk about all the things we've never had time ot talk about before, and I'll bake you blackberry-and-apple pies and gingerbread and the best plum cake you've ever tasted."

Her words were loving, happy, and full of confidence. Having committed herself, she would go forward with no aim other than to make him a good wife. That was her destiny. It was a path that had been set for her by circumstances, but one which she would tread lightly and with a glad heart.

The sound of a carriage coming up the drive made her spring to her feet and dart to the window. "It's papa! Now we can tell him! He will be surprised!"

"And pleased, too, I hope," Matthew said, coming to her side.

She looked up at him and was moved afresh by the devotion she saw in his eyes. He had waited long and faithfully for her. She would give him no cause to regret it.

"Papa has always thought highly of you, as you well know," she admonished lightly. "Didn't he as much as say that when you asked formally for my hand? He's not likely to put any obstacles up at this late hour."

Dr. Gilmore entered soon afterward. He was an erect, distinguished-looking man with shrewd eyes and a kindly mouth, his fairish hair brindled with gray. Through the open doors of the drawing room he could see his daughter and her betrothed standing side by side waiting for him. As he went in to them he could tell by Delia's deep curtsy and Matthew's bow that they had something of importance to disclose. It wasn't hard to guess what it would be.

2

DELIA turned up the lamplight in the guest room. Several weeks had gone by since she had received the news of Aaron Hart's coming, and now that he was due at any time she was making a final check as his hostess to see that everything had been made ready for him and nothing had been overlooked. Approvingly she noted that there were plenty of towels on the wooden rail by the washstand, a new piece of soap in the dish on its starched mat, and a lace-edged linen square was keeping dust-free the cold water in the freshly-fitted, rose-patterned ewer, which stood in its matching washbowl. The grate in the fireplace was laid with paper, sticks, and coal, which would flare to a welcoming blaze when a match was put to it. Moving to the bed, she smoothed out a crease in the spread and stooped to twitch a valence-fold into place.

Would the American be resting his head on that pillow the next night or the night after? His ship, a packet of the Black Ball Line, had been due to dock at Liverpool earlier in the day, but that was no guarantee of its arrival, for the Atlantic winds could play havoc with sailing schedules. Yet her father had been optimistic that there would be small delay, pointing out that vessels of the United States usually kept remarkably good time, that country's insurance companies insisting that the captains be tip-top, and the ships of other lands were sometimes put to shame.

21

At least she knew that whenever he did finally arrive at Sycamore House he would be more than tired, the journey from Liverpool to Penghyll being a most awkward one necessitating several changes of trains, transport by coach and horses where no railway link had yet been laid down, and a final stretch of road that would have to be covered in any vehicle he could find that was available for private hire. When the branch line was built to Penghyll it would make traveling much easier, but that day was still distant, no site for it having been settled upon yet by the Lancashire & Yorkshire Railway Company, and in the meantime Aaron Hart would have to make his own way as best he could.

She gave thought to Matthew's impatience at the delay in the company's decision. He could be decidedly short-tempered when things did not go exactly his way and it did not suit him to drag his heels. No area viewed seemed just right, and more than once she had combined house-hunting with a trip in his curricle to yet another possible siting. While she had collected keys and walked through empty rooms, her footsteps echoing, he had been engaged in the arguments that always seemed to spring up whenever the railway representatives got together to view a particular layout, their maps and notebooks fluttering in the wind, their expressions becoming more exasperated and irritable. It was during one of these sorties with Matthew into the countryside that she had found in the village of Fellfoot a charming little house called Wisteria Lodge with a view of the river. Matthew had liked it as much as she, and once he could be sure that the new line was not to go across the land nearby, that particular route having been considered for far longer than the others, he purchased the property and decorators moved in. Only that morning she had driven the wagonette over to Fellfoot to see how the work was progressing, and had been delighted with the silk panelling and pastel-colored paint.

Turning out the lamplight she went from the guest room, closing the door behind her. At a leisurely pace she went to the head of the stairs and started down the flight. It was a wild evening, with the wind howling around the house, making it cozy to be indoors and out of the heavy rain. Halfway down where the staircase bent at right angles she stopped and held back the curtain to look out on the drenched garden. A gasp escaped her. A hackney cab was entering the gates from the lamplit street beyond, baggage piled on its roof. Instantly she guessed the identity of the passenger within the cab. Aaron Hart had arrived!

She hastened down the rest of the flight, thoughts racing through her head. Her father was out! Nothing special had been planned for dinner! She would have to receive him on her own! If only Matthew were here, but he'd had to go out of town for a few days again and wouldn't be back for a week! She flung out a hand, cupped the newel post, and whirled herself with a hiss of frilled petticoats from the last stair.

Anxiously she checked her appearance in the looking glass on the wall above the hall table, wishing she had had time to change into one of her best outfits. With frantic impatience she tidied a stray ringlet around her finger while outside in the rain-damp air the clop of hooves drew nearer, the wheels of the hackney cab spitting aside the gravel of the drive which encircled the lawn in front of the house. She could picture the horse taking the curve of it and from the dank, leather-upholstered interior of the hackney cab Aaron Hart would be seeing her home as a black, rectangular shape with tall chimneys and a slate roof, the fanlight above the entrance a spread of jewel colors, the drawing room windows with their closed curtains glowing crimson. The tall trees, which made a windbreak at the side of the house, would be a wild tumble of tossing branches against the scudding sky.

Wheels scrunched to a halt and the sound of a voice told her that the passenger had alighted. As she smoothed down the plaid silk of her bodice in a final touch, the rattle of the bellpull was followed by the jingle of the bell far away in the depths of the house, and she started violently when it was followed unexpectedly by the sudden thunder of the brass knocker, which made the whole door vibrate. Darting forward, she pressed down the handles of the vestibule double doors with their colored glass panels, and even as she opened them she heard the squeak of a shoe's sole on the stone steps outside the entrance door, which told her that Aaron Hart had swung back after announcing his arrival to supervise the unloading of his boxes.

She had her hand on the latch to lift it when behind her in the long hall there came footsteps hurrying up from the kitchen regions, accompanied by the pristine rustle of a newly-tied apron. She spoke, not turning her head, determined not to share this moment of importance in her life, for it was as if she were about to let Halewood itself into her own home.

"Mr. Hart has arrived from America, Ellen. See that the groom knows which guest room has been prepared when he carries the visitor's boxes up the back stairs. Also inform Cook of the gentleman's arrival at the same time and ask her to serve the best dinner possible under the circumstances."

"Er—yes, miss. But—er—t'door?"

"There's no need for you to wait. I'll admit Mr. Hart."

Ellen's face became sulky and she dawdled, not departing, resentful at being dismissed from a duty that would have enabled her to catch a first glimpse of the visitor whom the whole household had been awaiting with interested anticipation for weeks. She thought it surprising that the front door had been reached before her coming into the hall, for she had moved sharply when the bell rang. What was more, her inquisitive nature was aroused. Her mistress's face was hidden from her, but there was something odd in the way she was

24

standing, alert and poised and almost on tiptoe, and making no attempt to push up the latch.

"Is it stuck again?" Ellen optimistically look a step forward, thinking her help might be needed. It did happen sometimes that the wooden panels of the door became swollen and difficult to open when the rain pelted ceaselessly for days and weeks on end, beating in to turn the lanes to liquid mud and crown the summit of the fells with leaden clouds that never lifted.

"No!" Delia spoke firmly. "Go and do as I told you."

Ellen had no choice but to obey, which she did with little grace, flouncing off down the passageway. Delia tightened her grip on the latch, slowly exerting pressure until it went upward with a sharp click. Unaware that she was holding her breath, she wrenched the door open in one swift movement, a cold draft blowing in on her, her shadow stretching out before her across the step in the golden patch of light thrown down by the lamp in the hall. She had expected to find Aaron returned again to the threshold and facing her, but the moment of meeting had yet to come.

He was paying the cabbie his fare, his broad-shouldered back toward her while he dived into his pocket for more change and brought out a fistful of sovereigns and silver coins, which he sorted out on the palm of his hand. Two pieces of baggage had been unloaded and set down on the ground beside him, a large, brass-cornered trunk bearing a steampacket label and a portmanteau of good leather which was much scuffed by long journeying.

There was a purposeful air about him, a powerful litheness to his tapered body, his clothes well cut and having the sheen of good cloth. She could not see what his features were like, his face being directed toward the cabbie, but there was every reason to suppose that when he turned around he would prove to be extremely personable. Under the tall stovepipe hat, which added to his already considerable height, his hair was blue-black, thick and vigorous, curly as a bearskin rug.

The cabbie accepted the fare, which appeared to have been crowned by a large tip judging by his pleased expression and the flourish with which he touched his cap. "Thank 'ee, sir. Good neet, sir."

"Good night," the newcomer replied in a deep voice that held an unmistakable Yankee intonation. He picked up the portmanteau, turning as he did so, and his gaze swept up and over the house before lowering to settle on her slender-waisted, bell-skirted silhouette in the doorway.

In those few seconds of his appraisal of her home she had looked on his face and gathered in an impression of it that she knew would stay with her until the end of her days. It was not a handsome face in the classic sense, lacking symmetry, but molded strongly and the more arresting because of that. The wide brow glowered over the long, narrow eyes vizored by their lashes, and the nose was large, but wonderfully shaped with winged nostrils unmistakably aggressive, the rocklike chin a stubborn thrust, and the mouth, full-lipped and sensual, did not look as if it smiled often or easily. Even in her innocence she knew she was meeting a man who would be a formidable adversary, a dangerous enemy, and without doubt a passionate lover, whose desires would reach out into the dark distances of which she knew nothing and did not dare to contemplate.

"How do you do, Mr. Hart," she said, relieved to hear no tremor in her voice. "I'm Delia Gilmore."

"I'm honored to make your acquaintance, Miss Delia." He removed his hat and took firmly the hand she extended to him. "I hope my being unable to give the exact time of my arrival has caused no inconvenience."

"Not at all. Come in, do. My father is out until later, but in his absence and on his behalf I bid you welcome to Lancashire and to our home!" She drew aside with a swish of her skirt to let him enter, the gas-light casting a running gleam over her shining hair, well aware of being scrutinized by that steady gaze of his, but not, she thought, with anything more specific than an alert and intelligent interest in all he was seeing in this country that was entirely new to him.

"I thank you. Your kind words are much appreciated." He set down the portmanteau and his voice took on a clipped, wry note. "I believe my late grandfather would turn in his grave if he knew that his disinherited son's son had come home to roost."

She caught the undertone of outrage and defiance in his words. If he had the stiff, fierce pride of the Hart family—and there was every indication of it in his face and bearing—the humiliation of having to bid publicly against all comers for his own birthright would be harder for him to endure than for the ordinary run of men; a savage, running sore that might never heal. And what if he did not get it? That did not bear thinking about! She took his hat from him and put it on the hall seat.

"Did you have a good journey?" she inquired. He had slipped off his traveling coat and she would have taken it from him, but he would not let her wait on him further and put it with his gloves over the arm of the seat.

"It was a rough passage, but the wind was with us all the way and we docked ahead of time. I contacted Mr. Radleigh's Liverpool representative as arranged and left him to see to the crates in the hold. The most difficult part of the whole journey from Boston has been getting from Liverpool to Penghyll. When I got as far as the nearest railroad depot I took a cab to cover the rest of the way. I must say I'm exceedingly glad to get here at last."

"I'm afraid the rough weather you spoke of has followed you to our doorstep. We barely saw the summer this year and autumn is proving wild and cold. Lancashire weather will be harder on you than any-

27

thing you have known in the United States, I'm sure."
She went ahead of him and paused with her fingertips against the drawing room door, ready to open it
when he reached her side.

He had observed with some surprise that she
walked with a slight limp and wondered if her dis-
ability were permanent or if she had recently sprained
her ankle. She was like a dainty, fragile little bird
dragging an injured wing, but the carriage of her head
and straightness of her back suggested that she was
not without courage or determination and would reject pity for her condition out of hand. He found this
combination of gentleness, timidity, and high spirits
extraordinarily appealing, arousing as it did both a desire to protect and to challenge. He thought her quite
lovely, this scrap of a girl with her neat, sparrow-
brown head, long neck, and small breasts.

"I doubt whether the climate has much that is new
to offer me," he replied easily. "I've lived through a
tornado that tore a town into plank-wood and I've
survived a flood. Should I expect worse than that?"

She smiled, inclining her head. "I think not. I just
wanted to prepare you."

He glanced again at the hall before following her
into the drawing room. The house was much as he
had expected it to be, large and comfortable, not unlike the residence of any small-town but prosperous
physician back in the United States. Obviously he had
caught the household unprepared, Dr. Gilmore being
out and Delia herself somewhat taut and tense beneath the polite facade. Had they thought he would
dally in Liverpool seeing the sights or some such
nonsense? He had not traveled all these miles to waste
time when Halewood was so near. If it had not been
too dark to see anything he would have gone to get
his first glimpse of it before arriving at Dr. Gilmore's
door. As it was, he could hardly wait till morning.

The drawing room was warm and inviting, a multicolored Turkish carpet on the floor, the furniture

rosewood, and the lamplight cast a pleasing glow over the apple-green upholstered sofa and the embroidered tapestry cushions on the fringed chairs. Opposite the fireplace, a pair of white-painted doors had been folded back to reveal an adjoining music room graced by a piano and a gilded harp. Delia invited him to take a comfortable-looking chair by the fire.

"Do you play?" he asked, gesturing toward the music room as he seated himself.

"A little," she replied.

"I look forward to hearing you."

"May I offer you some refreshment?" she asked, crossing to a cabinet embellished with marquetry. "A glass of claret perhaps? Or would you prefer Madeira?"

He chose the claret. She took a crystal decanter from a shelf and poured it for him. When she gave it to him he saw that her hand shook slightly. Wanting to put her at her ease, he waited until she had seated herself on the scroll-ended sofa and then raised his glass to her.

"To you, Miss Delia—and to Halewood."

She put her hand to her throat. It was an involuntary reaction to being linked with the house, but he did not notice. "I—I hope you will be happy there."

He held his glass as though studying the color of it before putting it down on the small table at the side of this chair. "I haven't come seeking happiness. According to my father there is no place on earth where one is less likely to find it. Legend has long held that there is a curse on the Harts of Halewood."

She was astounded at his words. "You know that! Why then have you made up your mind to live in it?"

He gave an easy little shrug. "I grew up believing that one day it would be mine. My father talked to me about Halewood from the time I was first able to understand that somewhere far across the sea there was a house that one day would belong to me. He fed me tales of its bloodthirsty past that excited my imagination—my poor mother couldn't bear to listen to them. How much was myth and how much the truth I've no idea, but all the adventure I even dreamed about as a boy was linked to a place I'd never seen."

"Did it never occur to your father that Sir Harry might marry again?"

"I don't think so, but even if it had he would have lost no sleep over it, for in matters of inheritance the only son of the eldest son is—or should be!—secure. Even if the second Lady Hart had had a dozen boys not one of them would have had any hereditary right to come between the house and me. That I should be cut off with my father was a possibility that occurred to neither of us."

"I did explain that Sir Harry never opened the letter giving him the news that he had a grandson."

"Yet my father was careful to make sure it was received into my grandfather's own hands." His lip curled wryly. "Not wanting to send such an important piece of information in the mail, he entrusted the letter to a church minister visiting England, who delivered it to Halewood himself. Had Sir Harry returned the letter unopened to Boston my father would have understood that all was not as it should be. As it was, he took for granted that it was read and that my grandfather harbored no ill will against me." He gave a long sigh. "I know it was homesickness as much as alcohol that killed my exiled parent, one cause aggravating the other. Through me he dreamed vicariously of returning to Halewood, and it was a longing that kept him from making a new life of any worth in a new land."

"Would you have preferred to grow up in ignorance of Halewood's existence?" she questioned with interest.

"Indeed, no! My childhood, as I explained, was the richer for it, and there is such a sense of belonging to Halewood inherent in me that I'm convinced I should have found it out had the name of the place never been spoken in my hearing." He turned to a point gaining preeminence in his mind. "I have much to thank you for. By notifying me in good time of the present Lady Hart's intention to sell you gave me fair chance to arrange my affairs and get here for the auction."

She glanced down at her hands folded in her lap. "Lady Hart instructed me to write."

He leaned forward, looking directly at her, one elbow resting on his knee. "I still believe you had much to do with it." Then he sat back again, crossing one long leg over the other. "Do you enjoy the time you spend at Halewood?"

She pondered before she answered. Mostly she was as happy there as she could be, but it was the curious rapport she had with the house that was often deeply disturbing, and she always avoided going near the sward in the courtyard for reasons of her own which she had never discussed with anyone.

"It's been wonderful working in such splendid surroundings," she answered carefully, "and Lady Hart has always been most kind to me."

"Tell me how you spend your time there. Where do you deal with correspondence? In which room were you when you wrote to me?"

He listened with rapt attention while she answered him as fully as she could. Finally she asked him another question in turn. "How can you be sure that you will settle down in this part of the world?"

"Why shouldn't I? I've come home."

It was a statement of fact that he appeared to think brooked no argument, but she wondered how much he knew about the husbandry of land and livestock, for Halewood was more than just a property to live in; the estate stretched out to encompass the homes of tenants and acres of good farmland. It was the second time he had referred to his arrival as a homecoming. Home to roost, he had said before. Yet was it so strange that he should think of Lancashire in such a way? After all, his roots went far back into local soil. Perhaps to the time when the Vikings had swept inland in their longboats out of the mists of the Irish Sea. Or even before that.

"Wasn't it hard to leave Boston and all that was familiar to you?" she wondered aloud.

He considered before he answered, taking a sip of claret and putting the glass down again. "Hard? No, I can't say it was hard. You must remember that I've always had my sights set on this side of the ocean. Naturally I'll miss many of my old friends, but most of them expect to take vacations in Europe at some time, and they'll visit me. I should have liked to keep my mother's old home, which my maternal grandparents left in trust for me to prevent my father getting hold of it in their daughter's lifetime and selling it with everything else he could lay his hands on for his gaming and his drinking and his—well, his other extravagances. It became mine when I was sixteen. I lost both parents the same year."

"What was your house like? Was it called Lincolnshire Hall because Boston's first settlers came from the English county of the same name?" She had read all she could find about his country in her father's collection of books and in the local lending library, refreshing all that she had learned at an earlier age and gaining new facts, having been determined that he should not find her ignorant on any points.

He gave a nod. "It was a small house compared to Halewood, with no more than a dozen rooms, but it was graciously designed, and in my opinion one of the most interesting old houses in the Boston area. But"—here he let his hands rise and fall—"it had to go with its land and all else I possessed in that field to help finance my venture here in Lancashire. I've burned my boats. There'll be no looking back over the shoulder for me."

"Did you run the estate yourself?"

"I did. I figure there'll be no great difficulty in running Halewood on more or less the same lines."

"You'll have no slave labor here," she pointed out innocently.

His brows snapped into a deep frown. "I'm aware of that, Miss Delia. I'll have you know that only free men have ever labored for me, and those I employ in this country in my house and on my land will receive fair wages for their toil and see their wives and children properly fed and clothed, safe from the squalor and misery that I've glimpsed from train and cab window since landing in Liverpool. I can assure you that slavery will eventually be abolished in the United States as it has been here long since and in the British colonies. Attitudes are changing toward the slave trade. Not so many Americans are as far behind the times as you appear to imagine."

She saw she had needled him. For a man who professed to have left the country of his birth without regrets, he was highly sensitive to even the most veiled criticism of it. In future she would guard her words more carefully. But words were easy to guard. The heart was more vulnerable.

"I'm sure you would like to see your room before dinner," she said, rising and going across to take hold of the bellpull and giving it a tug.

"Thank you." He emptied his glass and stood up, but his gaze had dropped to her left hand. "You're betrothed, I see. Who is the fortunate man?"

She looked down at the ring on her finger as if she had forgotten it existed. "His name is Matthew Shaw. He's a civil engineer at present with the Lancashire & Yorkshire Railway Company. His work takes him far afield." She turned, hearing the door open. Ellen stood there, her eyes wide with curiosity, going straight to the visitor in an unblinking stare. "Show Mr. Hart to his room, Ellen. Has a fire been lit there?"

"Yes, miss. This way, sir, if you please."

On her own again, Delia met her own reflected gaze in the nearby looking glass. Slowly she put up her hands and rested her fingers against her cheeks. She did not look any different, but something was happening to her over which she had no control. No matter that her mind cried out against it, every nerve and fiber of her being was attracted to Aaron as though to a magnet. It was her own fault through associating him too much with Halewood, which had such a hold on her affections. There could be no other explanation. Never before had she experienced such a violent onslaught upon her senses. She had not known that such an urge could exist in the female form and she was frightened and shamed by it. This wild turmoil of emotion was alien to her and somehow she must crush it down and forget that it ever threatened her.

Dr. Gilmore returned shortly before the dinner hour. Ellen, helping him off with his coat, was full of the foreign gentleman's arrival, and the words came from her with the speed of peas popped from a pod. Delia, changed into her best blue silk, had been making sure that the table had been laid as she wished it, and she came from the dining room to greet him.

"Thank goodness you've returned, papa," she exclaimed. "Aaron Hart has arrived."

"So Ellen informed me." He patted the hand that she had tucked into the crook of his arm, turning with her toward the drawing room. "Where is our visitor now?"

"He is still upstairs and hasn't come down yet. I was taken quite by surprise when he came, and there is only soup, fish, and hot-pot with pickled red cabbage for dinner. It should have been a much grander meal."

"I think not. The main course is an honest-to-goodness Lancashire dish. If he is to become a member of our community, what better way to start than partaking of a traditional culinary delight?"

They had reached his wing chair by the fire and

she threw him a smile as she removed her hand from his arm. "You're right, of course. In any case I don't think him to be a man to g.ve himself unnecessary airs."

"I'm glad to hear it." He sat down in his comfortable chair with a sense of relief, linked his hands across his waistcoat and set both his feet on the footstool that Delia had pushed forward, folding his legs neatly at the ankles. He had had a long and busy day, traveling to visit a number of patients in outlying districts, and afterward in his surgery, which was always busy, he had dealt with many poorer and less fortunately placed patients to whom he gave as much consideration and care as to those able to pay lavishly for attention. He had dealt with his partner's patients as well when the younger man had answered an emergency call to a man crushed under some machinery in a workshop, needing an amputation to set him free. Until a few years ago when he had first taken a partner, he had felt able to take everything in his stride, but now, at the age of sixty-three, although to all appearances a well-preserved and still remarkably young-looking man, he was not as fit as he might be, and he thought as he listened to his daughter telling him about her conversation with Aaron Hart from the chair opposite him that he would be thankful to see her safely married and settled. There had been a period when he had suspected she was having second thoughts about marrying Matthew, her willingness to let the betrothal drift on being in sharp contrast to the young man's natural ardor, and he had felt that more lay behind it than her contentment at home and the solid relationship that she shared with him, but whatever uncertainties she could have been experiencing over the matter had passed over safely. He approved the match. No prospective son-in-law was ever faultless, but young Matthew Shaw would be as good as any and considerably better than most, having advanced quite swiftly in his chosen career as well as being due to inherit handsomely from elderly grandparents. In addition, he had seen the lad grow up under that couple's excellent care and knew him to be a young man of principle. He could see by Delia's expression that she had something to ask him and he tilted his head inquiringly. "Yes?"

"Why did Aaron Hart's father quarrel with Sir Harry, papa?"

"There are plenty of versions of what happened in circulation," he answered with a slight smile. "Have you heard none of them?"

"Indeed I have." She hesitated. "It is most generally supposed that father and son quarreled over a—woman."

"That is correct."

"Is it true she was a humble mill-girl? What happened to her?"

"I regret to say that she died in the Penghyll workhouse some years ago. Now I suggest you leave the matter there and trouble your head no more about it."

She realized that he had no intention of discussing the unsavory scandal with her, having a distaste for anything remotely connected with gossip, and she respected his attitude, which was much like her own, but she could not resist questioning him further. "Were you well acquainted with Edward Hart?"

"I never met him. He had left for the New World before I moved to Penghyll. As my predecessor had been physician to Halewood I was invited to carry on in his place and I attended Sir Harry from that time forth."

"Was the first Lady Hart alive then?"

"No, she wasn't. She died while still young, which was the reason why Sir Harry had no other children."

"Did he ever talk about Edward to you?"

"Never. From the moment Edward left home Sir Harry considered himself childless, cutting off all connection with his son as when a man lops a branch from a tree, not caring whether it ends up as firewood

36

or rots where it falls, he himself having no further use for it."

"Why then did he keep that unopened letter from Edward in his desk?" she queried.

"Knowing Sir Harry, I'd say that it gave him a certain perverse satisfaction to know that Edward had sought to offer an olive branch by contacting him and he was casting him off anew, not once, but every day that the letter lay with its unbroken seal in his desk."

"How cruel! Edward could have been in dire straits! Dying, for all Sir Harry knew. If only he had read that letter!" She thumped a fist on her knee. "How different everything would have been for Aaron Hart."

"In what way?"

She looked surprised that he should ask. "Halewood would have been left to him! Sir Harry would have divided his fortune between his second wife and his grandson, which would have enabled both of them to live in comfort for the rest of their days—Aaron at the house and Lady Hart, if she'd a mind to it, could have stayed on. As it happens, she wanted to leave, but that is beside the point."

Dr. Gilmore gave his head a shake. "I must disagree with you. It's my opinion that it would have made no difference at all if Sir Harry had known he had a grandson. The Harts have always been a proud, unforgiving family, and Sir Harry was a true Hart in that respect. He was a stubborn, cantankerous man who could be extremely difficult—as you saw for yourself at the house on more than one occasion before he died of that attack of apoplexy—and I'm convinced he would have considered the bequeathing of Halewood to any child of Edward's as a gesture of reconciliation, which was a move he would never have made, not even if he had been told that his estranged son was dead and gone."

"You really believe that!" She looked sadly incredulous. Then she added on a sigh, "What a sorry business it all is."

"I agree. I feel heartily sorry for our guest at present upstairs. If he has the true Hart pride—and from your first impression of him that you have given me, I should say he has—he is not taking kindly to the humiliating position in which he finds himself. I'm extremely glad that we're able to do something to ease the way by showing him hospitality."

"There will be another diversion for him soon. Before long Aunt Rachel will arrive with Melissa to stay until the Penghyll Ball."

She saw that her reminder of his sister's annual visit with his niece had depressed him, but there was no time for more talk on the subject, for upstairs a door had opened and closed and footsteps were coming downstairs. Their guest was about to join them. Every part of her body seemed to tingle with a strange excitement.

"He's coming, papa," she said with a throb in her voice. "You are about to meet Mr. Hart."

Dr. Gilmore rose from his chair and when Aaron entered the room greetings and handshakes were exchanged. Aaron had gifts for them both, which he had unpacked from his baggage, and he presented his host with an antique tobacco jar inlaid with silver, while Delia unwrapped a white silk shawl delicately embroidered with roses in every shade from palest pink to deepest crimson and trimmed with a heavy fringe.

"It's beautiful!" she exclaimed, swirling it into place about her shoulders and looking down to admire it. "Such exquisite handiwork!"

"I'm happy the shawl pleases you. It was bought in Boston, but is Spanish in origin. However, I've another gift for you, Miss Delia, which is of Massachusetts and nowhere else."

He handed it to her. It was a book of very fine prints of Boston, showing the city streets, individual houses and gardens, the harbor and quayside, and historical scenes from the past. One print showed his own home, and from what she could see of it there was no doubt it was a charming residence of character and elegance.

"I've never received two more delightful gifts," she said sincerely, holding the book to her. "I shall treasure them."

She kept the shawl looped around her during dinner. Her father and Aaron found much to talk about, which enabled her to sit quietly listening for most of the time. But in the drawing room afterward Aaron made a point of addressing himself more to her, and several times she caught his gaze resting keenly on her for a reason she could not comprehend. It made her pulse quicken and her color come and go. It was with a sense of overwhelming relief that she was at last able to slip away to bed, leaving Aaron answering questions from her father about President James K. Polk's handling of the affairs of that brash young nation on the other side of the wide Atlantic Ocean.

৩ 3 ৫ৎ

It was barely six o'clock when Delia emerged
fully dressed from her bedroom to go downstairs, having spent a restless night, getting little sleep, and she
was thankful to be up and about.

"Good morning, Annie," she said to the housemaid
polishing the landing on hands and knees.

"Good morning, miss."

She carried on down the stairs and to her astonishment she found that Aaron, who was dressed to go
out, had stopped at the vestibule door at the sound of
her voice and come back to the foot of the flight to
meet her.

"Mr. Hart!" she exclaimed. "You're an early riser
indeed."

"I'm heading for Halewood!" His whole face was
alight and eager, and he reached out and caught both
her hands in his. "Come with me! I can wait no longer
to see it!"

Her first instinct was to cry out a refusal, but following hard upon it was a rebellious longing to be
with him at such a momentous time in his life.

"You won't be able to view the place," she felt
forced to point out. "That's to be by appointment only,
and yours is on Monday next."

"It's the exterior I'll be content to see for the time
being! The rest can wait! Put on your coat and bonnet
and come!"

41

She laughed shyly, carried away by his enthusiasm. "I'll come!"

"Good!" He pressed her hands hard and went hurrying out into the fierce, windblown morning.

Before returning to her room to get her outdoor clothes she hurried to the kitchen and told the cook to pack some food into a basket, having decided she could not let a guest take off on an expedition that might mean a couple of hours or more before he could sit down to breakfast.

She was fastening the tiny buttons of her gloves in the hall when he darted back into the house for her, having hurried the sleepy groom into harnessing two horses into the shafts of one of the vehicles in the coach house.

"What have you there?" he asked, seeing her pick up a wicker basket with a double-hinged lid.

"A snack for you to eat on the way."

"That's most kind of you. Later, perhaps. Are you ready?"

He took the basket from her hand and hastened her outside. He had chosen the phaeton, which was built for speed, and when he had helped her into the seat he took his place beside her, whip and reins in his hands. Then they were off, bowling down the drive and out into the quiet, residential avenue, deserted except for a milkman with a handcart.

She gave him directions, explaining that they would go through the center of town where she would point out buildings of interest. He had not been able to see much of Penghyll in the darkness of the previous evening, but as they drove along at a spanking pace it was revealed to him as a busy, thriving market town, a deal more prosperous than it had been in his father's day. It was built of mellow stone with dark slate roofs and was as yet unsullied by the grime of industry that had blackened whole areas of Liverpool and other places that he had glimpsed from the train windows on his journey the previous day. Its streets were cob-

bled, some with pumps providing a public source
of water for the humbler dwellings, and there were a
number of quite grand-looking municipal buildings,
which Delia pointed out in turn as being the Town
Hall, the courthouse, and the corn exchange. When
they entered the market square they drove past the
whitewashed eighteenth century frontage of the Red
Lion Hotel in order that Delia could show him the
next house, which was her father's surgery, and directly opposite, on the far side of the square, adorned
with Doric columns and a tall flight of stone steps,
were the recently completed Assembly Rooms in
which, Delia told him, the auction of Halewood would
take place, some posters announcing the sale adorning
its walls.

In the square itself the market was already in full
swing, with stalls and awnings erected and people mill-
ing about. From wagons and carts garden produce
was being unloaded, as well as fowls in crates, pots,
pans, rag rugs, rush baskets, bales of cloth, and furniture, all of it being borne away and set in place for
the day's selling. The sticky-sweet aroma of gingerbread and brandysnaps mingled with the more pungent
odors of leather, raw meat, strong cheese, and new
clogs. He noticed that amidst all the bustle there
were plenty of signs of the abject poverty that existed
side by side with high wealth in this cotton-, coal-,
and ship-booming county in the northwest of England,
most of the people being poorly clothed, the women
bleakly attired with gray shawls over their heads, and
many of the ragged urchins running barefoot. The
more well-to-do shoppers and the discerning house-
wives had yet to appear, but affluence was there in
the presence of a number of businessmen and land-
owners in loud checked coats, money jingling in their
pockets, who were laughing and talking together as
they converged on the inns in the vicinity of the square
where drinking was already in progress and pints
were being pulled.

They left the square, passing down narrow streets lined by tall, small-windowed buildings and sounding with the rhythmic clacking of looms, and Aaron thought of the mill-girl whom his father had lusted after and his grandfather had seduced, bringing about a quarrel of such magnitude between the two of them that only by the merest chance had it stopped short of patricide. Indeed, when Edward Hart had been thrown bodily out of Halewood by servants at their master's orders it had not been known for certain whether Sir Harry would survive the violence received at his son's hands.

Delia's soft voice interrupted his train of thought. "Turn left when you come to the next corner."

They passed a church, a few mean terraces where women were scrubbing their doorsteps in a foam of suds, and then the street petered out into a lane. Soon Penghyll was behind them and grazing cattle and small farmsteads were spread out around them. When the countryside became more deserted the wind, sweeping down the clough between the rolling hills, beat into their faces, sharp and cold, and not far away a flock of hardy fell-sheep flowed through a broken gap in one of the low stone walls as though driven through it by the invisible buffeting that never ceased. Delia huddled closer into the traveling rug that covered her, not liking the feel of the weather, for she had caught the first faint rumble of thunder over the hills and the sky was pressing down.

"What a strange light," Aaron commented with curiosity, observing the odd, almost eerie glow caused by the storm clouds diffusing the daylight. It was like looking at the scenery through pale green bottleglass. In the distance lightning flickered and thunder rolled again.

They were approaching a crossroad. The road they were following led straight ahead, but to left and right there were narrow, water-logged lanes. Delia indicated which turning he should take and with mud splashing the wheels shot along in the wake of the horses, which he was keeping to a fast and steady speed. All the time he kept his eyes strained ahead to catch the first glimpse of the gates to the estate, which he knew to be less than a mile away. To a rapid thudding of hooves the last curve in the lane was taken and ahead he saw them, flanked by great, dragon-topped pillars, but they were closed against him. Impatiently he urged the horses to a swifter pace and they covered the remaining distance in record time.

He had forgotten the girl at his side. Yanking the horses to a slithering halt, he leapt out and almost hurled himself at the gates. Gripping the cold iron bars he looked through at his ancestral home for the first time, fixing his hungry gaze on the mansion topping the rise of the hill, its shape curiously clearcut against the dark, bruised sky.

It was as though the ink-sketch that his father had once made had taken on form and color, but the impact on his senses was beyond anything he could have imagined. Its magnificence stunned him. His longing to possess the house, to know himself master of it, was akin to frantic desire at the height of passion. A fiery adoration went out from him toward Halewood. Suddenly he could not bear that the gates were locked against him. He shook them in a fury of frustration and shouted toward the lodge on the other side.

"Open up! Open up!"

The lodge was occupied, a thread of smoke rising from the chimney, but although the curtains at the windows twitched nobody came to do his bidding. He roared his demand again, crashing a clenched fist against the gates and making them rattle.

"Damn you, lodgekeeper! Open up, I say! Bring your keys and let me in!"

When no response was forthcoming he took a few steps back and stared wildly upward and about at the gates and spike-topped walls to see if they were climbable, but they had been constructed to keep out intruders and there was no easy way to overcome the formidable barrier presented.

A touch on his sleeve made him turn sharply. Delia had alighted from the phaeton and her face within the frame of her bonnet-brim was strained and tight, her cheeks hollow.

"It's useless, Aaron. You won't be let in. Even if I asked—and the lodgekeeper knows me well—Lady Hart's orders can't be flouted."

He was trembling in every limb and he almost cast her hand from him, but there was something in the look she was giving him, eyes luminous with unshed tears, and in the whole drawn-bow tautness of her slim figure, that he found peculiarly touching, impossible to reject.

"Why should they not!" he demanded fiercely. "I have every right to be admitted!"

"It doesn't matter who you are or why you're here," she insisted tensely. "Apart from myself Lady Hart receives few people other than my father, her priest, and her lawyer. Strangers are never welcome at Halewood and never were in Sir Harry's time either. He was suspicious of everyone, but that is not in Lady Hart's nature. I believe she cut herself off from her past life when she married Sir Harry and wants never to meet anyone from it again, whether by chance or design. At the present time when hosts of idle sightseers are wanting to get into the grounds of Halewood on the pretext of wishing to purchase the place she is being even stricter about who is to be admitted, and nobody—not even you—can gain admittance except when expected at an appointed hour. If you stay on this spot all day you'll never get the gates opened up for you."

His brows had drawn into a frown, but he gave a reluctant nod. "I'm letting my eagerness run away with me," he conceded. But although she had succeeded in cooling his temper somewhat, his anger at the injustice of the situation did not abate. Reaching out, he put an arm about her narrow shoulders and jerked her with him in one swift movement to the gates, so that they both stood pressed against them and the angle at which he was holding her forced her to look toward Halewood.

"That's the house where I should have been born, Delia!" his voice grated harshly. "That's where I'm going to live for the rest of my life and where I intend to die—and my children after me!"

She made a faint sound that was a dry sob in her throat. His arm tightened about her and he half-lifted her off her feet, feeling the need to put some seal on the vow he had made, and crushing her between the gates and his own hard body he bent his tall head swiftly and took her defenseless mouth with his in a kiss of such ferocity that it sought the very heart of her.

He released her more gently than when he had snatched her to him, lowering her back on her feet but continuing to support her. She stared at him dumbly. Overhead a curlew cried, winging its way across the morning sky. There was a drowning warmth in his gaze fixed on her and slowly he brought up his hand to touch her face with his fingertips, almost in tender reassurance, as if he believed her to be afraid of him. She could have been a tiny, injured bird, stunned with fright. She heard herself speak, her voice oddly tremulous.

"Come away from the gates now. Please."

He obeyed after one last sharp and resolute look toward the house over his shoulder, taking her by the elbow at the same time and leading her back to the carriage. While he had not spoken on the last lap of the way to Halewood, he talked volubly as he drove back, his mood completely changed, his exultation in the house taking over. He told her what he knew of the different rooms there and how he had had all his own books indexed and crated before leaving Boston in readiness for when they would fill some of the emptied shelves in the great library.

"Halewood will be in a barren state when the present owner has departed and all the contents gone. I'll go to the London saleroom and buy whatever I can afford of them there, which will insure that some of the house's own furnishings don't fall into other hands." He gave a quiet, good-humored laugh. "At least they'll help to stop my rattling about in forty empty rooms like a solitary pea in a pod."

"Don't you mind that the best of everything will be going from Halewood?" Delia asked, speaking for the first time since they had left the gates behind them.

He shot a look at her, his eyes glinting behind their lashes. "I mind! Make no mistake about that! I mind that portraits and furniture, porcelain and sculpture, tapestries and family silver were left to a woman who considers them only in the light of their monetary value! But I have the house!" He seemed to forget that the business of the sale had yet to be gone through. "Halewood itself is mine. That's all that really matters."

"Shall you close up a wing or two for the time being?"

"I guess I'll have to. Fortunately I should be able to furnish all the rooms I'll need for my immediate use with the furniture and goods I had shipped over with me, which are being stored in a Liverpool warehouse until such time as I'm ready to have them removed. Most of the furniture is French—family pieces from my mother's side that I didn't care to sell."

They had reached the crossroad, but instead of turning left onto the road that would take them into town he drove straight across, making for the lane on the other side, which took a rambling route through wilder moorland and over a hill.

"You're going the wrong way!" she exclaimed.

"I know, but I thought we'd stop somewhere out in

48

this beautiful countryside and eat that picnic you brought along."

"There's going to be a storm!" she protested faintly. The purple clouds were pressing down on all the hilltops and there was a faint rumbling that seemed to come from all around them.

He waved her argument aside with a curling flick of his whip. "The rain's holding off. We'll find some trees to give us shelter if it should start before we've finished the picnic." Jubilantly he tilted his face into the bitter wind. "This is true Halewood weather! My father mentioned often enough the damp, icy atmosphere of the bedrooms and the drafts that sweep permanently down the corridors."

She looked at him wonderingly. "Is nothing able to put you off the house?"

Unexpectedly he grinned at her. "Nothing! Enough fuel will banish the cold, and drafts can be stopped up. I intend to bring the house up to a high degree of comfort that's probably unknown in these parts."

"It's a very old house. It could prove more difficult to make it comfortable than you anticipate."

"You have reservations about Halewood, haven't you, Delia?"

The directness of the question caught her off guard. She glanced at him and away again, recovering herself. "The name of the hill on whch it stands is chilling enough," she said evasively. "It is known locally as the Howling Hill."

"So I learned from my father. But how could such a hill be called anything else? The howling of the wind never leaves the house in winter and at other times of the year the sighing never leaves the chimneys. It was probably one of my distant ancestors who named it the Howling Hill."

"There are other theories," she replied, looking ahead at the winding road.

"What are they?"

"This district was notorious for its witches in days

49

gone by. Some say a witch put a spell on the hill to prevent it from ever knowing the gentleness of summer again. That's why the house suffers."

"That I don't believe." There was amusement in his tone.

She did not say whether or not she shared his opinion. She was simply stating the facts. "My father has done a lot of research into the history of this district. It's his hobby. He holds to the theory that a dwelling-place on the same site in centuries gone by was known by a Norse name that meant a wolves' den. Hence it was a short step to the hill's present name."

"I remember hearing something about that. It's as good an explanation as any in my opinion." He pulled on the reins, bringing the horses to a halt, for he had spotted a copse of rowan trees forming a natural windbreak. "We'll have our picnic over there."

He carried the basket and the tartan traveling-rug from the phaeton, walking with her across to the trees. Gorse grew thick on all sides and the heather went down with a rustle under their feet and sprang up again behind them. Everything was astir in the wind, all foliage restless, the berry-laden branches genuflecting dementedly before the ceaseless buffeting. Resilient cobwebs, wet with dew and strung like swaying gossamer sails between the stouter blades of grass, collapsed before them, small scraps clinging to the light gray checked cloth of his trousers and to her deep blue skirtfolds. She glanced skyward, wondering how long it would be before the storm broke. The light was fast fading as if the day were dying almost before it had been born, the weird, greenish glow having surrendered to an oppressive gloom which steeped the undulating landscape in darkening shades.

A felled tree-trunk made a seat for them and he spread the rug over it for her. She lifted the lid of the basket and took out a folded, starched white napkin, which contained some slices of cold partridge, chicken, ham, and tongue. In another were oatcakes and some newly baked rolls which had been delivered from the bakery at the first light of day, and a container of tea that had been wrapped around with a special piece of flannel for insulation and was still warm.

She did not feel hungry, but he settled down to enjoy the food, the fresh air and the outing having stimulated his appetite. He sat with his elbows on his knees, taking hearty bites from the pieces of meat, which he held between the fingers of both hands. His high-crowned, round-topped hat was tilted slightly forward over his eyes as he let his gaze wander over the wide stretches of heather and the hump-backed slopes of the surrounding landscape, an expression of vast contentment on his face.

"What else do you know about the Vikings who came to Halewood?" he inquired with interest, reaching down to pick up the cup that was lodged conveniently on a jutting slab of limestone and taking a sip of the lukewarm tea.

"Only that they must have arrived with their fellow Norsemen in the dragon-headed longboats that invaded the estuaries, coming first to plunder and then to settle. The Norwegian Vikings penetrated inland along the rivers, and those who took over land in these parts probably came part of the way up the Ribble. The warriors and sea-rovers became farmers and landsmen—and the names they gave their settlements are with us today. Anything with *wick* is a derivation of *vik,* which means an inlet in Norwegian, such as Salwick and Urswick, and there are countless other examples. We call our hills the *fells* because the old Norsemen called them *fjells.* My father can list hundreds of place-names that are Norse in origin. That's how he knows the summit of Howling Hill boasted one of them."

Aaron stood up and stepped briskly away from the copse to stand amid the waving grass, looking toward Halewood, which he could see clearly on the prominent hilltop, his hands set low on his hips, coattails whipping in the wind.

"Now I know why there are stone dragons on the gate pillars! They're links with those longships. It could be that my forebear who set them up for all to see was as proud as I am of Halewood's past glories!"

A great crack of thunder followed hard on a blue flash of lightning that greeted his words, and the first heavy drops of rain began to fall. Delia sprang up and scrabbled at the picnic things, snatching them up to thrust them into the basket. He made no move to help her, apparently oblivious to the rain, his expression rapt, enchanted, set toward the house as though he were gazing at a woman he loved.

She paused in what she was doing, straightening up to stare at him, a linen napkin trailing from her hand, and a chilling sensation akin to foreboding wrenched through her as violently as if she had been pierced by one of the shafts of lightning darting across the sky. On his own admission he did not look for happiness at Halewood. He was prepared for the shadows that lurked there. But would he know how to defend himself from the strife and hate and bitterness that had accumulated there over the centuries? The curse of Halewood! One title was as good as another for the tricks that fate played, but none could deny the evil that haunted the great house. She herself had not been left unmarked by her contact with it, but, as a loving parent forgives a child that strikes out in the throes of a tantrum, she bore it no malice. But how would he fare? Alone?

A helpless fury surged up in her, the reason for it completely escaping her at this moment of tempestuous stress. She was angry with him, with Halewood, and mostly with herself.

She hurled aside the napkin and dashed across to him. Seizing him by the arm, she jerked him around to face her, catching him off guard. His eyes expanded in baffled astonishment at the rage and anguish tearing at her face.

"Glories! What glories?" she exclaimed tormentedly, echoing his words. "Brothers have fought and killed each other for possession of Halewood! Women have been wed into the family against their will for the riches they could bring to that handsome house! It has split asunder father and son! You talked to me of the Halewood curse! There *is* a curse on it! Some awful, indefinable curse that hits out without warning! No one is safe from it. Least of all you—unless you discover how to free that poor, suffering house from it and set a new future for yourself and your children after you!"

He grabbed her by the arms and held her hard, thrusting his face toward hers. "What's behind all this? What haven't you told me?"

The rain was lashing them, running down their faces, making strands of their hair stick wetly to forehead and cheek, the curled brim of his hat collecting the drips that ran in rivulets from the crown and becoming awash like a roof-gutter. When she did not answer him at once, biting deep into her lower lip, he shook her in his impatience, determined to have the truth out of her.

She reacted instantly, tearing herself away from him with elbows awhirl. Again the thunder rumbled deafeningly and the horses whinnied in fright, jerking their heads violently. Having withdrawn a couple of paces from him, she stood with her arms against her sides and her hands pressed flat against her skirt, her attitude defiant and defensive.

"Something happened to me eighteen months ago at Halewood! This!"

With a single movement she hoisted aside her stiffened petticoats and extended her left foot in a froth of lace. Then he saw why she limped. Her leg above the ankle was cruelly scarred. There was no mistaking the cause of such lacerations.

"You were caught in a trap?" he exclaimed on a note of appalled disbelief.

"Correct!" She threw down her skirt-hems, which fell swishing into place. "Sir Harry had man-traps all over the grounds to keep out poachers and other intruders! A clever surgeon saved my leg, but it was a long time before I learned to walk again!" She cupped her elbows in her hands, flinging herself into a half-turn from him, chin jutting. "I only tell you this to warn you to be on your guard at Halewood. Anything can happen here."

"No," he stated stonily. "There's more to it than that. You haven't told me everything."

She shot him an angry glance. "What do you mean?"

"What were you doing in the grounds of Halewood in the first place?"

"Trespassing! That was Sir Harry's judgment!" She gave a jerky, intensely unhappy laugh, and without another word she bolted past him, making for the phaeton, but she did not get back into the vehicle. Instead she went to the horses and spoke soothingly to them as they flared their nostrils and tossed their heads in alarm at another clap of thunder.

Aaron watched her. He did not know if it was rain or tears on her face. When she moved to pat the rivulet-streaked neck of the horse nearest to her he saw that her eyes were closed tightly as though she were struggling to regain control of herself. He turned and went back to the copse, rescuing the linen napkin from a bush before packing all that was left of the picnic into the basket. Swinging it in his hand, he walked across to the phaeton where she had taken her seat. In silence he stashed the basket aboard, climbed in, and took up reins and whip. At his signal the horses plunged forward, eager to get home to a dry stable.

"How did the accident occur?" he questioned. It was as though there had been no break in their conversation, except that she was calmer now, with a dignified air of resignation.

"Through unlucky chance. Up to that time I used to go riding a lot out from Penghyll into the surrounding district. As much as the riding itself I loved feeling at one with the open air and the countryside. Sometimes Matthew or a friend or two came with me, but usually I was alone. I liked best to ride across the moorland not far from the boundaries of Halewood. There's always much to see when one comes along quietly without talking. Gambolling hares. A pheasant strutting. Leverets chasing around in circles. And so many birds —my father taught me to name most of them, from a dipper's bib to a kingfisher, when I was still a child. I went riding in all seasons, when there was heather as far as the eye could see or snow on the ground. The only days I had to watch out for were those when the weather threatened to be really treacherous, but a light rain never stopped me, although it's probably the reason why I rode alone more often than not. I was on my own the day it—happened."

She paused. The drops were thudding relentlessly on the carriage hood above their heads and although they were no longer exposed to the torrential downpour he noticed in a glance that she looked pinched and colder than she had previously; whether it was due to her soaked condition or what she was about to tell him he could not be sure. He thought the latter.

"On this particular day there was some low-lying mist when I set out," she went on, "but there often is in these parts and I thought nothing of it. Later, however, it thickened without warning when I was far from home, closing down as swiftly as if a gray blanket had been flung over everything. Then my horse stumbled, almost threw me, and went lame. Visibility was no more than a few yards, but I reached the lane and it was only a short distance to Halewood. I knew well enough that visitors were never welcome there, but I thought that under the circumstances, and considering I was daughter to Sir Harry's physician, I could expect help to be forthcoming and a carriage and a groom provided to drive me home. The gates were open when they finally loomed up before me, and I remember glancing up at those stone dragons with their curling tongues on the pillars and thinking that was how the figureheads of the Viking ships must have looked coming in to the coast with the sea-mist swirling about them. I led the horse through the gates, but I hadn't gone more than a hundred yards when the mist became so dense that I could only tell I was still on the drive by the uphill slope of it and the gravel under foot. When the ground leveled out again I knew I couldn't be far from the house, but then for no apparent reason my horse took fright and was impossible to control. I tried to hang onto his bridle, but he swung away and I lost my grip and fell to my knees while he was swallowed up in seconds by the mist. I discovered I was kneeling on grass!"

"You'd gone under the archway without seeing it and entered the inner courtyard," he explained. "I know it's made up of green sward surrounded by a flagged drive."

"That's exactly what had happened," she said. "Even if I hadn't been struggling with the horse I wouldn't have noticed the archway, because of the mist, but I remembered how the hooves had clacked noisily and guessed it had been on flagstones. It was then that the nightmare began." She clutched a fold of the rug over her knees. "I got to my feet and decided to walk with hands outstretched until I stepped on the flagstones again and reached a wall. I intended to feel my way along to a door or a window and knock to try to get attention from a servant. If the worst came to the worst I was prepared to open a window and climb in. But I'd lost all sense of direction and I suppose I walked in circles in the grass—and suddenly I knew I was no longer alone."

"What do you mean?"

"There was—something else with me in the mist. A—a presence that I couldn't see. A powerful, dreadful presence that was all around me, near enough to be almost tangible. I snatched back my hands, terrified that I might touch whatever it was that pressed in on me. The atmosphere had become icy cold. Demands were being made on me that I couldn't understand. A yearning that was angry and frantic and terrifying was getting through to me. That's when I gave way to panic. I ran—blindly. I could have gone crashing into a wall of the house or into any other obstacle, but I had no thought in my head but to get away from—whatever it was there in the heart of Halewood. By some miracle I must have passed back under the archway and I ran on and on in that blanket of fog, conscious of going downhill and knowing it meant Halewood was rising away behind me. When I was almost out of breath, trees began to loom up on all sides and I knew I had stumbled into woodland within the grounds. I was slowing down, my breath rasping in the silence, when a sudden, awful clash of iron jaws threw me into excruciating pain and I fell headlong, my leg caught in that fiendish trap! Whether I fainted with shock or hit my head I don't know, but I didn't recover consciousness until long after a gamekeeper had found me and I'd been carried into Halewood. Lady Hart nursed me herself until I was able to walk again. It was she who paid the fees for a surgeon expert in such matters to attend me—not Sir Harry."

His expression was grim. "Halewood has much to answer for. It shall make amends."

She showed surprise. "I didn't expect you to say that."

He frowned. "I'm not sure I understand you."

"I was certain you'd suggest that the mist had played tricks with my imagination—or that I lost my head foolishly and it was really all my own fault. Things I've told myself many times."

"That's what you expected, is it?" He shook his head. "My father fed me with tales of things said to have been heard and seen at Halewood. A house so old must bear heavily the conflicts of the past. The very walls are surely permeated with all the living and dying that has taken place within them—and you yourself reminded me that it has known violent times. Who's to say you didn't brush against a manifestation of some ancient, long-forgotten tragedy that came seeping out to you?"

She considered what he had said and waited until he had overtaken a lumbering horse and wagon before she spoke again.

"There's something else."

"Yes?"

"I've always been convinced that my running into the trap wasn't by chance." She made a quick, emphatic little gesture. "I don't mean that spectral hands dragged it in my path or anything foolish like that. I'm simply convinced that the house didn't intend that I should leave it that day."

"I don't disbelieve that at all," he said.

She was grateful for his patient listening, his matter-of-fact acceptance of all she had confided to him. "I've never told anyone else about that eerie experience—or my feelings about it," she admitted. "Everybody thinks I simply lost my way in the grounds. You're the only one to share my secret."

"Not even Matthew knows?"

"Not even Matthew," she repeated.

"Why have you kept it to yourself,"

"I wanted to forget it. Never to have anyone remind me of it. Instead it has haunted me ever since and I never enter Halewood without feeling that the request demanded of me—whatever it was—has yet to be fulfilled. So you see, instead of putting that experience behind me I've stayed linked to it—a kind of prisoner through my own silence."

"Not any more."

"What do you mean?"

"You're released. You've told me about it."

"So I have." She gave a faint half-smile. "I wish I could say I feel liberated and free, but I can't. Instead I've involved you."

"I welcome that." He turned his head and their eyes met, binding her to him in a look that brought her to the edge of a precipice. She knew with every nerve and fiber in her body that he was about to say something tender and endearing that would drive a wedge between her and Matthew for ever. "Delia—"

She made a little fluttering movement with her hands as if she would have clapped both of them across his mouth to hold back his words. But in the same instant the sky cracked with such violence that the whole atmosphere seemed to shudder, and this time the horses in blind, eye-rolling terror bolted, the phaeton careening after them. Delia clung on with all her strength, gasping as each jolt made the vehicle totter anew, and it took every bit of Aaron's exceptional skill to wheel the horses on to the soggy moorland where eventually they slowed their frantic pace and came to a halt, steam rising from them. She relaxed back in the seat, quite breathless.

"No harm done," Aaron said with a laugh, exhilarated by his mastery of the reins, and he turned the horses homeward.

Delia put her hand across her racing heart. The moment of danger, greater than the possibility of being thrown from the phaeton, was—for the moment— past. But she had another fear to add to it, which sprang from her own turbulent emotions. She understood the reason why she had given way to anger. It had come from the frustration of denying a wildness of love and desire that had filled her heart and possessed her trembling body even more powerfully than before. If only he had not kissed her at the gates!

He had unleashed from the deepest fount of her being a sweet and passionate madness that must be crushed down without question or consideration. But how—oh, how?—to do it!

4

AARON set off for Halewood on Monday morning. His appointment was for eleven o'clock, and as far as Delia knew and was able to tell him, nobody else would be viewing the house that day. With a sense of occasion he had decided to be driven in style, and he sat back in the elegant hired carriage with his gloved hands folded together over the gold top of his cane, which he held propped at an angle. He had dressed with care in a double-breasted frock coat and trousers of gray broadcloth, his fold-over cravat fastened with a pearl-headed pin, his tall silk hat at a debonair angle.

He had the intense satisfaction of seeing the gates of Halewood being opened for him when his carriage drew near. He was not to be kept waiting like a pauper at the gates this time! Remembering what Delia had said he looked at the approaching dragons on the gate pillars and it seemed to him those gaping, fork-tongued mouths were set in a grin of welcome. He smiled to himself at his flight of fancy and then forgot it as the carriage swept through the gates and far on the rise of the hill Halewood awaited him, its Elizabethan splendor glorious in the pale morning sun.

Taking notice of the grounds slipping past beyond the beech trees, which stood sentinel-like on either side of the drive, he caught the silvery gleam of a lake and spreads of lush woodland. Nearer the house terraced gardens rose to meet the open balustrade that bordered the forecourt, the parapet embellished with stone dragons similar to those at the gates, some moss-stained, others half choked by ivy. But oh! the house! The mullioned windows winked at him in golden colors that became lost in shades of violet, olive, and sapphire when the carriage took a wide sweep and passed under the richly ornamented archway into the courtyard, where it followed the inner flagged drive that bordered the sward and came to a halt with timed perfection. Aaron found himself exactly level with the entrance, which was a superbly carved porch that ran clear through two stories. The groom, leaping down from the back of the carriage, opened the door for him with a flourish, lowering the step at the same time. In the same instant the great main door of Halewood itself was flung wide for him by a footman.

Aaron alighted without haste and stood observing his surroundings while he savored every moment of his homecoming. It was in this courtyard that Delia became frightened in the mist, but he had no time to think of that now, his gaze dwelling appreciatively on all he saw. He felt at one with it, as if his own life's blood flowed within the arteries of its walls. Now he knew that all else he had ever known was alien to him; here on this isolated hilltop in a bleak corner of England his roots were snaking down to mingle with those that had been lying there for a thousand years.

"Good-day, Mr. Hart. How do you do. My name is Marsden—I'm agent to Lady Hart and in charge of all matters concerning the sale."

Aaron turned to face the man who had emerged from the house and saw he was dapper in appearance, hair slicked down from a center parting, coattails swinging.

"Good-day," Aaron replied. "I understand that I'm to view at leisure and that no one else is coming today."

"That is correct, sir. Should you wish me to accompany you I will gladly do so, but her ladyship thought you might prefer to go around on your own."

"That's most considerate of her."

"She wishes you to wander freely. Only her own apartments are sacrosanct."

Aaron's face tightened at the snub. So the woman would not see him! It was a deliberate forestalling of any wish he might have expressed to pay her his compliments in person. Was it possible that it troubled her that she, who had lived a mere handful of years at Halewood, should be offering his rightful inheritance in the open market to all comers? In spite of Delia's praises of her, he thought not. Delia in her innocence had mistaken an idle woman's whim to play nurse to her as evidence of a bountiful nature, but he held a different opinion of Berenice Hart. To have married his old rake of a grandfather was enough evidence to show she was avaricious and without principles. No woman of gentle breeding could have given herself to Sir Harry, whose first wife—his own unfortunate grandmother—had been married for her fortune and driven to an early grave through the misery and humiliation she had suffered through her husband's countless cruelties and infidelities.

The agent was waiting for him to enter the house, but Aaron was determined not to be hurried. He let his gaze sweep over the inner courtyard and its enclosing walls once more before making a move to mount the steps. Then his sharp eye caught a shimmer of movement in an upper window in the west wing as someone drew back quickly out of sight. Ah! Berenice Hart wanted to see what he was like, but he was not to be permitted to look upon her!

Passing through the porch he was uncomfortably aware of the intense chill given off by the stonework of it, and when he entered the hall the almost icy air seemed to hang about him still, in spite of the warmth given off by a fire of logs burning in the wide fireplace.

63

Then behind him the entrance door slammed shut with an echoing thunder, causing the smoke to billow forth. He half-turned, startled that Marsden should have used the door so violently, but the agent was at his side and a footman was standing by it, one white-gloved hand outstretched as if he had been about to close it in the normal way. Seeing that he was being observed, the footman gave an embarrassed shrug.

"Beg pardon, gentlemen," he stated uncomfortably. "'T' draft caught it."

Marsden uttered some pernickety reproof, but Aaron turned his back on both of them, strolling forward to stand with feet apart and survey with a hard and challenging eye the magnificence of the vast hall with its grand staircase, its walls bedecked with fine tapestries and displays of ancient arms, the pikes arranged in enormous fans, the muskets slotted at a level, and the swords crossed. In that first moment of startlement he had forgotten the old tale told him many times by his father that when the huge main door slammed by itself the dreadful curse was about to take a new twist, but now he recalled it vividly. So Halewood knew he had come home to it! He welcomed its awareness of him, but—by God!—he would show it who was master! Had he been alone he would have shouted his resolution aloud in a voice that would have echoed among the rafters and in every corner. But the house knew anyway, he was sure of that. It understood that here was the one Hart who would love it more than all the rest that had borne the family name, but who would not be crushed, no matter what dire misfortunes it released in his path.

"Mr. Hart. Er—Mr. Hart."

Aaron realized that the agent had been addressing him. "Yes? I'm afraid my thoughts were concentrated on the house."

"That's not to be wondered at. The hall is quite splendid, is it not?" Marsden held out a sale pamphlet opened at a printed plan of the house, which he had picked up from one of several stacks of them ranged on a side table. "This will enable you to find your way about. Luncheon will be served for you in the dining hall at one o'clock. When you have seen all you wish of the house you may want to inspect the stables and the coach houses and the grounds. A steward will be waiting to show you around and answer any queries that might arise. If time runs out he will either ride with you tomorrow—or arrange for a carriage if you prefer it—to take you to look over the rest of the land and the tenanted property that make up the estate of Halewood. Is there anything you would like to ask me now?"

"Yes, there is one point. I was informed that everything in the house is to be sold in London. I would be willing to make an offer for anything I see today that I feel should not be removed from Halewood."

The agent's face remained bland. "I have been instructed by her ladyship to reject any such offers."

Aaron clenched the pamphlet in his hand until it crackled, but he set his jaw and gave a curt nod, not trusting himself to speak. All that had been collected and treasured by his family throughout the centuries was to become nothing more than a job lot in a saleroom, no matter how grand a reputation the saleroom enjoyed, no matter how distinguished the buyers who gathered there.

"Is there anything else, sir?"

Fiercely irritated by the agent's obsequiousness, smarting under the injustice of the situation, Aaron answered on a staccato note. "No. I'll start with the library."

"Yes, sir. This way, if you please."

The agent went in front of him to show him through. Then he was alone in the great library, which was a full hundred feet in length with a spiral staircase on either side rising to meet the railed gallery that gave access to the books on the upper shelves, which reached to the ceiling. His feet made no sound on the Aubusson carpet, and although brass-grilled glass doors protected the hundreds of volumes, all had been unlocked to enable him to pick out at random any book that caught this interest, a privilege he knew would not be extended to outsiders viewing the house after him.

He began looking for the three volumes of the history of Halewood, which he knew should be housed there; when he failed to find the category that would have included them he glanced upward, wondering if he would find them on the top shelves, and mounted one of the spiral staircases. He strolled right along the gallery and had encircled the end of the library, returning on the opposite side, when he sighted them. Three huge volumes, numbered I, II, and III. *The History of Halewood*. Eagerly he opened the grilled door and took out the first volume, leaning back with it against the protective railings of the gallery, but even as he opened it the mahogany top rail began to sway, giving him the sickening sensation of being about to plunge backward into space. Instinctively he threw himself forward against the bookshelves and, being already off balance, fell to one knee. To his horror he saw the railings against which he had leaned disappear over the gallery's edge, dragging with them the neighboring struts, which were tilting crazily, in their turn to go plummeting down, setting off a chain reaction that resulted in a thumping and thudding and crashing on the tabletops and chairs and the floor many feet below. When the final boom of the last falling strut faded to silence, a long gap in the railings left several yards of the gallery completely unguarded.

The doors of the library burst open. Two footmen entered at a run, black coattails flying, and in their wake came a wide-eyed parlormaid with Marsden following behind. They stared aghast at the damage, their gaze traveling up to him and down again. The agent spoke first.

"Are you all right, Mr. Hart?"

"Yes." Aaron stood up, the book he had been holding still in his hand; he tucked it under his arm. "As you can see, the railings gave way."

"You could have been killed!"

The parlormaid gave a little moan and clapped her hand over her mouth in alarm when she saw Aaron move to the unguarded edge of the gallery and crouch down to examine the place where the struts had been torn away. He frowned, able to find no trace of crumbling wood or worm; nothing but an ancient, time-darkened crack that should never have given way, especially since he had not even lodged his full weight against it. Compressing his lips thoughtfully, he moved on to examine the length of the remaining railings and found many other such hair-fine cracks in the woodwork, but although he shook the top rail vigorously each strut remained solid as a rock.

"Hadn't you better come down, sir?" The agent hovered anxiously at the foot of the nearest spiral staircase, too nervous to mount it. "The whole gallery could be unsafe."

"I think not," Aaron replied, unaware that he spoke in a voice of authority, as though Halewood were already his. "Let the servants clear up the mess. There's no danger."

"Aren't you coming down?"

Aaron indicated the book he held. "Not yet. I have a little reading to do first." Deliberately he opened it as he had done before. Let Halewood learn that he was not to be intimidated! Let it know that he meant what he had said!

He could have spent all day in the library with those three volumes alone, but for the present time he could do no more than leaf through them, absorbing new scraps of information here and there, recognizing facts that he had learned from his father in early days. Halewood Hall had been built by a certain Raoul Hart on land already belonging to the family, funds for the grand edifice having been forthcoming from the royal purse of Queen Elizabeth, who rewarded generously all those who served her well. A hand-blocked print of the original plan for the house also showed the date on it, which had been written in the architect's own hand: *Halewoode whereof ye first stone was layd 1569.* Nineteen years later had come the destruction of the Spanish Armada, when Raoul Hart had sailed with Drake and met his end with an enemy musket-ball through the throat.

After returning the volumes to the shelf, Aaron descended from the gallery. He passed the servants brushing and sweeping and carrying out debris, and went on through another pair of double doors into a small drawing room which had been converted into a billiard room, and from there he strolled on into other finely proportioned rooms where almost all the ceilings were of wood with intricately carved bosses. He was studying a portrait of Queen Elizabeth hung in acknowledgment of her munificence by Raoul Hart when a footman came to lead him to the dining hall where luncheon awaited him.

Under a canopy of stone vaulting he took his place in a high-backed chair at a long table that would have seated forty in comfort. The food served to him was excellent and the wines superb, but it was a lonely meal. He wished Delia were with him. He had been on the point of asking her to accompany him at breakfast, but—almost as if she had divined his thought—she had mentioned that she had an appointment at the dressmaker's and would her father drop her off there in his brougham when he set off on his rounds.

"Didn't you tell me last time that your dress for the Penghyll Ball was finished?" Dr. Gilmore had remarked mildly.

"So it is," she had replied, "and it's hanging upstairs ready to wear. Today I'm to have the second fitting of my wedding gown. There may have to be another. It must be quite perfect. Everything about my wedding must be quite perfect."

She had made her declaration a trifle too vehemently. There had been an undercurrent of defiance in her voice directed toward—no, not her father—himself. He had watched her steadily, and although she kept her attention on the plate before her she had shown she was aware of his gaze by the way her color came and went.

He had wanted to speak his mind to her. Wanted to say that she might as well drop the farce of so much wedding talk because she knew and he knew that she would not be able to go through with it. It was sheer pretense on her part to make out that she was prepared to go to the altar to marry another man.

He loved her and he meant to have her. He didn't know exactly when he had fallen in love with her, but he believed it was when he had turned from the hackney cab at his arrival and had seen her standing in the doorway. He had been conscious of a curious fusion of spirits, as though something within him had gone out to her, and when she had drawn back into the lamplight and he had looked fully on her lovely face for the first time, he had known it was not only for Halewood that he had come to England. Everything about her enchanted him. The way her face glowed when she laughed, her chin tilted upward, both eyes closed in merriment. And those contented, fully absorbed looks that held her face in tranquil repose when she was reading something that interested her or was engaged in some small domestic task, such as the arranging of flowers, which gave her particular pleasure. In anger? Ah, he had seen her wrathful and in despair on the day of the storm, and he knew that in passion she would blaze like a beacon under his touch, fiery in desire, tender in love.

But since that stormy day she was assiduously careful never to be alone with him. This in itself was an acknowledgment of awareness, although perhaps she did not realize it. By her own admission she believed

Halewood had laid claim to her, and through belonging to Halewood she belonged to him. That, apart from anything else, sealed her fate.

Sitting there in the dining hall he was not quite sure when he became aware of being watched, but gradually he sensed something more than the impersonal gaze of the footmen who were waiting on him. Raising his head, he looked toward the row of arched apertures high in the far wall and there, staring down at him with a look of sullen hatred in his eyes, was a boy aged about eight years, a handsome child with chestnut curly hair, thick brows, and a stubborn mouth. Even as Aaron lowered the piece of pear he had been about to eat, taken aback by the extraordinary ferocity of that youthful glare, the boy darted back from the aperture and vanished. Somewhere in the distance a door closed after him with a bang.

It was an incident of no importance, but he had never seen such enmity on a child's face before and found it impossible to dismiss the affair without some thought. No doubt the boy was one of the gardeners' children who had slipped in to take a look at a prospective buyer of the property which provided one parent—and probably both—with a livelihood, and their talk of the uncertainty of their future had aroused fear and dislike in the child. It was the only possible explanation.

He finished his pear, put down his starched linen napkin, and rose from the table. Refusing coffee, he left the dining hall and continued his inspection of the house.

In his late grandfather's bedroom he stood by the enormous four-poster bed where the Hart brides had been bedded, their children born, and the heads of the house—at least, those who had not died elsewhere by violence or treachery—had drawn their last breaths. Turning on his heel he went across to the window and released a long sigh of satisfaction at the view. This would be his room. In this room he would make Delia his own.

There was a door half hidden by a draped curtain leading off the room. He knew that it let to Berenice's apartments. When she left the house and the rooms were stripped bare, he would leave them as they were until Delia had time to chose her own decor, select her own furniture, and stamp her own delightful personality on that traditionally feminine sector of the house.

Leaving the bedroom, he wandered on until he came to the portrait gallery, where he strolled from painting to painting, halting before each one to study the visages of his ancestors looking down on him. The men were hard-eyed, hard-mouthed, who had fought bloody battles down through the centuries, sometimes in the service of the royal throne and sometimes against it, and always with each other. As Delia had said, brother against brother, father against son, uncle against nephew, but never before—until his own grandfather had struck the name of the rightful heir from his will—had a Hart failed to inherit Halewood. Aaron looked long on the face of Sir Harry, which had been painted when he had been no more than thirty, but debauchery had aged the arrogant features even then and gluttony had swollen the bulge of the waistcoat buttons.

An empty space showed where the portrait of Edward Hart had hung. Well, it was no matter. There was one in the boxes being stored at Liverpool which had been painted by an American artist of no mean repute, and it should take its rightful place in the gallery even though the rest of the portraits would have been taken off to a saleroom. Aaron's jaw tightened. He'd start his own dynasty. In time to come his children and his children's children would look down from these walls at their descendants.

He had reached the end of the gallery and turned to study the portraits of the Hart women which lined the wall on the opposite side of their menfolk. Again

Delia's words came back to him and he was forced to admit that those faces, framed in caps and curls and standing ruffs, lacked gaiety or spirit. There was one exception, a defiant-looking woman with a mocking glint in her eye. This was Alice Hart. He knew what had happened to her. She had been burned as a witch shortly before the famous trial of other Lancashire witches in 1612 when another gentlewoman with the same Christian name had also been condemned to death, the law against witchcraft taking no account of a woman's station in life.

Wandering on from the gallery, he came to a place of embrasured windows that looked out onto a flat section of roof which was flagged and set with wrought iron seats. Then he saw her. Berenice! She must have been taking a stroll on the terrace, for she was coming from the far end, making her way back toward the house, her face veiled from his direct gaze by the filmy lace mantilla she wore draped over her head against the chilly outdoor air, the day having long since clouded over. But the breeze was strong as it blew across the terrace and suddenly the mantilla was lifted, wafting down onto her shoulders. As she sought to retrieve it she saw him through the panes of the mullioned window and her eyes met his.

He had been surprised to see how tall she was, not reaching his height, but tall nevertheless. Although older than he was by a number of years, she was still an incredibly beautiful woman, and even as he stared at her she drew the lace back to shield her face. Making a conventional pretense of not having seen him, she went out of his sight through a recessed door that let into another part of the wing.

It had happened in a matter of seconds, but he had seen enough to both partly confirm and partly disprove his original conception of her. As he had expected, she was unmistakably a woman of the world, but she had none of the hardness and greed stamped on her features that were the hallmark of such females. Instead she had retained a glacial hauteur as if her true self were locked away within her, safe from all sordidness, no matter how much she might have been physically abused. Therein lay her mystery, her eternal allure with its promise held out of passionate depths lying secret and undiscovered and unconquered. In all, she possessed a sexual magnetism that must have been hers since she first grew to young womanhood, with all the misfortunes attendant to the path in life she had followed through choice or force of circumstances.

His curiosity was keenly aroused. Such a woman could not be dismissed lightly from one's thoughts for there had been in her every movement, in her very walk, an age-old invitation to pursue, even though it had not been intentional, as she was keeping herself and her door barred against him, but if such an encounter had taken place before he had ever come to England and Halewood he would have swept aside all bastions and taken the citadel by storm.

Yet as he continued his tour of Halewood his mind was distracted from thoughts of Berenice Hart, for he found himself unable to pass a single piece of the fine old furniture without stopping to feast his eyes on it, straining his memory to recall anything his father might have said about it. The beautiful clocks particularly affected him, giving him pain to think of them being removed from the gracious rooms where they had languorously ticked away the hours for a century or more. He took careful note of repairs needed and damp patches where the roof leaked, and he tested with the pressure of his foot the many places where the floor sagged. He could see himself up to his eyes in debt at Halewood until all the restoration work was done and the house made truly habitable.

He was coming from one of the upper drawing rooms when he saw the boy again. The child was standing under an archway at the head of a short flight of stairs, his whole stance defiant, fists clenched, feet set stoutly apart.

"Go away!" the youthful voice rang out shrilly. "You don't belong here!"

Aaron was more curious than annoyed. "Who are you? What's your name?"

The boy ignored the questions. "This is my house! Halewood is mine! Go away and never come back! I order you to leave!"

Aaron's tolerance went before such a show of ill manners. He was about to rebuke the child when a sudden suspicion darted into his mind. "What grounds have you for such a claim?" he demanded grimly, wondering why—if this should be a son of Sir Harry's old age—he had not been forewarned about him by Delia or the lawyer or even Dr. Gilmore himself. "My name is Hart. Can you match that?"

Tears burst from the boy's eyes, although not a muscle of his angry little face acknowledged the drops that ran down his cheeks. With dignity, he chose to ignore the unmanly weakness that had overtaken him. "No, I can't!" he retorted furiously. "I'm Roland Alexander Newman, but Lady Hart is my mama, and I've always been told that one day Halewood would be mine!"

"Then I regret you've had to suffer a disappointment, which—although you couldn't begin to comprehend the circumstances—is similar to mine. I also expected to have Halewood bequeathed to me. Nevertheless your rudeness of manner can't be overlooked. I suggest you behave in a gentlemanly way and say you're sorry."

"Never!" The boy raised both taut fists and shook them. "I'll see you damned first!" Then to Aaron's shocked surprise the boy spat contemptuously at him. An instant later, perhaps realizing the enormity of his misbehavior, the boy had turned and gone bolting through the nearest door, slamming it shut behind him.

Aaron, reaching the door after him, half expected to find the key turned or the boy's inadequate strength attempting to keep it closed to avoid expected retribution, but it opened easily and he found himself in a silk-paneled anteroom with an archway hung with velvet drapes in the same soft shade of apple green, which led into a drawing room beyond. Even as he held back the drapes to pass through he realized he had entered Berenice's private apartments. There was no sign of the boy, who could have disappeared through some double doors into the other room and those linked to it, but Berenice herself sat in a high-backed chair, her feet on a footstool, some embroidery in one hand, a needle with crimson silken thread poised in mid-air in the other.

"Mr. Hart!" Her exclamation was chilly, reminding him in no uncertain way that he was an unwelcome intruder, but at the same time he had the extraordinary impression that she was not so averse to his unannounced entry as she would have him believe. He saw she was as beautiful at close quarters as she had been when viewed at a distance through the window, although he was able to see now that there was an almost transparent pallor to her skin, which suggested extreme tiredness, and tiny lines etched her forehead and magnificent eyes.

"I ask your pardon, ma'am, for bursting in here, in such a fashion," he said, watching her closely, "but I was in hot pursuit of your insolent son who had the audacity to order me out of Halewood."

"I'm sorry indeed! And this on top of a high-fatal occurrence in the library, which was reported to me!" She showed her distress and put aside her embroidery, throwing a harassed glance toward the door, not realizing that she was giving away the escape route that the child had taken. As she stood up some of the rainbow skeins with which she had been stitching tumbled from her lap and clung to the cinnamon velvet folds of her skirt like a fall of twisted flower petals. "Roland ran through with such haste I thought he was playing some game. He shall be punished, I promise you."

"What did you have in mind?"

"I'm not sure." Her hands were agitated. "He's never

been beaten. I couldn't bear to have him beaten and I've never allowed it. But he does deserve some punishment."

"I wasn't thinking in terms of any chastisement for the child," he said, seeing that he had her at a complete disadvantage, for his disclosure of her son's waywardness had made it impossible for her to dismiss him, however politely, from her presence without making some amends.

"What do you suggest?" she asked helplessly.

He thought her singularly inept at managing her own offspring. No doubt the boy had been left to the care of nurses and tutors, she seeing him no more than an hour or two a day. "I'd be satisfied with an apology from Roland," he said crisply. "If you can extract that from him I think it will teach him a well-deserved lesson in respect and courtesy toward his elders."

She sat down again and almost absently removed her silver thimble and put it with her embroidery. "He'd never do that, I know," she confessed unhappily. "No matter what happened to him. He thinks Halewood should be his."

"He made that perfectly clear," he remarked wryly, reaching out for the back of a rosewood chair, which he swung into position near her, for she had indicated that he should sit down. He settled himself leisurely, well pleased with this unexpected opportunity to study her at close quarters after that brief and tantalizing glimpse of her on the terrace. He was aware again of being strongly stirred and attracted by her, a wholly basic and healthy male reaction to the sheer physical onslaught of her beauty. Under his lashes his gaze roved speculatively over her, taking in every detail. The pretty lobes of her ears adorned with jet droplets. The milky curve of her throat. The deep fullness of her breasts straining against the seams of her high-necked, lace-collared bodice. In the well of her velvet lap her right hand twisted the rings on the third finger of her left, causing a sparkle of emeralds and diamonds. The tip of a neat, soft shoe showed under her skirt hems, plain with a narrow silk bow. Discreet. Ladylike. But to him it was an intriguing charade. She had come a long way from her days of scarlet slippers with brass heels. Where on earth had old Sir Harry found her? In some better-class bordello?

She knew the query in his mind. There was nothing she did not know about the thoughts of men. It was plain to her that in another place and in another time he would have tossed a handful of golden sovereigns on the table beside her and made demands on her that she would not have been at liberty to refuse. She had learned long since that poise, refinement, gentleness of manners and voice, all natural to her, could never camouflage her origins or the profession she had followed through wretched, unhappy years. She had deliberately contrived the conception of her only child in a last throw to keep the protection and affection of a man who was tiring of her, but it had been in vain. She had not loved the man, but she had been terribly afraid of the future. She would always be grateful to Sir Harry for taking it into his head to marry her instead of acquiring her. She had since realized that his whim had been evil in its intent, for he had used her as an instrument to outwit his own son and deprive his grandson of a rightful inheritance, but he had given her a wedding ring and his name, and although Halewood had failed to be the home she had imagined it would be, she had gained independence and need never again call any man her master.

"I can't understand why Roland should feel so strongly about Halewood," she said uneasily. "He has spent scarcely any time here. Sir Harry had no wish that the son of my first husband should grow up at Halewood." She knew that the lie about Roland's legitimacy would not be believed by the young American, but he would be well-mannered enough to bow to her pretense.

"Why was that?"

She had expected the question. "Sir Harry was old and irascible. He didn't want the sound of a tiny baby crying in the house, and so Roland was fostered out from the start of our marriage. I used to visit him sometimes, but Sir Harry would never allow me to have him to stay. In all Roland's eight years and a handful of months he's spent no more than a few hours at a stretch here now and again, and one of the conditions imposed on me by Sir Harry was that I should keep the child out of his sight. He had no liking for children at all. It was only a few nights ago that Roland slept under this roof for the first time." She paused, tilting her head a little as she looked at Aaron, wondering if he took the Halewood curse as seriously as she did. "After I had lived in this house for a little while I no longer wanted my son to be with me in it. For his own well-being I considered the less time he spent at Halewood the better. He wouldn't be here now if his foster mother hadn't been taken ill, causing me to take him into my charge earlier than I had intended. I wanted to wait until we were due to leave for Italy together."

"How did he get the idea that one day Halewood would be his?"

She linked her hands and lifted them up and down in a restless manner. "I blame myself. I used to talk to him of the home we would share one day, and I suppose he imagined it would be Halewood."

"Now you are taking that dream away from him by selling it."

Her lower lip trembled, but she spoke firmly, as if reiterating a statement that she had made to herself many times. "One house can be the same as another to a little boy as long as he can look upon it as home. I refuse to believe that Halewood has any special hold on him yet, but it soon would have if I let him grow up here. That's why I'm taking him as far away from Lancashire as I can get." Her voice took on the rising note of vehemence. "If good fortune is with me I'll see him reach manhood in the Italian sun among people who have never heard of this accursed place!" Her eyes were enormous, melting in their appeal. "Does all this sound foolish to you?"

"Not at all. I'm not ignorant of the curse of Halewood and I don't disbelieve it either—far from it. There hasn't been a Hart born yet who hasn't been saddled with the knowledge of it from the cradle. I heard my father say many times that when a Hart seemed strong enough to resist its force it would attack insidiously through those dear to him in order to bring him down—or her, as the case may be. You were wise to keep the boy away from the house."

"Wise?" she echoed dully. "Perhaps not wise enough. Maybe I should never have seen him again after he was fostered out, never let him come to Halewood at all."

He was still eyeing her keenly. "I had no idea until we had this talk that you loathed Halewood to such an extent. Delia never mentioned it."

She relaxed almost imperceptibly against the chair. "Naturally she wouldn't. Delia is a high-principled young woman. She would never betray a confidence or break her word. Her friendship has done much to ease the hours of loneliness for me in these bleak surroundings. Her father has also been a good friend to me as well as being my medical adviser. I shall miss them both when I leave." Then she seemed to recollect her duties as hostess of Halewood. "Perhaps you would care for some tea, Mr. Hart?"

He accepted her offer and she rang for it to be brought. When he watched her pour the tea from the silver Georgian teapot into the rose and gilt porcelain cups he realized that he was looking at other heirlooms that he would never see again. Over the tea, the tiny buttered scones with strawberry jam, and the rich fruitcake she questioned him about America, and he talked at some length, for she parried all further questions about herself and he understood that she had said more to him through the confusion over her son's ill-mannered behavior than she would have done if they had met in any other way. He found it sharply interesting that for a few brief minutes he had caught off guard this woman of delicate beauty who had married Sir Harry for the most mercenary of reasons. Yet he did not begrudge her one penny of his grandfather's fortune. Far from it. He was only glad that she was selling Halewood, or else the opportunity to own it might never have become his.

He rose to leave. Already it was dusk outside and the lamps in the room had been lit. He decided to put directly to her the request that the agent had refused on her behalf.

"There's one thing I feel I must ask you, Lady Hart. I understand that the contents of Halewood are to be sold, lock, stock, and barrel, by auction. There are many pieces that have been in the house since it was built. I'd welcome the chance to purchase them individually if you would get a valuer to set a price on them."

The long, deep look she gave him held out no hope, and yet she took her time before replying, her gaze seeming to search his features in a curiously guarded way.

"My decision has been made. There can be no changing the arrangements at his late hour. Everything must go to the highest bidder."

There was nothing more to be said. He hid his bitter disappointment in a bow, murmuring some conventional thanks for the hospitality received that day.

She gave him her hand. "I'll see that the library gallery is restored to its original condition by craftsmen without delay. Everything will be in order by the time of the auction. Good-day, Mr. Hart."

It was starting to drizzle when he went out to his carriage. He had had a final word with Marsden to say he would be back in the morning to view the remainder of the house and go over the land and other properties. When the agent pointed out that his private viewing time was at an end and that there would be other prospective purchasers in the house and grounds on the morrow, Aaron gave a shrug of irritated resignation.

Sitting back in the corner seat, his thoughts leapt with anticipation toward Delia, who would be waiting for him at her home, and his spirits lifted. He did not know that Berenice stood at one of the windows watching his carriage out of sight. Only when she could no longer see the flicker of its lamps did she let the curtain fall back into place.

⊰ 5 ⊱

WHEN Aaron arrived back at Sycamore House Delia failed to meet him as he had expected, and from somewhere upstairs there was the sound of female voices and the tap of heels. He frowned, handing his hat, cane, and gloves to Ellen, who had admitted him.

"There appears to be new company in the house," he remarked.

"Yes, sir. Dr. Gilmore's sister, Mrs. Barton, and her daughter, Miss Melissa, arrived this afternoon from London in good time for Penghyll's Annual Ball, which is a big night in these parts for t' gentry, sir. Mr. Barton, who's a member of Parliament, was unable to accompany them this time due to being a candidate in a forthcoming election."

Aaron's frown deepened. Delia had said something about guests coming to stay for the Penghyll Ball, but he hadn't paid much attention. Now he felt exasperated that he had lost all chance of a talk before dinner with her on her own. It would have been his only real opportunity in any case, for after dinner Dr. Gilmore liked to engage him in a game of chess or backgammon while Delia amused herself playing the piano, stitching some petit point, or writing yet another letter to Matthew Shaw. Usually there was some conversation with her, but it was always inconsequential, and she made a point of going to bed before he and her father finished the game, giving him no chance to be

83

alone with her. Now with strangers in the house making demands on her attention he would have even less chance of ensnaring some of her time to himself than before, and he had much to achieve in the short period left to him before the appointed wedding day. At the very least he must wring a postponement of the ceremony out of her, which might be all she would be prepared to commit herself to for the time being.

He made his way up the stairs in the direction of his own room and reached the landing as Delia emerged from another of the guest rooms, from which had come the sounds of female chatter. Her face lighted up when she saw him and she clasped her hands together.

"How did it go?" she inquired eagerly, absorbing every detail of his expression. "Were you pleased with Halewood? Did everything come up to your expectations?"

"Beyond measure," he answered with pleasure, "in spite of its urgent need of repairs, including some damages incurred during my visit there. I was looking forward to talking it all over with you, but I hear that there are other people staying." He nodded toward the door she had closed behind her.

Her forehead creased in a little frown. "Aunt Rachel brought Melissa up from London today instead of next week, because she herself can't stay for the Penghyll Ball this year. With all the business of the election Uncle Harry naturally wants his wife at home."

"I don't want to discuss Halewood with you in front of strangers. When may we talk alone?"

She glanced at him penetratingly. Halewood had made a tremendous impression on him, that was easy to see. But was there something more? A unique experience or a personal encounter that he would not easily forget? "This evening, after everybody else has gone to bed, I'll meet you downstairs in the music room."

"I'll be waiting there," he said with satisfaction.

Her gaze lingered on him for a fraction of a second longer before she went on downstairs, bound for the kitchen, which had been her original intention when leaving the newly arrived guests to change for dinner. An anxious look clouded her face. She had been able to tell from the first moment of seeing her aunt and cousin on the doorstep that there was some trouble in the air, for Melissa's face had been mutinous and Aunt Rachel had looked at her wits' end. They had not been in the house more than ten minutes before Aunt Rachel had seized the chance to disclose the situation out of her daughter's hearing. It was not an unusual state of affairs. Melissa had become infatuated with a most unsuitable young man. Uncle Harry had put an end to it, but he and Aunt Rachel had thought it best to get the girl away from London and into fresh surroundings where there would be no chance of further meetings, accidental or contrived. Aunt Rachel said enough to make Delia feel that there was some justification for their wishing to get their daughter away from the young man in question, but she wasn't sure that bundling Melissa ignominiously up to Lancashire against her will had been the right acton. Absence made the heart grow fonder, and there was nothing like parental opposition to make young love blaze. She must only hope that Melissa would accept her temporary banishment more graciously as time went by. In the meantime, she had to check with Cook in the kitchen that everything was under control.

Dr. Gilmore received the news that his sister and his niece had arrived several days earlier than expected with noticeable lack of enthusiasm, and when Delia gave him the details of the Bartons' present domestic upheaval, the nucleus of which had been transplanted into his own home, he rolled up his eyes in wearied and exaggerated despair, letting his hands rise and fall to his sides. Deila, who had gone with him into his study, gave him a little admonitory shake of her head.

"Papa! You should be thankful that we're able to help poor Aunt Rachel at this particular time. She's quite beside herself."

"My sister," he replied laconically, taking his long-stemmed pipe from its rack, "is always beside herself over something or other. She used to visit at a more civilized time of year when you and Melissa were younger and there could be picnics and outings and trips to the seaside, but since she has taken it into her head to parade her offspring annually at the Penghyll Ball, which in my opinion is nothing more than a marriage market with all the mothers bringing along their marriageable daughters like heifers to a cattle auction, she invades my house at a time of year when bad weather makes her loath to go out once she has arrived. As a result I must suffer her pent-up chatter whenever she sets eyes on me, and it's enough to drive a stronger man than I am to drink."

Delia hid her smile, knowing he sounded a good deal fiercer over the matter than he really was, but he was to be excused when he was as tired as she knew him to be at the close of a busy day. Stooping, she lighted a taper in the fire and handed it to him. He put it to his tobacco-filled pipe.

"I should have thought that you, a proud Lancashire man," she teased gently, "would have approved your sister's desire that Melissa should marry into one of the grander local families. I believe that's half the trouble behind the present upset. Aunt Rachel has had her eye on the eldest of the Whinlatter boys, who is rich *and* next in line for a hereditary title or two, as a possible husband for Melissa for a long time. She would like to see her married and settled away from London—and Uncle Henry. There has always been such friction in that household between father and daughter."

Dr. Gilmore drew on his pipe, coughed, and set the

flat of his hand against his chest as if the smoke bothered him. "Rachel is a fool," he stated tersely, "and Henry, even if he is in the Commons, is an arrogant dunderhead. My niece, being an only child, has been alternately browbeaten by her father, who's treated her harshly for not being the son he wanted, and spoiled by her mother, who is too weak and silly to cope sensibly with any situation. The girl has been full of sly tricks to get her own way and avoid trouble since she was first laid in a cradle. This latest escapade of hers is not the first bout of foolish nonsense she had landed herself into, nor will it be the last. I've no patience with her. You must admit she's been unkind to you many a time."

"She doesn't really mean to be."

"Pshaw! You're too forgiving—just like your dear mother. I'm not blind, you know. If Matthew had been a more susceptible young man she would have taken him from you without the least twinge of conscience last time she was staying in this house. Not because she wanted him, I hasten to add, but simply to score over you and chalk up another conquest to amuse herself until it was time to leave again."

"Now that's only your opinion," she answered him firmly, "and it could be unjust. I know Melissa likes to flirt, but so do most girls. Anyway, in normal circumstances I like having Aunt Rachel to stay—it's a treat for her to get away from Uncle Henry, too. The Penghyll Ball is more important than ever to her this year, even though she can't stay for it herself, because she's hoping desperately that it will help to distract Melissa and give her a new romantic interest to dull the pain of being parted once and for all from the young man left behind in London."

"What was his name again.?"

"Richard Dibley."

"He's well rid of the little minx."

She decided to turn the conversation, seeing that nothing was going to budge him from his present attitude. "I must go and change for dinner. You have time for a little rest here on your own before you need to do likewise. Be thankful that you find pleasure in the conversation of your other guest in this house. He was at Halewood today."

"He was well pleased with it, no doubt."

She hesitated before replying. "Yes, he was. Yet I had the impression he was curiously tense."

"Not having second thoughts about buying Halewood, is he?"

"No, nothing like that. There was a kind of excitement about him that I couldn't define." She made a quick little gesture with her hands, indicating her momentary self-exasperation. "I'm far too involved with Halewood. It makes me listen and imagine and probe and dissect as if I alone were responsible for it and those who come and go there. I must stop thinking about Halewood and concentrate my thoughts on my own new home that awaits me after my wedding day."

"How is the work progressing at Wisteria Lodge?"

"The workmen are due to finish this week." Her expression was serious and there was a troubled look in the depths of her eyes. "How swiftly the days are running out for me. I shall find myself a bride in no time at all now."

He knew she sought reassurance and he gave it. "Matthew loves you and you love him. He will be a good husband to you, I'm sure of it, or else I would never have given my permission for you to marry him in the first place. All will be well. It's natural to have last-minute doubts and fears. Try to put them aside. Few brides have known their grooms as long as you have known Matthew. Your union will be blessed with love and friendship. On such foundations are the best of marriages made."

She nodded and went to put her arms lightly about his neck and kiss him affectionately on the cheek.

"Thank you for those wise words. I was in need of such a reminder. I'll not forget again."

"I'm sure you won't."

She crossed to the door and looked back over her shoulder at him before leaving the study. "Take a nap now, papa. It was unfair of me to keep you talking, but I can't help but be glad that I did."

The door closed after her. Slowly Dr. Gilmore lowered his pipe and rested it on a ledge. He had been afraid when she had turned in that last moment that she had some suspicion about the true state of his health and had been about to throw some question about it to him, but as yet she did not suspect the existence of the constricting pains in his chest that had begun to afflict him almost daily.

Rubbing his chest with his fist, he took from his pocket a key to his dispensary, which led off the study, and went into it. Although the dispensary was not much bigger than a cupboard, the main one being at his surgery, he found it useful to have on hand everything he might need for an emergency call or for domestic accidents such as occurred in the kitchen from time to time, servants being singularly careless with the sharp blades of knives and scalding liquids. Taking down from a shelf a bottle of physic he had dispensed for his own use, he poured out a measure and drank it down. Knowing it took a little time to have effect, he sat down in a study chair, set his feet on the brass fender, and dozed as instructed for half an hour, undisturbed by the activities in the rest of the house. When he bestirred himself he felt much better, the opiate having soothed away his discomfort. Shortly afterward, bathed and changed, he entered the drawing room where he found Aaron, and together they conversed until Delia came with the two lady guests to join them.

Rachel Barton, a once-pretty, harassed-looking woman, came forward in a whisper of lavender shot-silk to embrace her brother, uttering a stream of complaints in greeting. "Charles! What a journey to get here! I declare the roads to Penghyll get worse every year! Delia tells me there's to be a railway branch line very shortly—and not before time. Think yourself fortunate to see your only sister as often as you do. Traveling without Henry made everything twice as difficult on this particular journey from London. I declare I'll never be able to do it again—"

Dr. Gilmore checked the moaning flow with introductions. After some general conversation Melissa was left with Aaron and the other three moved to sit down in grouped chairs. She looked about her and sank down gracefully into one half of a comfortably upholstered sociable, indicating that he sit beside her. She thought him handsome and because of that it was as natural to her to coquette with him as it was for her to breathe, but at the same time her innermost mood was at danger level. Before coming downstairs she had quarreled again with her mother, a more-than-daily occurrence over the past weeks, and there was a burning savagery in her that sprang from a helpless rage at having been compelled to leave London whe she least desired it.

"So you're from America, Mr. Hart," she said flutingly, baring her small, pearly teeth into a smile that brought dimples into play. "From which place exactly, may I ask?"

"Boston, Massachusetts."

"I declare!" She lifted her hands and put them together, prayer like. "Mama complains of the journey from London, but you've come from far across the sea. Tell me, do! What is it like to enter surroundings of a civilized and cultured nature for the first time?"

He eyed her with a sidelong glance, irritated and far from intrigued by her gibing attitude toward him, which—although sexually provocative—was insufferably rude and patronizing. He thought it lamentable that with her seductive looks she should have all the makings of a snobbish shrew. Without doubt her features, framed as they were with a luxuriance of dark, gold hair dressed in long ringlets that lay softly against her neck, would have been considered quite perfect by any fashionable artist of the day. Here was the smooth, rounded brow, the slightly long but exquisitely narrow nose, the mouth that was rosebud, and the alabaster complexion. Her china-blue eyes with her deep lids and curling lashes added to her look of ultimate feminine docility, but he noted the steel behind her gaze and the stubborn set to her hard little jaw.

He answered her question evenly. "I've been accustomed to a similar environment since birth. Boston is a fine city, not a frontier encampment."

"Indeed? But, of course! I was forgetting! You had an English father and he would have made sure that you had a gentleman's education in the most barbaric of settings!" She gave a tinkling laugh and tapped his arm lightly with her fingertips, finding it balm to her own searing emotions to do battle with him. On the other side of the room her mother sent a relieved glance in her direction, thinking that her daughter was responding in her customary flirtatious way to any young man of better-than-average looks, and hoped it was a sign that already the girl had found a new diversion to make her forget her former foolishness and that there would be no more rebelliousness or trouble. Delia also concluded that Aaron and her cousin were getting on well and was thankful for it.

"I find it regrettable," Aaron was saying wryly, "that such ignorance exists about the land I've left behind. The progress made *since* the War of Independence has been outstanding."

The point went home. She flushed, but in her dangerous mood she found his retaliation exciting. She was carrying on a deadly flirtation with him and enjoying every barbed word of it. Tilting her head to one side, she studied him deliberately with a narrow smile of her lips. "You're reminding me that you were born a foreigner. Pride centered in another country—and one that in the living memory of my parents' generation took up arms against our Canadian colonies—will not go down well here."

He had no intention of disclosing to her his awareness of completely belonging to Halewood, and he answered her on an impersonal note. "It's possible to harbor loyal and affectionate feelings toward the land of one's birth as well as one's land of adoption. America is made up mostly of such people."

"But this is England! If you're going to be a true squire of Halewood you must forget you ever knew another land."

"That I could never do."

She shrugged her pretty shoulders nonchalantly at advice rejected and leaned over to him, resting her elbow on the polished walnut arm between them. "What plans have you made? Do you intend to shut yourself away in that dreary old house or are you going to make it come alive again?"

He was saved from making a reply by the arrival of Matthew. Delia, who had expected him, sprang up and went forward to slip her arm through his and bring him into the center of the room. He knew Melissa and her mother from many years back, but Aaron, who had risen to his feet, he was meeting for the first time. There was no friendliness in Matthew's eyes, although normally he was agreeable and amiable to most people he met, but he felt that this American stranger from far away represented a further intrusion into Delia's life—and his, for that matter—by Halewood, and once again he experienced the sensation of jealousy. More and more he disliked her having interests that he could not or did not wish to share.

"I'm told you're a railroad engineer," Aaron remarked as an opening. "Before I left the United States there was already talk of the not-too-distant day when a railroad will stretch from the Atlantic to the Pacific coast."

They were on a topic that interested each as much as the other and from that point the conversation flowed freely between them. It was not until after dinner was over and the three ladies had left the gentlemen to their port that Matthew himself brought up the subject of Halewood.

"I understand you're hoping to purchase your family's ancestral home," he said through a haze of cigar smoke, leaning back in his chair.

"I trust I'll be able to meet the highest figure it reaches at the auction," Aaron replied, refilling his glass from the decanter before passing it on.

Dr. Gilmore took it from him. "Delia said you were well satisfied with all you saw of it today."

Matthew paid no attention to what Aaron said to the doctor in reply, but sat forward and leaned both arms on the table in front of him. "I think Halewood should be pulled down."

"Come, come," Dr. Gilmore said reprovingly. "It's a splendid example of Elizabethan architecture."

"It was, but now it has fallen to rack and ruin," Matthew persisted.

"You're mistaken," Aaron argued. "It's structurally sound and there's nothing that new roofing and the skill of craftsmen can't put right."

"But the cost—and for what?" Matthew went on. "Why not build a new house on part of the land? It will set you back less in pocket in the end."

"I think your suggestion is insane," Aaron stated bluntly, losing patience.

"I agree with Mr. Hart, Matthew," Dr. Gilmore said. "It's the family home he's come all these miles for! What pleasure would there be for him, even if he built the grandest house in England, to look out and see a barren hilltop where once Halewood stood as a landmark for the whole district."

"Then let him leave it to crumble and fall where it

stands. It will save him the expense of having to erect pseudo-Italian ruins or some other absurd edifice in his gardens to follow the popular fashion for such follies."

"I find your remark exceedingly offensive," Aaron said quietly, his eyes narrowed.

There was silence in the room. Matthew's jaw tightened, and he was conscious that he had allowed his suppressed enmity to come to the surface. "That wasn't my intention," he blustered truthfully. "I apologize to you—and to our host. I only meant to proffer good advice."

Aaron inclined his head with a complete lack of animosity, but he had seen that Matthew resented him and guessed that there could be only one cause. "I accept your apology."

"Yes, indeed." Dr. Gilmore gave a nod. "We'll let the subject of Halewood rest there. In any case, it's high time we joined the ladies."

Delia thought the evening went well. When it ended she picked up the Spanish shawl and put it about her shoulders to go with Matthew to the door and out onto the step to see him on his way. It being a fine night, he had walked to Sycamore House from his grandparents' house, where he had grown up and in which he stayed whenever he was back in Penghyll, and he would be walking home again.

"Has Aaron Hart unlimited funds?" he asked thoughtfully as if it were a question that had been much on his mind throughout the evening. "I mean, is he a really rich man?"

"Not at all. At least, judging from all he's said to me I gather he had some difficulty in raising the sum needed. Why do you ask?"

"Oh, I'm curious. That's all. Let's not talk about him any longer." He took her by the shoulders and smiled down into her face. "It won't be long to wait now before this kind of good-night parting for us is no more."

In spite of herself she stiffened and looked away from him, struggling to crush down the uncertainties which earlier that evening she had determined to dispel once and for all.

"Delia?" he inquired fondly, lowering his head to try to see her expression. "Is anything wrong?"

She couldn't lie to him, but she couldn't hurt him either. Better to seek the comfort of his arms as a protection against herself, for she was her own worst enemy. Impulsively she moved nearer and buried her face in his shoulder.

"Dear little sweetheart," he whispered, his arms enfolding her, his hands caressing her back and arms through the slippery silkiness of the shawl. "You looked lovely this evening. I could hardly take my eyes from you." The fringe slid over his fingers. "This shawl. I haven't seen you wear it before." He chuckled softly. "Did you buy it new for the Penghyll Ball and then find you couldn't wait to put it on?"

How well he knew her, she thought despairingly. Always she had adored new clothes. In childhood when a new and pretty hair ribbon had been purchased she'd had to wear it from the market, unable to wait until she got home. Yet in a way he did not know her at all. It was a stranger he held in his arms. Guilt and misery swept through her.

"Aaron brought it for me from the New World," she said, drawing back from him to gather the shawl about her. She was shivering. "It's cold out here. I must go in."

He looked displeased. "I'm not sure you should have accepted such a gift—or that he should have offered it."

Because he had put her own original doubts into words she answered him with a gust of heated impatience. "It's a beautiful shawl and was given as a token of appreciation for my being responsible for letting him know about the sale of Halewood. You can't object to that."

He knew she was right and he was being unreasonable. He sought to make amends in kissing her, but her response lacked warmth, which he blamed on their difference of opinion over the shawl.

He went over the incident carefully in his mind when he walked briskly homeward. It would all be forgotten when they met again. Delia had never harbored a grudge in her life. On the remarkably few occasions when they had had words, even in their childhood, she had always been the first to end the quarrel with a kiss and a hug and a gentle entreaty for all to be at peace between them again. Nevertheless it wasn't quite like her to be so quick to shut the door without waving him out of sight. He'd take her flowers tomorrow. A posy. And the prettiest shawl he could find. Then the Spanish one could be put away and never thought of again.

In her bedroom Delia was sitting with her elbows on the dressing table, her head in her hands. Somehow she must exert all her willpower and drive Aaron from her heart. She could not go back on her promise to marry Matthew. The pledge had been made and must not be broken for a wild and senseless longing that she refused to define as love. If only she could disassociate Aaron from Halewood she would feel nothing for him. Through the house he was too entwined in her thoughts and in her heart. How ironic it was that she had been given the responsibility of persuading Melissa out of an unsuitable infatuation when she herself was similarly afflicted and knew not how to break the bonds.

A tap came at the door. Hastily she straightened up and turned her head to the door. "Come in."

It was Melissa who entered, a beribboned peignoir over her nightgown, a candle in hand. She looked surprised to see Delia still in her gown with her hair untouched. Her own was brushed into a glimmering flow down her back.

"I thought you'd be in bed," she said. "I want to talk."

It made Delia realize how long she must have been

sitting motionless at the dressing table. She was also thankful for Melissa's intrusion, which gave her a legitimate excuse not to go downstairs yet to the music room where Aaron would be awaiting her.

"I've been—daydreaming," she said with a vague gesture of her hands. "Do sit down. I'm sure I can guess what it is you want to talk about."

Melissa set down the candle. Then with a choking sob she flew across to Delia, where she dropped to her knees in a flurry of rose-pink ruffles, flung her arms across Delia's lap and burst into a storm of weeping. "I can't bear it! I'll die without him! I love him and he loves me! No girl ever had a more cruel father or a less understanding mother!"

Delia had seen Melissa fall in and out of love with as many as three young men in the same number of weeks on previous visits to Penghyll, and if Aunt Rachel was to be believed it was not an uncommon occurrence at home, but never had she seen her cousin more distressed or more heartbroken. Was it possible that this time Melissa was genuinely in love?

"Why not tell me the whole story?" she asked compassionately. "All I know is that you met a young man named Richard Dibley, whom your parents regard as a scoundrel and a fortune-hunter, and—from what I've been told—not without reason."

Melissa raised eyes swimming with tears. "They don't know him as I do! All they can think about is that a stupid old great-aunt on my father's side of the family left a few thousand pounds in trust for me to inherit when I marry. Richard doesn't care about the money! Neither do I! We could be happy together in a garret!"

Delia doubted it. Melissa had been brought up in the lap of luxury, and although she would have learned how to run a house and manage servants it was doubtful whether she could cope with living in poverty, no matter how idyllic their love, for very long. Richard, too, appeared to have expensive tastes. According to

Aunt Rachel he spent his days escaping his creditors, while Uncle Henry, who had had him watched and followed, knew that he frequented gaming clubs and certain other notorious nightspots in London where gentlemen did not go for cultural entertainment, but this information had been divulged to Delia's unwilling ears in confidence and it was obvious that Melissa knew nothing of that side of Richard's life.

"How did you meet?" she asked, leaning over to slide open a dressing table drawer and take out a clean handkerchief, which she unfolded and gave to Melissa, who appeared to have come without one.

"At Caroline Hewett's coming-out ball." The words came muffled by the handkerchief and torn with gulping sobs. "He would have danced every dance with me if my program hadn't already been almost full. But I fell in love with him before our first waltz together had ended and he felt the same about me. Unfortunately mama was already looking down her nose. She upbraided me all the way home, saying that I should have known that he was *the* Richard Dibley who'd been involved in an unsavory scandal, and I should have refused to dance with him. But I didn't care! I knew then that he would never be received by either papa or mama, and he must have known it, too, because he had made secret arrangements to meet me in the park next morning. Within a week he had proposed to me and I had accepted."

"How did you expect to be allowed to marry him?"

"I don't know. I didn't think. All I knew was that I couldn't live without him. After that we had many perfect hours together. I used every kind of lie I could think of to escape chaperonage and meet him. We used to laugh at the tricks I played to get away, and he helped me think up what to say next time."

Delia suppressed a sigh. It was a familiar pattern of lies and deceit and trickery that Melissa had used all her life to get her own way, but this time it was on a dangerous level. The more Delia heard of Rich-

ard the less she trusted him. It was probably not unknown that Melissa was an heiress and to a young
man in desperate financial straits she would offer a solution to all his problems. Not least of all, marriage to
the daughter of a respectable and distinguished Member of Parliament could do much to wipe out indiscre-
tions of the past. Unluckily for Richard it also worked
the other way, and Uncle Henry, jealous of his good
name and that of his daughter, had made it clear
enough that he would consider such an alliance tarnish-
ing to say the least. Aunt Rachel when talking about
it all had passed quickly over the scandal in which
Richard had been involved, but unpaid gambling
debts had been mentioned.

"How was your romance discovered?" Delia questioned.

Again the pretty, tear-wet face was raised, but it
was a mask of bitterness with a sullen twist to the
mouth. "Somebody saw us and papa got wind of it.
Who it was or how it happened I don't know. He
called me into his study and demanded the truth." Her
eyes closed briefly on the fright and horror of the interview. "For the first time in my life I stood up to him.
I told him that no matter what had happened in the
past Richard had mended his ways and was full of
plans for a new beginning. When we were married he
intended first to settle his debts and then we'd travel
abroad for a while before returning to buy a house in
London that suited us. After that he'd invest in some
business venture on the highest level, and everything
would be quite wonderful." She drew a shuddering
breath and bit her lip until it showed white. "That was
when papa nearly exploded with rage, saying that I
was too stupid to see that if it were not for my inheritance Richard wouldn't give me a second glance.
But that's not true! I know I'm pretty and desirable—
enough men have told me that, heaven knows!—and
all Richard wants is to make me his own dear wife!
But papa forbade me ever to see him again!"

"Did you obey his order?"

"I had no choice! I was confined to the house and not allowed to go out without mama. All my correspondence was checked and opened. Then with the election coming up papa needed mama to dance attendance on him and see that important guests were properly received, which meant she couldn't keep an eye on me all the time. That's when they decided between them that I'd learned my lesson and would never dare disobey them again. Oh, how I had to humble myself before papa for that concession! I groveled! It was humiliating! I'll hate him for it for the rest of my life! Then all I earned from it was temporary banishment to Lancashire to give me more time to think over how magnanimous he had been. Ugh!" Her whole body shuddered with aversion to her parent. "Mama held out the Penghyll Ball like a carrot to a donkey—as if I cared about so provincial a social function any more!—and said that she knew I'd be welcome to stay on afterward until the wedding, because I could help you list the gifts you'd receive and all that. But it's banishment nevertheless!" The tears brimmed up and overflowed again. "I can't live without Richard! What am I to do?"

She gave a fresh tumultuous wail and bowed her head, her sobs coming with the uncontrolled abandonment of self-indulgence. Delia could tell it would take some time to quieten the girl and try to soothe her sorrow and despair enough for her to get some sleep that night. She must go downstairs and tell Aaron not to wait for her. It would be far too late before she managed to get Melissa back to her own room.

"You're uncomfortable there on the floor," she said. "Go and sit on the bed. I have to go downstairs for a few moments, but I'll be back at once."

"Don't leave me!" Melissa clutched childishly and pettishly at her skirt.

Delia unplucked the girl's hands and helped her to her feet and across to the bed where she collapsed forlornly, lying on her stomach, her face within the circle of her outflung arms. Delia had barely reached the door when Melissa raised herself to make a blubbering, self-pitying inquiry.

"Why *are* you leaving me alone like this?"

"Aaron was hoping to talk over Halewood with me. I'll only be away long enough to tell him not to wait for me."

Melissa threw out an appealing hand. "Don't tell him about Richard and me! I couldn't bear anyone to know how my parents have humiliated us and degraded our love for each other."

Delia returned to the bedfoot and spoke reassuringly. "You should know I'd never repeat anything you've told me in this room or anywhere else you might chose to speak to me in confidence."

"Promise?"

"I promise."

Melissa gave a satisfied nod and dropped her head to the coverlet again.

In the music room Aaron turned when he heard Delia's step across the drawing room floor and pleasure flashed into his face when she appeared in the frame of the open doorway. She could tell he had begun to be afraid she was not coming.

"I can't stop," she said hastily before he could speak. "Melissa is slightly indisposed and so I'll be sitting with her for a while. I came to let you know. I didn't want you to think I'd forgotten about coming down here."

He gave a rueful smile, showing his disappointment, but accepted her statement without question. "I'd many things to ask you, many things to tell you. I'm returning to Halewood tomorrow. Come with me."

Regretfully she shook her head. "There'll be too much to do here with Aunt Rachel and Melissa in the house. I have to organize everything to allow myself some free time to wait on Lady Hart the next day." She took a step backward to leave again. "I must go."

Swiftly he moved forward and blocked her way. "You mustn't neglect one guest for the sake of two others," he said, not entirely in jest.

"I know," she said sincerely. "I'm sorry."

"Then we'll meet tomorrow night instead. There'll be twice as much to talk about."

"Very well. Tomorrow. And now good night."

She flew back upstairs to her bedroom. Melissa, chilled by misery, had gathered about her the Spanish shawl that Delia had left lying on the bedfoot, and was sitting up, dry sobs racking her, tears still trickling down her cheeks. Delia was moved by pity for the girl's undeniable distress. She sat down on the bed beside her.

"I know it seems hard," she said sympathetically, "but such a liaison was doomed from the start. It would never—"

Melissa interrupted her. "I'm not giving him up. It's not over. I refuse to believe it. No matter what anyone says. Richard loves me. He really loves me. He said he did a thousand times."

She collapsed heartbrokenly against Delia, who simply held her in comfort, thinking that perhaps to cry it all out was the best possible remedy. Uncle Henry would never retract his decision once it was made. There was nothing to be done but to hope that Melissa would recover quickly from the whole affair. Normally her feelings were remarkably shallow, and it would be ill luck indeed if this should prove to be the first time they were otherwise. There was something desperate about Melissa's whole attitude that made Delia feel singularly uneasy, but she could not pinpoint the reason why. It was against her nature to be suspicious, but when dealing with Melissa it was difficult not to get wary of whatever she might be plotting for the future.

6

Aunt Rachel departed in the morning. She was much less anxious than when she had arrived, having decided that Aaron was the ideal person to turn Melissa away from her languishings, and if anything serious should come of it she herself would be more than pleased and Henry would not hesitate to give his permission there. Mistress of Halewood! Personally she didn't believe the place was as sinister as everyone said it was. Probably all it needed was up-to-date plumbing and new drapes.

"Good-bye, my dear," she said affectionately to Delia. "I know Melissa will be in good hands here at Sycamore House. It will take a few days for her to get over that highly unfortunate little *contretemps* in London, but I believe it's going to be a case of all's well that ends well."

"Good-bye, aunt," Delia replied. "Give my regards to Uncle Henry. I hope he wins the election."

Her aunt looked surprised that Delia seemed to think the result might be in any doubt. "He will, my dear," she said with innocent seriousness. "Nobody would dare defeat him."

When the carriage had left Delia went back indoors. The house was quiet. Her father was on his rounds, Aaron had gone to Halewood, and Melissa was somewhere upstairs. With a little sigh she thought of the innumerable small tasks that awaited her attention. After checking the day's menus with Cook she must set about them without further delay.

She was seated at the desk in her father's study, writing out bills for his patients before dealing with the household accounts, when Melissa appeared dressed in bonnet and sealskin cape, her hands in her muff. Relief that her mother had departed showed in her face, but she was pale, with purple smudges under her eyes.

"I'm going for a walk," she announced. "It will be the first walk I've had on my own for ages. I can't tell you what it means to me to have regained my freedom."

Delia smiled, hoping that this was a first indication that Melissa might be reconciling herself to the turn that events had taken after all. Last night's storm of grief could have been the climax and the shutting of the door on the past. She tipped her head in understanding, thinking that Melissa looked as if she had had little sleep.

"Some fresh air will do you good. You have no color in your cheeks, are you feeling well? I noticed you ate almost nothing at breakfast?"

Melissa hooded her eyes quickly, hiding the start in them. "I'm perfectly well. I intend to go as far as the market square and look around the stalls and the shops. Should I meet you at the dressmaker's?"

"That's an excellent idea. It will save you coming back here first. The appointment is at noon. I gave the dressmaker the measurements you posted to me long since, and your bridesmaid's gown will be ready for a fitting."

Delia was left alone with her ledgers. Melissa walked purposefully and with haste. At the first postbox she took a letter from her muff and pressed it impulsively to her lips before sending it on its way. It was addressed to Mr. Richard Dibley. She had given him her whereabouts, told him all that happened to prevent

104

her getting in touch before, and poured out her undying love.

As she continued on toward the market at a more leisurely pace she willed him to reply by return of post. Otherwise her future was too bleak to contemplate for any number of reasons. Not least among them were the first disturbing suspicions she was beginning to harbor about her physical state, although she took hope from the fact that she had never been really sure when to expect the times of inconvenience to come upon her, a truly regular pattern never having established itself. Resolutely she pushed the doubt down below the surface of her mind and let her spirits lighten at the sight of the bustling scene that met her in the market square. Her mood was even more greatly restored when she met two daughters of a local family with whom she was acquainted from previous visits to Penghyll over the years, and she accepted their invitation to drink a cup of chocolate with them in the ladies' drawing room at the Red Lion Hotel.

When Delia arrived at the dressmaker's she found Melissa being fitted in the rose-silver gown, her expression dubious although she had known what to expect, having been sent a fashion plate and a piece of the fabric. The dressmaker appeared to have made a mistake in taking too much of the silk in at the seams and a minor adjustment was being completed to ease the tightness about the waist and bustline. Delia hoped the error had not put Melissa off the garment, but she need not have worried on that point.

"I think the color suits me very well," Melissa conceded with a critical air, twirling before the full-length looking glass and making the skirt flounces, which were caught up by clusters of gauze roses, dip and float. Then she noticed that Delia was being helped into her bridal gown by two of the dressmaker's assistants and she stood back to leave space before the looking glass.

Delia viewed her reflection. For the first time she

was wearing the veil and circlet of wax orange blossoms to get the full effect with her gown of white lace and satin, which trailed into a train behind her. Thus would she look on her wedding day. She barely recognized herself. It was as though she were simply studying the appearance of a bride with whom she had only the briefest acquaintance. She had felt the same every time she'd had a fitting. There was no sense of excitement, no happy anticipation. She was completely cut off from that serious, white-cheeked, gray-eyed girl who faced her in the looking glass.

Then with a flash of revelation she understood the reason why. Never once had she truly believed she was going to wear that wedding gown! Not into church or anywhere else for that matter. It was a conviction that had laid hold of her from the start without her being aware of it. Now it had come to light and with it a terrible chill seemed to strike her. She swayed and dropped her face into her hands.

Only then did she realize that the others in the room had been talking to her all the time, Melissa leading the praise in how fine she looked. Now they were all concern and the dressmaker herself took charge.

"Nerves! Brides often get them," she stated, putting an arm about Delia's shoulders to guide her toward a chair, and she gave orders to her assistants. "Fetch the vinaigrette! Make some tea!"

"I'm all right. Really," Delia murmured, but she sank willingly into the chair and let her head come to rest on the back of it. The aroma of the vinaigrette cleared her head and brought her sitting upright, coughing and gasping.

Melissa smiled uncertainly at her. "That's better. You gave us quite a fright."

Delia gave a self-conscious nod, feeling she had made a fool of herself. The dressmaker had been right, echoing words that her father had said to her that evening in the study. It was only nerves. Nevertheless she was glad she didn't have to put the gown on again until her wedding day.

The tea was brought, and Melissa had a cup with her while the two assistants bore away the dresses and veil. The dressmaker made notes about the wedding day, saying she would be at the house by ten o'clock to help Delia dress and then would go on to the church to make sure the train was spread out correctly before she started up the aisle.

To Delia's relief Melissa did not chatter in the carriage on the way home from the dressmaker's establishment, but sat with her elbow on the armrest, chin in hand, looking out of the window in a subdued and thoughtful mood. Delia, whose head was aching, appreciated the chance to sit quietly, but she could not help wondering what it was that had caused her cousin's silence. Melissa seemed almost chastened.

After dinner that evening Dr. Gilmore was called out to a confinement and Melissa went early to bed, which gave Delia and Aaron the opportunity to be alone together sooner than they had expected. He moved from the sofa opposite her and drew up a footstool to sit by her chair.

"At last a chance to talk on our own," he said with supreme contentment, looking at her, his arms resting on his knees. "I've now seem the whole of Halewood, its land, and its properties. What a grand house it is. The interior doesn't disappoint me in any way. Those ceilings! The paneling! That great stone staircase with its molded arches and splendid columns!"

She gave him a warm, spontaneous smile, enjoying his pleasure. "At least none of those things can be ripped out and auctioned with the contents of the house."

He laughed quietly and somewhat sardonically. "I had the same thought. Yet some structural changes did occur yesterday in the library." Briefly he explained what had happened, playing down his own conviction that the malignant force of Halewood had thus made its presence known to him.

"How dangerous!" She looked disturbed, drawing her lower lip under her teeth. "Are you sure that—?"

He interrupted her quickly, able to tell that she did not believe that the railings could have been made faulty by age. "I can't be sure of anything. I must wait and see. If what happened was Halewood's warning to me of greater violence to come, I'm prepared for it and I'm not afraid. I believe I made the house understand that."

"You must take care!"

"I will, I give you my word. At the present time the atmosphere of Halewood is charged with change and upheaval, but I'm hoping that once the ownership has passed into my hands Halewood will settle again and nothing more will go amiss."

"Don't be overconfident," she begged.

"That's a mistake I don't intend to make. But let me tell you about the rest of the time I spent there. Have you ever seen the original plan of the house? I came across it framed most unsuitably and without the protection of glass in one of those dark little upper anterooms."

"I'm glad you saw it. Who would have expected the ink to remain so black after just on three hundred years?"

They talked on in the rose-gold glow of fire and lamplight, their shadows flickering around them. Then, not quite sure why he had not mentioned it before, he told her about meeting Berenice. "I was invited to take tea with her."

She showed her astonishment. "She actually received you!"

"Yes, she did—and I saw her again for a short while today. She came out in a cloak and hood to the stables where the steward was taking me through."

"I can't understand it. She never receives anybody, and she led me to believe you'd be no exception."

"Unluckily for her, whatever she had intended, she had no choice but to speak to me at Halewood yesterday." He went on to describe all that had taken place. "Her reason for going out of her way to see me this morning was to tell me that Roland had been sent to bed without supper as a punishment for his insolence to me. Apparently an apology was not to be had, and I let the whole affair rest there."

She remembered the impression she had gathered the day before when he returned from Halewood, and if the outstanding event had been his meeting with Berenice she did not want to pursue that thought. "So Roland is with her for good now," she said reflectively, looking into the fire. "She knew nothing of his coming when I saw her last. I expect I shall hear all the details tomorrow." She was silent for a few moments and then turned her head toward him. "Doesn't it strike you as odd that in spite of her son being kept safely away from Halewood since infancy, the very denial of his right to live in it with her has resulted in his developing an absurd obsession for the house—the last thing she ever wanted. It's as if Halewood is mocking her for her pains."

He held her eyes. "Do you mean that the Halewood curse is striking at her through her son?"

She nodded. "All along I've been scared that it would use some final trick to destroy whatever chance of happiness awaits her once she has gone from it. What could be worse than knowing the house she hated has fastened its talons into the one person dearest to her on this earth? The threat that Halewood may one day draw the boy back to it, even when he is full-grown, would hang over her like the sword of Damocles."

"The boy is young. He's going to a new country and to an entirely different environment. Gradually he will forget. Halewood will fade from his memory."

"Would you have forgotten it?" she challenged.

"No, but I happen to be a Hart. Roland is not. Tell me, how long have you known the boy?"

She rested her head against the back of the cushioned chair. "I first met him when I was an invalid staying at Halewood while my leg healed, and I've seen him since on the occasions when he's been at the house."

"How did you get on with him?"

"Quite well. He was never rude to me, but then I didn't represent a threat to him as your presence in the house must have done. I feel sorry for the boy. Lady Hart's idea of motherhood is to spoil him foolishly. Luckily he's had sensible foster parents, but the boy always wept bitterly when it was time to leave his mother."

"It appears now it was the house he didn't want to leave."

"Not altogether. His mother and Halewood must have seemed one and the same to him, and he felt rejected whenever he was sent back to his foster home. He is now secure in the knowledge that he's not to be parted from her again, and he wants to feel the same about the house. A logical explanation, but it still remains Halewood's vindictive triumph."

"You've given a great deal of thought to the boy's problems, haven't you?"

She inclined her head. "I'm fond of children. I'd like them all to have the sort of upbringing that I've had. A good home, discipline tempered with kindness and understanding, and lots of parental love. I'm the only one among all the girls I know who's not afraid of her father. He's never ruled me with a rod of iron. Unlike several of my friends, I'd never be expected to marry a husband who'd been picked out for me."

"Maybe you make your own mistakes." His comment fell like a stone in the silence of the room, which was broken only by the leaping dance of the flames in the coal fire.

Her face had swung towards him, startled and confused. "Are you suggesting I don't know my own mind as far as Matthew is concerned?"

"I'm suggesting you're not listening to your own heart." He reached out for her hand, but when his fingers touched hers she snatched her own away and placed them tremblingly against the base of her throat.

"I've known Matthew nearly all my life. I've loved him for as long as I can remember. Nothing can change that!"

"I agree nothing can or should change the fondness you feel for an old friend who was also your childhood sweetheart. But it's not love you feel for Matthew. Habit and obligation and a promise given before you and I met bind you to him."

"That's not true!" She sprang up from her chair as though she would flee from the room, but he was up in the same instant. He caught her by both her arms and held her, his head lowered as he looked into her frantic face.

"What are you afraid of? Of me? Or yourself?"

She knew the answer to that. Her fear sprang from the wild and senseless passion that had temporarily afflicted her, but it was nothing more than a storm in the heart, a storm that would pass. It was not to be listened to, not to be consulted, not to be allowed to disrupt the peaceful existence she had planned with Matthew, who would be a broken man if she went back on her promise now. He needed her! Aaron did not need her! He would have Halewood to fill his life!

"I hardly know you," she whispered brokenly. "You're a stranger in my home. I can count the days you've been here on the fingers of both hands."

"Time has nothing to do with it. It's something a man and woman know the moment they set eyes on each other. That sense of belonging. The miracle of discovering the other half of oneself. The knowledge that love is of the eye, mind, heart, and body, a combined force that cannot be denied. I knew when

111

you opened the door to me on the night I arrived at this house that it had happened. I'd found you."

"You mustn't say these things to me!" she cried.

He released her arms and cupped her face between tender hands, bringing his own so close to hers that his breath was warm on her lips. "To whom should I say them if not to you? I love you, Delia. I love you."

She could not move. She did not want to move, aware that this kiss would be entirely different from the time he had taken her lips with such fierceness at the gates of Halewood. Her eyes closed as his mouth, warm, moist, urgent, and alive, came softly down on hers and was exploratory at first, his lips discovering the shape of hers in a kiss that was many tiny kisses. Then his arms went about her and with a rush of passion he caught her body hard against his, arching her from the waist, holding her in an embrace that encompassed all she had ever imagined such a kiss of love might be, free of all restraint, released from all the confines of convention, given up to the joy of conquest and surrender.

Neither heard the clop of hooves on the drive. It was the sharp tap of a servant's heels going past the drawing room down the hall to open the front door that brought her back to reality and she thrust herself from him. She stood breathing deeply and he half-lifted his arms to her in a gesture of appeal, knowing that momentarily he had lost her.

"No!" she said agitatedly, making a little movement of her hands as if to keep him from her. "It can't be!"

Outside in the hall there was the sound of her father's voice. She heard Ellen answer, no doubt taking his hat and medical bag from him. Delia knew that he would be tired and he would come to sit for a while by the fire before going to bed. She had a few seconds left in which to withdraw so far from Aaron that he would never presume in such a way again.

"In two weeks' time Halewood will become yours at public action. Seven days after that I go to church to marry a man to whom I've given my promise. Our fates are settled. We are destined to go in opposite directions. Dismiss completely any hope that it can be otherwise!" The door opened and she turned quickly and with relief, greeting her father a little too effusively. "You're back, papa! Did all go well?"

"Mrs. Milner gave birth to her fifth son and wept, I regret to say, because it was not a girl, but her husband was content." He rubbed his chilled hands and held them to the warmth of the fire. "A brandy would not go amiss after being out in the cold night. Pour one for our guest, my dear, and another for your extremely tired father."

She did as he requested and then escaped to her room. There she shut the door and leaned against it for a few seconds with arms spread as if it were a barrier between her and Aaron. Then she went across to the bed and sat down on the foot of it, setting her hand against the post, her head bowed. Thoughts spun in her brain, her face reflecting her torment. If only she had met Aaron last year instead of this. If only she had never accepted without question that one day she would marry Matthew. If only she had never let him give her a betrothal ring. If only—if only—.

She heard the two men come up to bed. Some little joke passed between them and they laughed before parting company. Their respective doors closed. Immediately she sprang to her feet and walked up and down to assuage her restlessness of mind and spirit, hands clenched together. She would forget that kiss! Or, if she was never able to do that, she would thrust it away as a mere incident not to be thought about. When she and Matthew were married he would kiss her in that searing, intimate way and she would feel the same sharp flare of ecstatic longing. He would drive Aaron from her thoughts and from her heart!

She wrung her locked hands, giving emphasis to all

she had resolved. If only their marriage could be to-morrow instead of three weeks distant! She wanted to be safe with Matthew and given no more chance to lose all reason in Aaron's arms. How right she had been never to be alone with him since the day of the storm. Instinct had told her it would be dangerous, and then she had allowed it to happen. But not again! No, never again! Then, like the bursting forth of a mountain spring, the tears overcame her and she buried her face in her hands.

At Halewood the next day Berenice talked of how she had met Aaron and of her subsequent meeeting in the stables to relate the punishment that had been dealt out to Roland.

"He told me," Delia said briefly, not wanting to be drawn to any lengths on the subject of Aaron, but Berenice persisted.

"He seems quite spellbound over Halewood," she declared incredulously. "Not at all like his grand-father. Perhaps Sir Harry cared about the property in his younger days, but it's my belief he had come to hate Halewood toward the end of his life. It seems to happen to all who bear the Hart name and live under its roof."

For the first time the idea occurred to Delia that Sir Harry might have thought to end the curse of Halewood on the Hart family by deliberately avoiding any knowledge of a legitimate heir. Thus he would spare his descendants from all he and his ancestors had suffered. Certainly such a supposition put the old man in a more compassionate light. Delia made up her mind to pass on her idea to Aaron It was only right for him to have the chance to consider giving old Sir Harry the benefit of the doubt.

"I'll go and write these letters now," she said, collecting up the notes she had made.

"When you bring them back for me to sign we'll take tea," Berenice said, returning her attention to the embroidery she was at work on. "I'd like to hear what you intend wearing to the Penghyll Ball."

Making her way back along the north corridor to her east wing office, Delia considered the prospect of the ball with a heavy heart. She would not be able to avoid dancing at least once with Aaron. How would she react to being in his arms once again, no matter that it would be less intimate an embrace? It was not to be thought about. Not now. Time enough when the evening came upon her.

⊰ 7 ⊱

On the morning of the Penghyll Ball the postman's knock resounded as Delia was about to go into the study. She paused, watching as Ellen answered it and came from the door with a letter and two packages.

"More wedding gifts, miss!" the parlormaid exclaimed, her round face beaming.

"Yes, I'm sure you're right." Delia expected the letter to be handed to her with the packages, but Ellen withheld it. Normally Delia would not have given the matter a second thought, but something slightly furtive about Ellen's action made her give the girl a second look.

"T'letter isn't for you, miss." Ellen pressed it down out of sight in her pocket, making it crackle. "It's for me. From my ma."

Delia inclined her head and went into the study to unwrap the gifts, wishing that she could receive the well-meant kindnesses without being assailed afresh by depression, each one a reminder of her rapidly approaching wedding day. There were silver teaspoons in one package and a fine damask cloth in the other. She sat down to write letters of thanks and was sealing the second one when she heard Melissa return from the dressmaker's. Her cousin had decided on a last-minute alteration to the gown she had made up her mind to wear to the ball that evening.

Picking up both letters, she took them with her into the hall, intending to have them sent to the post, but she came to a standstill in surprise. Melissa was whispering to Ellen, their heads together. There was the clink of money being put in the parlormaid's hand. Melissa herself was holding the letter that Ellen had taken from her pocket. It was Melissa who noticed Delia first, and Ellen, following her gaze with a startled glance, flushed scarlet to the roots of her sandy hair and went scurrying away in the direction of the baize-lined door.

Melissa waved the letter tauntingly at Delia. "Have you guessed who it's from?"

"Yes. I believe so. It's from Richard Dibley, isn't it?"

Melissa nodded with a thrilling little laugh and ripped open the letter to read it through. With a smiling sigh she came to the end of it and held it to her breast, her eyes twinkling triumphantly at Delia. "I told you it couldn't be over between us. As soon as I was able to let him have my address he has been writing to me."

"It's none of my business whether he writes to you or not," Delia replied, "although I think you're being extremely unwise. But I do object most strongly that you should coerce Ellen into deceit. She felt compelled to tell me a lie. In most households she would be dismissed instantly."

"I don't care what happens to the stupid girl!" Melissa retorted crossly, throwing her hands up in the air. "I paid her well for keeping her mouth shut and it's her own silly fault if she gets discovered. I didn't want Uncle Charles to find out that Richard and I were writing to each other, or else he would most surely have stopped it."

Delia gave a nod. "You were right in supposing that. Papa would have done, I know. Aunt Rachel told him exactly why she and Uncle Henry wanted your romance with Richard to come to an end, and although normally he hasn't much patience with your parents, in this case his sympathies are entirely with them."

"Are you going to tell him?"

"You know I won't," Delia said with a sigh, "but I beg you not to make any promises to Richard. Wait. Take your time. It might not be the kind of everlasting love that you think it is. Let things ride for a while."

Melissa had picked up again the dressmaker's box containing her ball gown, which she had rested on a chair, and her little mouth smirked maliciously, her eyes mocking. "As you wish you had done?" she inquired, her tone silky. "Not knowing that Aaron was to come upon the scene?"

Delia could not answer her, her whole face taut. Had all the emotional turmoil she'd been going through shown up so obviously? With effort she managed to parry the question with another. "Why do you say that?"

"Keeping away from or deliberately avoiding contact with a man is a sure sign of being attracted to him against your will. You won't even meet Aaron's glance if you can help it. His eyes go to you as soon as he comes into a room. He sits looking across the table at you. Did you think I hadn't noticed that you've stopped me leaving you alone with him on some pretense several times?" She stepped nearer and thrust her face toward. "Well, I'm not like you, thank God! I'm prepared to risk everything for the man I want, and I wouldn't care who I walked over or knocked down to achieve my aim! Nothing on this earth is going to stop me marrying the man I love!"

With a flounce of petticoats she stalked away. Delia pressed the back of a trembling hand against her mouth. Nothing would have stopped her either if it had not been Matthew standing in her way. She could not trample him down, not he who had shown her so much love and kindness through all the years they had known each other. She thought of the dolls he'd mended for her, the time on a picnic when she'd got lost on the moors and he had hunted on his own far into the night, not knowing she'd been found by another child's nursemaid and taken home, and the way he had dried her tears and bandaged her cut head when she'd fallen from her pony. Then there was her first kiss. No one but Matthew could have kissed with such sweetness, shy himself, and she was moved to wonder by the enchantment of the moment. After that their relationship had developed and changed, reaching a different level. Always love had bound them together, for she knew his faults as well as he knew hers and neither imagained the other to be perfect. Even when frustrated and angry he would use her as a verbal whipping post, lashing out with hurtful words which later he wanted her to forgive. She had forgiven and forgotten, for the causes of his temper had been brief and passing things of no real importance, nothing serious enough to sever their affection for each other and invariably brought about by some outside trouble or annoyance that had had nothing to do with her in the first place. No matter how she stacked up against him his jealousy, his possessiveness, his shortness of temper, none of it outweighed the other side of his character, which had shown itself in gentleness a thousand times, or the fact that she knew herself to be the pivot around which his life turned.

Wearily she went back into the study and rang the bell. As she had expected, Annie had been sent to answer it. "Send Ellen to me, Annie," she instructed.

"Yes, miss." Annie's anxious expression showed that in the kitchen quarters it was already assumed that Ellen would be dismissed without further ado.

While waiting for the girl to appear Delia rested her elbows on the desk and held her head between her hands. She would reprimand Ellen severely, but that was all. Ellen's two years of faithful service entitled her to a second chance. Second chances didn't often come to people. She would have liked one herself, but that could never be.

That evening she was almost ready for the Penghyll Ball when Melissa came into the bedroom, wanting the back of her gown hooked up. It was iris blue tarlatan, which suited her coloring and the richness of her hair. Underneath she was well-laced, but she pressed her hands onto her waist as Delia fastened one tiny hook after another.

"That stupid dressmaker," Melissa grumbled. "She hasn't altered the gown as I wished. I can hardly breathe. It's a pity mama's lady's maid isn't here. She's French and *knows* how to sew. I miss her helping me dress. Mama always lends her to me for special occasions."

In spite of her complaints Melissa was not in an ill temper. On the contrary, she was singularly high-spirited and, to Delia's mind, quite astonishingly excited about the ball they were to attend, considering she had no interest in any of the young men who would be there.

"How do I look?" she demanded, taking Delia's vacated place before the dressing table's looking glass to touch a ringlet into place. Pearl drops swung from her ears and around her throat she wore a matching strand.

Delia paused in pinning a cameo brooch to the bodice of her cream bouffant gown, its stiffened underskirts holding out its rows of ribbon-edged frills. "Do you want my candid opinion?" she asked.

Melissa met her eyes in the glass, a secret, anticipatory look on her face. "Yes! What is it?"

"You look like a girl dressing to meet her lover."

Melissa gave a squeal of delight and swung around on the stool, her gown catching the sheen of the lamplight. "You've guessed!" she exclaimed delightedly. "Richard is going to be at the Assembly Rooms this evening! I'm hoping he'll be there waiting for me

121

when I arrive! Nobody knows him! Luckily Uncle Charles told me several days ago he wouldn't be attending the ball, and so I was able to go ahead and make plans with Richard for this night!"

Delia had not been looking forward to the ball, knowing that she must dance at least one dance with Aaron, uncertain how she would react to his nearness, and now she dreaded it even more. "It's madness," she said helplessly. "Penghyll isn't London. Newcomers are always noticed. All the older ladies sitting around the room will ask each other whose guest he is and if anyone knows his name. Tomorrow when my father goes on his rounds at least half a dozen people will ask him who the young man was who danced with his niece."

Melissa laughed, the color bright in her cheeks, and she leapt to her feet, flinging out her arms exuberantly as if she would embrace the whole world. "I don't care! Nothing matters except this wonderful night of reunion that awaits me!

Left alone, Delia draped about her shoulders the new shawl that Matthew had given her, feeling obliged to wear it. She liked it less than the Spanish one, although it was of delicate lace fine enough to pull through a wedding ring. Taking her furlined cloak from the mahogany wardrobe, she looped it over her arm to carry downstairs with her, knowing she would need its heavy warmth for protection against the truly bitter night with it buffeting wind, which held the peculiarly intense iciness that presages snow.

She found that Matthew had arrived and had joined Aaron and Melissa in the drawing room, where her father was comfortably ensconced in his favorite chair by the roaring fire, a book on his knees and several others, all on the subject of local history, stacked on the small table beside him. Delia was struck afresh by the handsomeness of the two young men who were in love with her. Matthew's tawny fairness and Aaron's darker good looks were set off by the formal black of their evening clothes and the sharp whiteness of their high collars, the cravats neatly tied, the gleaming edge of cuffs, and the snowy gloves smooth and unwrinkled. Neither could take his eyes from her when she pirouetted for her father's benefit, making her wide skirt sway and billow.

"You look very fine indeed, my dear," Dr. Gilmore commented warmly.

"The belle of Penghyll Ball, I'd say," Matthew endorsed, proud of her and grinning hugely in his pleasure.

Aaron said nothing. He did not have to. His eyes boldly paid her a greater compliment and she pulled her glance from his glittering gaze, fussing with her cloak. Then he was there, taking it from her and putting it about her shoulders before Matthew could reach her. It was Melissa whom Matthew found himself waiting on.

"Enjoy yourselves," Dr. Gilmore said, settling himself even more comfortably against the cushioned back and arms of his chair, folding his hands across his waistcoat. "I cannot say I wish I were coming with you, because it would not be true. This is the best place for me this evening—by the fireside."

"I hope you don't get called out," Delia said, bending to kiss him lightly on the cheek. She could tell he was looking forward to an evening on his own. They all bade him good night and went out to ride in the same carriage to the Assembly Rooms, the girls ·sitting side by side, the young men facing them. Melissa and Matthew did most of the talking. Once in the passing rays of a streetlamp Delia looked toward Aaron and their eyes met and held until darkness took over the interior of the carriage again.

Their vehicle soon joined a stream of others crossing the market square, wheels rumbling over cobbles, horses snorting and harnesses jingling as the drivers maneuvered into position to bring their passengers alongside the steps and pillars of the Assembly Rooms.

As the two girls and their escorts alighted, the freezing air bit into their faces and they hastened inside. After leaving their outdoor clothes, the four of them went up the side, curving staircase to the ballroom. It presented a spectacle of light and color, garlands hanging from the ceiling, flowering potted plants ornamenting the dais where the musicians were playing, and the mirrored walls and polished floor reflected the glow of the new gaslamp chandeliers and the swinging, bell-shaped skirts of the ladies rotating with their partners. All around the floor and on the balcony above, others were seated on gilded chairs and sofas, the buzz of conversation blending with the music.

Melissa, after looking about quickly and in vain for Richard, made a rueful little grimace at Delia to confirm that he had not yet arrived and then to pass the time she started renewing old acquaintanceships from her previous visits to Penghyll, including Tom Whinlatter, of whom Aunt Rachel had treasured such high hopes. Delia and Matthew were greeted on all sides by their friends and acquaintances, and Matthew presented Aaron, who found himself immediately in demand. To Delia it was obvious that to every mother there with a marriageable daughter—to say nothing of the daughters themselves—he was the catch of the season, for word had long since spread around the district that Edward Hart's son was to be among the bidders for Halewood, and tales of his supposed wealth had been enormously exaggerated.

Delia danced most of the time with Matthew and saw Melissa take the floor in turn with a variety of attentive young men, all showing their delight at seeing her again, laughing with her as they swept her into waltz, mazurka, polka, and polonaise. She was alive with happiness, her face glowing, her curls swinging. No doubt each young man imagined that it was for him alone that she sparkled, not noticing how she kept an alert and constant watch for another, glancing toward the arched entrance whenever fresh arrivals appeared. Aaron had one pretty partner after another, blonde, brunette, and redhead, their topknots and ringlets adorned with ribbons and flowers, each girl exuding the scent of violets or attar of roses, using every feminine art to attract, to intrigue, and to ensnare.

Delia danced several times with others to whom she had promised dances, but she was back with Matthew again when there was a stir among those standing near the head of the staircase, and the suddenly aroused interest spread like a ripple throughout the whole room. Delia, following the direction of the turning heads, gasped with amazement when she recognized the woman who had entered the ballroom.

"Matthew!" she exclaimed in disbelief. "It's Lady Hart! She's never once attended any social function in the county in all the years she's lived at Halewood! This is the first time ever! We must go to her!"

Berenice had not chosen a sober gown suited to widowhood but one of rich red velvet that was severely elegant over its supporting petticoats, and around her throat she wore a necklace of garnets set in gold which matched the earrings that flashed little sparks of crimson light as they swung from her ears. Over her face and head she wore a gilt-gauze shoulder-length mantilla of gossamer fineness, which was fastened to her burnished hair with golden combs.

Aaron, having decided to dance no more until he could take the floor with Delia, turned his head and saw her poised there on the threshold. Compassion moved him. She had tried for one brief, glorious night to play the lady of the manor, her gown tasteful, her choice of jewelry correct, but to him—and surely to every man present with some knowledge of the world —there was a sharp-edged brilliance about her that was unmistakable. Without hesitation he decided to make an amendment to his decision not to dance again except with a certain partner.

He moved toward Berenice, a tall figure threading

a passage through those clustered around the floor. When he reached her he closed his heels together and bowed deeply. "May I have the pleasure of this dance, Lady Hart?"

Relief showed in her eyes and he saw that she was as nervous as a young girl at a first ball. He wondered, remembering all that Delia had told him about her secluded way of life, why on earth she had ventured out into society at this late hour, when her departure from Halewood was almost imminent.

"Thank you, Mr. Hart." She let him lead her onto the floor and looked up into his face as she glided with him in the dancing steps. "I suppose everyone is much surprised to see me."

"They are, I'm sure of that." He was as much aware as she that all present were following their rotating progress down the floor.

"I saw how the word spread," she confided, a tiny smile pulling at her mouth. "Somebody at a window recognized my carriage even as I stepped from it, and in so many seconds there was a crowd of faces staring down."

"I guess few in this ballroom have ever set eyes on you before."

"Only from a distance." She acknowledged Delia as they passed in a bell-swing of their wide skirts.

"We had no idea you were coming," he remarked. "You gave Delia no hint."

"There was no point. I might have changed my mind at the last moment."

It was an insight into the torment of indecision she had gone through before eventually making the move to come. He could feel her trembling tautness as he held her. Around them the ballroom turned like a carousel, gaslamps and mirrored walls and the other dancing couples blending together in rainbow lights and textures.

"I hope you'll enjoy the evening now that you're here," he said.

She tilted her head. "I don't intend to stay more than a few minutes. It was simply a whim to see one Penghyll Ball before leaving Halewood."

"Surely you will stay to supper?"

"No, indeed. I should be forced to speak with local dignitaries and their wives whom I've no desire to acknowledge."

He was not deceived. She was fearful of being snubbed. By ignoring them it was she who was doing the snubbing. Her brief but glorious appearance at the ball was in itself a derisive gesture. She was showing herself to them as though they were peasantry.

"Do you intend to live as secluded a life in Italy as you have at Halewood?" he inquired courteously.

"I trust so. I seek peace and solitude. In Florence a villa with a walled garden awaits me. I shall paint and read and bask in the sunshine. When I emerge it will be only to visit a gallery or to go to church."

"What of Roland? Should he not have young company?"

She raised disdainful eyebrows. "I've no intention of mixing with the English émigrés there for his sake. He'll have lessons from a tutor to occupy him for most of the day. I'll buy him a pony. He can ride."

"Would it not be better to leave him at a school in England?"

"I want him to be with *me*," she said with sudden tragic emphasis. "Sir Harry kept me from him far too long."

He saw there was the glint of tears in her eyes. Again the sharp curiosity about her rose in him. When had this sensitive, vulnerable woman first taken on that defensive outward shell that was like a proclaiming mark on her? When had she first stepped onto the mercenary path? What had been the circumstances? Who was the first man to have corrupted and debased her into a way of life that she must have followed until Sir Harry in his dotage had offered a means of escape? He would never know. Such women never

127

talked about themselves. With her secrets she had come to Halewood and with them she would leave again.

The dance came to an end. Delia and Matthew were no more than two feet away and greetings were exchanged. "Now I'm going," Berenice said, and gently she waved aside Delia's protests. "Mr. Hart will explain why. Good night, Delia—Good night, Mr. Shaw."

"I'll escort you to your carriage," Aaron said.

Downstairs in the entrance hall the attendant, who must have been given instructions, was waiting with Berenice's sable cloak. Aaron took it and enfolded it about her shoulders. Then he walked with her down the steps to her waiting carriage. It had started to snow. Pale, silvery flakes were settling like a mantle over the town. The groom had sprung forward to open the carriage door for her. She gave Aaron her hand.

"I think we shall not meet again, Mr. Hart, I leave for Florence next week—the day before the auction. I wish you joy of Halewood. It brought none to me. But you love the house already and I never did. I pray that it will love you in return and soften its hard hearts toward you. Good night—and good-bye."

She stepped into the carriage. The groom slammed the door and jumped up behind, taking his place even as the carriage started to move, the horses with their breath steamy in the bitter night air obeying the flick of the coachman's whip. The wheels left dark tracks across the white square. Only when the carriage had vanished from his sight did Aaron turn and go back into the warmth of the building.

The call had come for the supper-dance. Melissa hastened across the floor to speak to Delia, her face desperately anxious. "Richard is late! He hasn't arrived yet!"

Delia tried to reassure her. "Don't worry. It's difficult to judge exactly how long any journey will take and it's many miles from the nearest railway station, remember. If there's been snow, a drift across the road could hold up a coach or force the driver to follow a longer route. Delays can happen all the time."

"What's that? Who's delayed?" Matthew asked, not having caught what was said.

Melissa shot Delia a warning glance and answered for her. "My partner for the supper-dance." She indicated the bare space on the little program dangling from her wrist. "I forgot to write it down."

Almost everyone was dancing. "We'll stay with you," Delia said, seeing that Melissa was distraught. Matthew would assume that the reason was that she was reluctant to leave Melissa a wall-flower for the supper-dance, which was every girl's nightmare.

"No need," Aaron said, catching her words as he came up to them. "Nobody should miss the supper-dance." He did not turn to Melissa as she had expected, but took her firmly by the hand while he addressed Matthew. "You, Matthew, can take Melissa onto the floor. I haven't had a chance to dance with Delia yet. This is my opportunity."

He swept her into the waltz before she could make any protest, one white-gloved hand holding hers, the other placed firmly on her waist. He did not speak, his eyes did not leave her as the dance took them around the floor. She felt compelled to break the silence of his stare.

"It won't be long now before you're back in these Assembly Rooms again," she said lightly. "But you'll be in the big hall downstairs, and an auctioneer will be on the rostrum."

A smile touched his mouth. "I'm counting on your coming to the auction with me. You'll bring me luck, I know."

"I'll attend with pleasure."

"It's right and proper that you should be there when it becomes mine. It is no longer only for myself that I want Halewood.'

She could not pretend not to understand his meaning.

There could be no pretense between them ever again. She sometimes felt that if she willed it she and Aaron would be able to read each other's very thoughts. An awareness of the devastating consequences of such revelations made her keep a tight mental barrier of restraint whenever she was in his company.

"Don't make everything harder for me," she implored unashamedly.

"I intend to give you no respite until you tell me once and for all you've finished with this masquerade that is deceiving neither of us," he replied, giving emphasis to his words with a tightening of his hands on hers.

Her betrothal ring was cutting into her finger under his grip and she welcomed the pain, taking it as a fierce reminder of where her true path lay, but the tears that stung the back of her eyes did not come from that small agony. It was from the greater hurt she was inflicting on her own heart and his.

"It's too late," she exclaimed despairingly.

"No, it's not!" He drew her closer to him than convention allowed. "The wedding can be canceled. Gifts returned! The chapter closed and another opened!"

The waltz was almost over. He spun her with slowly decreasing speed to the final notes of the music, and she found a way of answering him that could be no more to either of them than the tiny glow of a fading candle in a well of darkness.

"If Matthew should release me from my promise of his own free will, then I would listen to all you want to say to me. But the chance of that happening is too slight to be considered." The dance had ended, and she dipped her curtsy in a sea of rippling frills.

"It will happen!" He did not release her fingers. "It must happen! Without each other we shall both be destroyed."

She felt herself whiten, hearing the terrible ring of truth in his words. His face, which she had adored in her heart from the moment of meeting, was set, the mouth firm, and his eyes held such love for her that she wanted only to hurl herself in his arms, forgetful of all else, engulfed beyond recall by the answering wave of passion that was sweeping through her. She was actually teetering on her toes, her arms half-raised, when Matthew's hands gripped her by the shoulders and spun her round toward him.

"Stop daydreaming here! Everyone's going in to supper!" He was not smiling. He had been annoyed at Aaron's highhandedness in taking her away and leaving him with Melissa, for whom he had no liking, and now instead of joining the flow toward the supper-room Aaron had kept her on the floor in some serious conversation which—to judge by her startled, almost shocked reaction to his own intervention—had been upsetting her.

"Are they?" she gasped vaguely. "Where's Melissa?"

"Waiting for us. Come along."

In the supper-room Melissa had more than her fair share of young men wanting to wait on her, but she was offhand with all of them, taking no refreshment. "What's the matter?" Matthew asked when she refused the custard-ice he had brought for her with the one he had fetched for Delia. He thought she had seemed oddly detached and nervous when he had danced with her, and there was a pinched look about her mouth.

"Nothing's the matter!" she snapped back irritably. "Except you stepped on my foot while we waltzed. I don't know that I can dance any more." She sprang up from her chair like a released spring and swept away out of the supper-room.

Delia left her own untouched ice and followed after her. Melissa went hurrying down the stairway to the entrance hall. By the time Delia caught her up she was at a window looking out at the square, where a dusting of snow had fallen. She was quite frantic.

"He hasn't come! Oh, mercy, Delia! He should have arrived long ago! He must come! He must!"

"Give him time," Delia urged persuasively, genuinely concerned for Melissa, whose voice had become shaky and high-pitched, showing she was not far from hysteria. "Remember what I said about the snowfall? See the layer that has come down since we arrived at the ball? It will be much thicker on the hill-roads, and they could be impassable."

Melissa tossed herself around to face Delia, arms taut and fists clenched together. "Suppose he doesn't get here tonight or tomorrow or ever! Suppose something has happened to him! Something really dreadful! How shall I know? What shall I do?"

"If there was any kind of disaster anywhere along his route we should read about it in the newspapers tomorrow, and then we'd soon find out if Richard had been involved or not. But that's highly unlikely. I think you'll find that he's had to take shelter in an inn or hotel tonight."

"I don't know." Melissa gnawed her lip. "I wish I could believe that, but I can't. He should be here. He swore nothing should keep us apart a day longer. Only a catastrophe beyond anything imaginable would have stopped him coming to take me away at the hour we planned."

"What do you mean?" Delia demanded in hushed tones.

Melissa did not answer her, for her attention had been caught by a hackney cab which had turned into the square and was making for the steps of the Assembly Rooms. It was still some distance away, but it was the way the occupant, his face a misty oval, was peering through the cab window, conveying a sense of urgency, which succeeded in convincing her beyond a shadow of a doubt that her time of anxious waiting was at an end.

"It's Richard!" she breathed, her whole face becoming radiant. "He has come!" She grinned trium-

132

phantly at Delia, her eyes sparkling, her cheeks flushed with excitement and relief. "Now I'll tell you the rest of my secret, but you mustn't say a word until tomorrow! Richard and I are eloping! We had planned to disappear while everyone was having supper! I'd not have been missed until you were all ready to leave in the early hours of the morning. But, as you said, Richard must have been delayed by the weather. He will have picked up at the coaching-station a packed valise that I smuggled out of the house yesterday. I'll send for the rest of my boxes as soon as we're safely abroad and married. Then papa can do nothing to prevent my receiving my inheritance! Don't look so serious. Rejoice with me! I'm going to get my cloak and you get yours. I want you to come out to the hackney cab with me and wave me farewell. It's a pity you haven't any rice to throw."

Giggling excitedly, she shot another glance out at the approaching cab and hustled Delia with her into the anteroom to get their cloaks. Delia, fastening her clasp, was not averse to meeting Richard. She would be able to judge him better for herself than from such diverse evidence as that which had been provided by Melissa and Aunt Rachel.

The cab came to a halt as the two cousins emerged from the building. Melissa ran down the steps, followed at a slower pace by Delia, who was trying to pull up her hood. When she heard Melissa give a cry she lifted her head sharply and saw to her astonishment that her own father and a middle-aged man, a stranger to her, were alighting from the vehicle.

"Uncle Charles!" Melissa gasped hoarsely, able to tell from his expression that he knew whom she had been expecting to find in the cab.

"Melissa," he began, breathing heavily as though having difficulty in inhaling the ice-cold air, "I have to tell you that Mr. Dibley, who is in good health and has come to no harm, will not be arriving to fetch you. Allow me to present Mr. Foley, who has been sent by your father's lawyers and will explain what has happened as soon as you have returned to Sycamore House with us."

"Good evening, Miss Barton." The man was thickset and coarse-featured, plainly dressed in tweed traveling clothes.

Melissa stood as though transfixed, looking from one to the other of them, her eyes enormous in her blanched face. "I want to know now!" she demanded harshly. "Where is Richard? Why isn't he here?"

"Get into the cab, Melissa," the doctor said. He would have assisted her, but she snatched herself back, throwing off his hand.

"No! It's a trick! Somehow you've found out that he's on his way to Penghyll and you're trying to get me away while there's time!"

Delia, who had come to her side, spoke up. "Is that true, papa?"

"No, my dear. Help me to persuade Melissa that we have only her good at heart. This is no place for her to receive the news that we have to tell."

Delia turned to her cousin. "I don't know what it can be, but take papa's advice." She was equally concerned for her father, whose face looked drawn, his color patchy. She could imagine how his peaceful evening had been shattered by the arrival of this stranger out of the blue to tell him that his niece had planned an elopement and that it was being stopped.

Melissa spoke through gritted teeth. "I'm not moving a step until I know what's happened!"

Dr. Gilmore rubbed an anxious hand across his forehead at her insistence, and although he ignored the nod from Mr. Foley encouraging him to answer her, he did capitulate. "Very well," he said with regret. "It is my sad and painful duty to tell you that you have trusted and believed a young villain who cares nothing for you. He has been watched and followed. When he purchased rail and Channel packet tickets from London to Calais it was not difficult for Mr. Foley to deduce what he had in mind."

Melissa turned like a fury on Mr. Foley, her eyes glazing. "So you're a spy! A despicable little spy sent out to snoop on your betters!"

Mr. Foley's immobile face remained impassive. Abuse was nothing new to him and he merely tilted his head attentively at the doctor, waiting to hear what he would say next.

Dr. Gilmore was finding the whole affair upsetting and exceedingly distasteful, not least of all his brother-in-law's use of a paid spy or private detective, as Mr. Foley chose to call himself, and he tried to find the words to ease the blow that must befall his unfortunate niece, for he could not allow the unpleasant Mr. Foley to be the bearer of the news. "I have not inquired into Mr. Foley's methods of investigation, nor do I intend to, but it suffices to say he was able to obtain sufficient information to discover the day that Mr. Dibley intended to spirit you away from my present care into the unknown. Whereupon your father gave instructions that Mr. Dibley be approached with an offer of financial reimbursement in return for signing a certain document."

"Why? For what reason?" Still Melissa had not grasped the terrible fact that was only too clear to Delia.

"Your father realizes that to thwart his elopement attempt would not be enough in itself. Unless he kept you locked up, which was impossible, or kept you under constant surveillance indefinitely, there was nothing to stop another more cunningly planned elopement being attempted and perhaps carried out successfully."

"He's right in thinking that!" Melissa retorted defiantly. "Nothing shall—"

Dr. Gilmore interrupted her. "Hear me out, child. Mr. Dibley left yesterday for a destination abroad that is not to be made known to you. He has agreed never to see you again."

Melissa collapsed without a sound. Dr. Gilmore and Mr. Foley picked her up between them and lifted her into the cab. Delia would have gone with them, but her father bade her return to the ball.

"At all costs we must keep this affair quiet. There must be no scandal, Delia. Make some excuse to explain her absence to Matthew and Mr. Hart. I'll tell you all the details later."

Delia hurried back inside to find Matthew looking for her.

"Wherever have you been?" he asked in amazement, seeing her in her snow-covered cloak.

"Melissa has gone home in a cab," she answered as calmly as she could.

"Hmm. Making a fuss about my stepping on her foot," Matthew grumbled. "I barely touched her toe. Come along. Let's go back to the dancing."

They stayed until the early hours of the morning. Delia would have left long before if the decision could have been hers to make, but Matthew was enjoying himself, the fun having become faster and more furious, and she could not leave without him. She and Aaron danced several more times together, but they no longer talked except with their eyes, he saying such loving things to her that at times she could not bear to receive his silent messages and danced in his arms with her eyes downcast.

She had grasped the consequences that would result if she did go through with the marriage to Matthew. As Aaron had warned, she would destroy not only her life and his, but Matthew's too. Sooner or later, no matter how she tried to disguise the fact from him, Matthew would discover that she had married him out of loyalty and affection and not through love. Then he would not know how to cope with his anguish and misery. She, understanding him as she did, had no doubt as to the form his frustration would take. She, whom he would love no less, would become by her very presence in their home a constant

136

thorn in his side, and never again would there be harmony between them, his resentment increasing as the love he desired from her slipped ever from him.

The ball came to an end at last. She sensed that Aaron was as thankful as she that it was over. Matthew had offered two acquaintances a lift and the carriage was crowded. When it reached Sycamore House she was swift to bid him good night and hurry indoors, where she went upstairs at once, leaving Aaron to enter after her and lock up the door.

Her father's bedroom door stood ajar and a candle flickered. She pushed it a little wider. "Papa?" she whispered, uncertain whether he was awake.

He had taken to sleeping propped against his pillows in recent months and he rolled his head around toward her, lifting his hand, which had been pressed against his chest, to beckon her forward. "Have you looked in at Melissa? I gave her a sleeping draft to calm her or else she wouldn't have closed her eyes this night."

"Do you want me to check on her?"

"She'll be all right, but you can put your head round her door before you go to bed."

"Why aren't *you* asleep?" she questioned with mock reproof, sitting down on the edge of the bed.

"I have been, but I heard the carriage come up the drive."

"Have you a pain?" she asked with a frown of concern, seeing how he rubbed his knuckles against his chest.

"A touch of dyspepsia. Nothing more."

"Can I fetch you a drink of sugared water?"

"No, no. I've taken something for it. It will soon go off."

"Where's Mr. Foley?"

"He's putting up at a local hostelry for the night. We shall not see him again, thank God! Deucedly unpleasant fellow. He arrived saying that Melissa had planned to elope direct from the ball and we must get there and bring her away before she gave way to distress or hysteria when Dibley failed to arrive. My brother-in-law's chief consideration in all this, has been his fear of scandal, which would ruin his chances in the election. His concern for his daughter had been of secondary importance, although there's no denying Melissa is well rid of the young scallywag. He would have brought her nothing but misery."

"How was Richard Dibley persuaded to give up Melissa? Surely her inheritance was more than any sum Uncle Henry would offer?"

"But Dibley wasn't going to get his hands on her money. Henry has a couple of clever lawyers. It's a long and complicated will and they'd managed to pinpoint some tiny clause that could mean withholding payment through some counterclaim from Henry himself. A ridiculous situation, but it was enough to make Dibley realize that even if he pressed on and eloped with Melissa it could be a long wait before her money was finally in his hands. He accepted a cash settlement and agreed to go abroad for an indefinite period. He was glad to do it. Henry had been pulling other strings and there was the possibility of a charge of embezzlement and subsequent imprisonment. The young man's affections for Melissa just melted away."

Delia let her shoulders rise and fall in a long deep sigh. "What a sad and sordid business. Poor Melissa. What happens now?"

"Henry and Rachel want her to stay with us for a while. They're too busy with the election to cope with the gloom and tears that are bound to follow. I can keep a professional eye on her, but I'm afraid it's a lot to expect you to manage with the wedding on your mind."

"I think it's best she stay with us," she agreed, "but as to my wedding"—she fell silent. She wanted to talk to him again about her dilemma, but this was not the time for it. He had had a most exhausting night with

138

little sleep and it was almost morning. She rose from the bed. "I'll look in at Melissa. Good night, papa."

Melissa was sleeping soundly, tears wet on her cheeks. Delia went into her own room, and by the time she climbed into bed and slid down under the covers there was already a stirring in the servant's quarters in preparation for a new day. Somewhere in the distance a cock crowed.

8

DELIA seemed hardly to have closed her eyes before she was roused from heavy slumber by someone shaking her shoulder. Ellen's voice came through to her. "Wake up, miss! Something horrible's happened!"

Her first thought flew to Melissa and she bounced up in bed, thrusting back the hair from her eyes, her heart thumping. "What is it?"

"Your father, miss!" Ellen's face was ashen. "Annie took his shaving-water and couldn't get a reply. She opened the door and found him lying face downward on the floor!"

Delia flung herself from the bed. On bare feet with nightgown flapping she raced to her father's room and the anxious Annie drew back from the door to let her pass. She saw at once he must have fallen from the bed while reaching for a vial on the bedside table, for it lay by his hand, the liquid it had contained spilled into a pool. Dropping to her knees beside him, she felt for the pulse in his neck and found it was beating, although weak and irregular. He was alive! She looked over her shoulder at the two servant girls.

"You, Annie, wake Mr. Hart and fetch Cobby from the stables to help lift my father back into bed!" She snatched down a blanket from the bed as she spoke and covered him. He was cold through his linen night-shirt and she had no idea how long he had been lying there. "You, Ellen, send the coachman on horseback

141

posthaste to my father's partner, Dr. Pomfret! He's to come at once! Understand?"

"Yes, miss!" they chorused together and ran off on their errands. She heard the pounding on Aaron's door and Annie's anxiety-pitched voice was answered by his deep tones. Seconds later he came hastening into the room, tying the cord of his dressing gown, his feet as bare as hers.

"Is it a stroke?" he asked quickly in deep concern, going down on one knee beside the prostrate man and feeling immediately for the pulse in the limp wrist that he lifted from the floor.

"I think so. I don't know. I've sent for the doctor."

"I'll get him back into bed."

"The groom will be here in a minute to help you." The words came shakily. Shock had set in and she was shivering. Aaron put a hand on her shoulder.

"Go and put on a robe. You'll take cold."

"Not yet. I must see papa into bed first."

He reached for another blanket and folded it about her. She put her head on one side and rested her cheek against his hand as he did so, her eyes closing tightly. "Thank God you're with me!"

The groom came clattering up the stairs. Swiftly he lent a hand and together he and Aaron lifted the doctor back into bed. Only then did Delia realize her father was still conscious. He opened his eyes and looked at her, whispered something she could not catch, and gave a long groan of pain.

She sat by his bed, holding his hand between hers, and left him only to complete her morning toilette and put on the clothes that Ellen had brought her in his dressing room, where she could keep an eye on him through the half-open door. Slipping a last hairpin into her tresses, she returned to the bedside and once more slid her fingers under her father's hand on the coverlet and held it. He lay perfectly still with his eyes closed, breathing with difficulty. She hoped that she was giving him comfort through contact, as

Aaron's presence in the room had been succor to her in her hour of need.

Dr. Pomfret wasted no time in coming. He was a youngish man, brisk and capable in his manner, and he diagnosed a seizure of the heart. He did what he could for the patient, who was to have absolute quiet, and having administered a dose of laudanum to ease the pain, he gave Delia instructions about giving further doses.

"I'll be back later," he said, picking up his bag, "and in the meantime I'll send along a nurse whom I know to be clean, conscientious, and reliable."

"But I want to look after my father myself!"

"Come, come, Miss Gilmore. We can't have you at the bedside twenty-four hours of the day, or else I shall have a second patient in this house. Be advised by me. Your father needs constant and careful nursing, and if you're tired out you cannot give it. You want the best for him, don't you?"

"Indeed I do!"

"That's settled then."

He left, and she went back to stand by the bedside, pressing trembling fingertips against her mouth. Aaron, after speaking to Dr. Pomfret in the hall, returned to the room. She turned when he reached her, throwing herself into his arms and burying her face against his neck. He held her hard and tight in wordless sympathy.

When they drew apart he put up his hands and gently stroked her face from cheekbones down to chin. "There's always hope," he whispered. "Your father is a strong man. He'll fight this attack if we do all we can to help him. Don't despair, my love. Don't despair."

She gave a little nod, managed a glimmer of a smile in response to his encouragement, and went back to her chair at the bedside to take up her vigil again.

It was after midday when Melissa came to see her. Delia gave a start, ashamed that she had forgotten all about the unfortunate girl in the midst of her own troubles, and she was relieved to see that Melissa had not surrendered to tears and apathy but wore her hair neatly dressed and had on one of her prettiest afternoon gowns in striped blue merino. Her face, although pale, her still-swollen lids bearing evidence of much weeping, was composed and set in hardness. It was easy to see she would not give her heart again with reckless abandon. All that was frivolous in her nature seemed to have been consumed in bitter resignation and all that was ruthless had turned to steel. Observing that she was about to speak, Delia put a finger to her lips and rose to draw her away from the bed and into the dressing room.

"Papa mustn't be disturbed," she whispered. "How are you? Have you eaten?"

"I've spent the morning in my room and I've had nothing, but I'm not hungry. Oh, don't worry about me. You've enough to think about with Uncle Charles. Is he very ill? Annie told me all about finding him."

"Yes, he is."

"I thought there was something the matter last night, although I was in such a state myself I could hardly think. He went into the dispensary to fetch me a special kind of medicine to calm me down, because I was quite beside myself, and I heard a crash. When he came back to the drawing room there was powder all down his jacket. He held on to the back of the chair when he passed me the medicine and his hand shook more than mine—and I could hardly hold the glass, which rattled against my teeth. Then I went up to bed feeling strangely light-headed, almost tipsy. I remembered nothing more until this morning."

Delia found herself trying not to blame Melissa for being the cause of her father's heart attack, but it was impossible not to take into account all the upsetting events of the previous night and stack them together. Determinedly she reminded herself that he must have been in poor health for a considerable while, and it could have happened at any time and anywhere.

"You must try to eat luncheon," she said. "Aaron will eat with you. I'm staying in the sickroom."

Melissa looked disdainful. "There's no need to suppose I'm going to pine away. I've no intention of doing that." Then her voice became acid, her mouth tightening to control the tremulous lips. "Richard was paid off, you know. My dear father paid him off. And do you know what was in the letter that my devoted parent had delivered to me by that hateful Mr. Foley? He wrote that if ever I went against his wishes again he would turn me out and fight his claim to my great-aunt's money through to the High Court to make sure that not a penny of it came to me."

"Oh, Melissa—," Delia said unhappily.

"Don't pity me!" Melissa flashed sharply, interrupting whatever she had been about to say. "I won't be pitied! Never mention last night's affair to me again. Uncle Charles agreed to that last night when we talked after he had sent Mr. Foley away. I'm putting Richard out of my mind. Will you agree to forget that he ever existed?"

"Of course I will."

"It's a relief that I can stay on here. I feel I never want to see my home or my father again. Now I'm going to send a groom to collect my valise from the coach station for me. After that I'll come and take a turn at the bedside if you like. I don't mind what I do to help. In any case I'll be glad of a chance to sit and think."

On her own again Delia went over all that Melissa had said, and she frowned uncertainly. She could tell Melissa had spent the whole morning alone in her room coming to terms with the situation. It had not crushed her, which was admirable, but there was something odd about her abrupt severing of the past that seemed to spring more from desperation than from courage. She talked as if she had some other matter on her mind that she must plot to see through. Could she be planning some revenge against her father for putting an end to the romance? That was unlikely, but what else could it be?

There came a moan from the bed. Delia sprang forward to lean over her patient and forgot about Melissa once more.

Nurse Baker arrived in mid-afternoon. She was not a stranger to Delia, who knew her from the times she had been called in to attend to some of the practice's more well-to-do patients. She was plump and straw-haired, neat in her appearance, and always wore on duty a starched apron and a tiny cap that tied under her chin.

"What a sorry state of affairs this is," she said, clucking her tongue as she smoothed the sheet over the patient. "Now you take a rest while you can, Miss Gilmore. I'll call you if I think you should come—and I'd appreciate a tray of tea."

Delia, after giving the order for the tea, which was to be the first of many such trays borne up to Nurse Baker, ignored the well-meaning advice to rest and went instead to check on the state of the dispensary, wondering what her father had broken to cause the crash that Melissa heard. She was opening the locked door of the dispensary with her own key when Melissa, who had heard her, came drifting into the study.

"How is Uncle Charles?" she inquired listlessly.

"No change," Delia replied with a suppressed and deeply anxious sigh. Then she stepped into the dispensary and gasped at the mess. A smashed jar lay on its side at her feet and the powder it had contained had spread out and settled dustlike over the entire black-and-white checkered floor. "I must get Annie to come and clean this up!"

As Delia pulled the bell rope Melissa picked up a blue glass bottle that stood on the table and removed the stopper to sniff the contents. "This is what I was given last night," she remarked. "I slept like a stone. Do you think I could have some more tonight? I don't want to lie awake."

Delia took the bottle and set it back in a glass-fronted cabinet where it belonged. "I can't let you have that. I wouldn't know the dosage anyway."

"It was about a tablespoon, I'd say."

"*About* is not accurate enough with anything on these shelves. I'll ask Dr. Pomfret to prescribe a sleeping draft for you." To Delia's relief Melissa did not argue the point and accepted her suggestion.

Annie was quick to fetch a bucket of soapy water and a cloth to clean up the mess. Delia stayed in the dispensary to wipe the powdery dust from flagons that she knew her father would not want the servants to touch. Melissa wandered out into the study and looked unseeingly along the bookshelves, fingering the collection of volumes of local history and folklore without really taking note of what she was doing, her thoughts turned inward. She intended to get her hands on that bottle somehow for use in what she deemed to be an emergency. The audacity of what she had thought out that morning almost frightened her, but somehow it had to be done. She had only to watch and pray—to the devil if need be!—for the right opportunity and seize it when it came. She had nothing to lose and everything to gain. The whole scheme had come to her while she had wept, not shedding tears for her lost love or the dream that had been shattered, but only for herself. She, who could have had the pick of men, had made a fool of herself and been duped like any foolish servant girl. Had her humiliation become public knowledge in London among her friends and acquaintances she would not have been able to face it. Never had she thought to look upon the Pendle district of Lancashire as a haven. She envied Berenice, who was able to keep locked doors between herself and inquisitive intruders. No longer did she think of Halewood as a gloomy den, for in her present state of distress she saw it as a shining refuge.

Delia was locking the dispensary door and her voice broke in on Melissa's thoughts. "That's papa's favorite reading when he's not taken up with new writings on medical matters."

"What?" Melissa turned toward her.

Delia, seeing her cousin's completely blank expression, indicated the leather and gilt-lettered spines along which Melissa had been running a finger. "Those books are papa's treasures."

"Oh, are they?" Melissa remarked dully.

"He has files of his own notes on the research he has done throughout the years while he's been in practice in Penghyll," Delia continued as they went from the study together. Then, seeing that there appeared to be no chance of arousing Melissa's interest in that subject or anything else, she parted from her at the foot of the stairs. "I have to put the dispensary key away in my room, and after that I'll be sitting at papa's bedside. Don't be alone. Aaron talked of taking a stroll about the town to look at some of the old buildings. Why not go with him?"

Melissa dipped her head, a closed look on her face, her eyes hooded. "I think I will." She went off to find him, her hard little mouth set in a thin, determined smile that Delia did not see.

Matthew came to the house that evening. He had been told of the doctor's heart attack by his grandparents. Delia received him in the study, away from the drawing room where Melissa had asked Aaron to play a game of chess with her.

"I came as soon as I heard," he said, putting his arms about her. He was genuinely upset. He liked and respected Dr. Gilmore, and in addition there was another side of the matter which had to be discussed.

She moved away from him and sat in the swivel chair by the desk. "You realize what this means." She picked up a quill pen from its stand and played with

Hart mentioned the surprising number of seriously interested purchasers, many of whom—to her relief—have been devoting more time to pacing about on the land in rain and mud than trailing through the house itself."

"But you told me that Aaron isn't a rich man."

"He isn't. But he has been given the top figure that Halewood is likely to fetch and has no qualms about being able to meet it."

"He *had* the top figure," Matthew pointed out pedantically, "but I should say that in the past few days it's soared to a much higher one."

She froze. Frightened. Frightened for Aaron. Frightened for the house. "Are you telling me that the railway company wants the land?"

He nodded. "Part of it. There is an alternative siting, but to lay tracks across a section of the Halewood land would cut the distance by several miles. No mean consideration in terms of labor, steel, blasting, and tunneling."

"It's sacrilege!" she expostulated, horrified.

"The house won't be touched. Admittedly its views will be changed to the north and west because the woods must be thinned out and many of the trees felled. Some of the old cottages and a farmstead will have to go, too. Whoever lives in the house will be able to see the railway from most of the windows, but there's no danger of it being turned into a signal box."

"That's not funny!" she slammed a hand down on the desk.

"It wasn't meant to be," he retorted, suddenly as heated as she. "You think too much about that damned house and if I had my way I'd have it razed to the ground!"

"Such an act of vandalism could take place if it isn't kept in the Hart family!" she cried, her color high, her eyes flashing, and she wrung her hands. "Aaron must be told of this new turn of events. Perhaps if he's forewarned—"

"What difference could it make now? Remember the auction is only four days away. If he's already scraped the barrel, where could he raise any more at this late hour? The property is expected to reach a record figure, I've heard. A really great sum involving thousands and thousands of pounds."

"So much!" she exclaimed distractedly.

"Do you want me to tell him?" Matthew's expression showed he would not be averse to the mission.

"No!" She calmed herself with effort. "I'll do it. It won't be easy, but it's better that it should come from me."

"Why?" He poked his face towards her with aggressive curiosity. "What makes you take on such an unpleasant duty when you've so much else to think about?"

Her shoulders slumped and she bowed her head, holding her brow in her hand. "Because I'm the one responsible for having brought him here in the first place. It was I who raised his hopes falsely and let him imagine for such a brief spell that one day he would be master of Halewood."

Matthew looked slightly shamefaced. He hadn't meant to lose his temper with her today of all days, when her father lay practically at death's door in a room above. But always when he wanted to be closest to her she seemed to hold back some part of her whole nature from him, keeping him at a distance even when his arms were about her. As well as her body he wanted to possess her every thought, her every feeling, sparing nothing for anyone else, and sooner or later he would do it. Surely that time would come when Halewood had passed into hands other than those of Aaron Hart, and when its lands were dissected, engine smoke drifting across to hasten the decay of its stonework with soot and to ruin its gardens. In his own way he could destroy Halewood, and he could do it guiltlessly in the name of progress.

"I'll be going," he said, picking up his hat.

"Yes," she answered vaguely. "We must talk again. Another time."

She walked with him to the front door. He would have kissed her, but her face was averted from him. He stepped into the porch and clapped his tall hat on his head.

"I hope Dr. Gilmore is better soon. I'll look in again tomorrow evening. When he can have visitors I'd like to see him."

"Of course. You shall be the first." She was already closing the door.

She went into the drawing room. The game of chess was no longer in progress. Melissa had seated herself at the harp in the adjoining music room and was plucking the strings in a gentle, romantic little tune. She looked exceedingly pretty in her graceful pose, only the heaviness about her eyes an indication that all was not as well with her as she wanted it to appear, but the lamplight was flattering and made a golden aura of her hair. Aaron, listening from the large wing chair by the fire, chin in hand, did not notice Delia's approach, but he turned his head quickly when she sat down on the sociable nearby and gave her a warm glance and a smile. When the last sweet notes of the music faded away they both applauded Melissa.

"Thank you," he said to the girl. "I enjoyed that immensely."

"I only hope I'm not disturbing Uncle Charles," Melissa said a trifle shortly, showing Delia that she resented her intrusion, "but I couldn't concentrate on chess this evening."

"No, I'm sure you're not," Delia replied. "He wouldn't be able to hear the music upstairs. I'm afraid I'm the one to disturb you." She made a little placating gesture with her hands. "I'm sorry, but I have to ask you to let me speak to Aaron alone. It is an important matter."

Melissa sighed somewhat petulantly, but she rose from her seat at the harp. "I had intended to retire early anyway. Good night."

When she had left them on their own Aaron's mouth twisted in amusement, his eyes twinkling. "Melissa has been uncommonly civil to me this evening. I can't begin to fathom the reason. Until now she's taken a vixenish delight in goading me about my American accent, my way of expressing myself, and anything else American that she can find fault with."

Incredulously Delia considered what he had said, although she was careful not to show it. Surely Melissa wasn't setting her sights on Aaron! Was she so determined not to return to her home and parents that she was prepared to try to ensnare the very next man who seemed suitable as a husband? Were Melissa's feelings even more shallow than she herself had suspected? Delia drew in her breath and released it again. This was not the time to think about Melissa. She had a much more serious matter to deal with. Promptly all other thoughts went from her.

"I've bad news," she began. Hastily she shook her head when she saw he believed she was referring to the condition of the patient upstairs. "It's to do with Halewood."

"Yes?" His eyes narrowed at her.

"Matthew just told me. The railway company has expressed an interest in the land. It will make the price soar at the auction."

The bones of his face showed white, but not a muscle twitched. He spoke quietly and levelly. "Then I must find the extra money somehow."

"But where?" she exclaimed. "I have a litttle money of my own and you're welcome to it, but it will be no more than a drop in the ocean."

"You offer touches me, my darling, but I'll not accept it. I must consult a banker in the morning and also visit Mr. Radleigh. Time is against me. Had I known such a catastrophe was likely to occur I could have pressed for a greater loan before leaving Boston, but Radleigh assured me that he had quoted a figure that was above anything the property was likely to fetch."

She reached out and rested her hand on his sleeve. "When the sale was just an ancient house and a good spread of land you had only to compete with those seeking the prestige of such a dwelling-place, the men who've made the money out of Lancashire's coal and railways and cotton mills—but now the auction will attract a wider field. Matthew says the price will soar by thousands. The speculators are moving in."

"Dear God!" he exclaimed hoarsely, leaning forward to let his elbows drop to his knees, his head falling into his hands. "Thousands! Now! When it was almost mine!"

She moved swiftly across to him and his arms received her, drawing her onto his knees, and they sat enfolded in each other's embrace, she comforting him as earlier that day he had comforted her. They had no need for words. The understanding beetween them was absolute. They spoke only in lovers' touches of the brushed cheek, the caressing hand, the soft balm of lips in traveling kisses over the face, the gentle pressure of arms, and the sensuous snugness of bodies molded together.

"You may find someone willing to give you a loan to bridge the gap," she said hopefully, stroking a strand of hair back from his forehead. "If only papa were well I'm sure he'd speak on your behalf to someone—"

"Oh, I haven't lost Halewood yet," he answered with determination. "If it's humanly possible I'll raise the money somewhere, but it will make a pauper of me for years to come." He looked into her face, compressing his lips in a wry smile. "How will you like living on bread and cheese at Halewood and wearing patched gowns?"

She knew he was exaggerating the outcome of his poverty, but she answered him seriously. "If fate allows me to become your wife I ask for nothing more in life."

His hand slid up the back of her neck under her hair to cup her head, bringing her forward to meet his kiss, and she gave up her mouth to his in its loving passion.

A long, sweet sigh escaped her when she slid from his knees. She turned to face her flushed reflection in the gilt-framed looking glass that hung on the wall above a rosewood cabinet, and put up her hands to tidy her hair. He came and looped his arms about her waist, standing behind her as he put his face against hers, meeting her reflected eyes in the looking glass.

"Did you speak to Matthew about us while he was here?" he asked.

"I tried, but then he told me about Halewood and that put an end to it."

"He must learn the truth of the matter. I've never associated with any man yet under false colors and I'm sure that Matthew is the same. I'll have it out with him myself without further delay."

"No!" She swung around within the circle of his arms and took his face between her hands. "Please be patient! I thought this evening the right moment had come for me to break it to him, but he swept it aside. I believe that in his heart he knows that I've drifted from him—he admitted it in so many words —but as yet he can't bring himself to accept it. Somehow I must bring him face to face with the realization that we could no longer be happy together. Tomorrow I must write to all who were coming to the wedding to tell them that due to my father's illness it will not take place. That's as far as I can go until Matthew has taken back the ring."

"Make it soon," he implored, tightening his arms to crush her against him, and she saw by the tautness of his face that he was desperately afraid of losing her and would know no peace of mind until she was his. Some of his fear touched her, and it was to hide the fact that she was also afraid that fate might yet tear them apart that she now kissed him until they were lost again in their own private wonder of each other.

She wrote the letters on her writting box at her father's bedside, letting Nurse Baker free of her duties for a while, He knew she was there, for he had whispered her name once, but he slept most of the time, drugged by laudanum. She had no heart for the task in hand, not because she was not overwhelmingly thankful to be released from a set marriage date, but because it was hard to concentrate on anything but the suffering of her parent, and time and time again she held the pen idly in her hand, watching him anxiously, until she forced herself to continue.

Aaron had gone to consult the two sources from which he hoped to gain guidance on the speedy raising of funds, but she could see no hope for him. She thought of him as part of Halewood, part of Lancashire but in the sight of others he was an alien with an unfamiliar accent who had nothing to offer for collateral security on this side of the Atlantic Ocean and no time to obtain proof of backing from the other side of it. The auction was the day after tomorrow. Already the hours were running out against him.

Although they had not talked about it, she knew he would not stay in England unless he were the owner of Halewood. He had nothing else to hold him here and he would never be able to endure living under an English sky while another occupied the house that should have been his. She realized she would have to go with him to Boston and start a completely new life as the wife of an American citizen. Adapting to new ways and new customs would be easy compared with another aim to which she would be dedicated, for she must be all in all to him, driving away the memory of Halewood and what might have been, filling his life with love and companionship until at last his thoughts no longer slid away from her back to a great house on a hill around which the wind never ceased to moan.

But as yet such plans were only dreams. She took up her pen again and the scratch of a nib and the breathing of the patient became the only sounds in the quiet room.

The last letter was written. She closed her writing box as Nurse Baker returned, bringing a small glass of egg wine and a spoon to feed the patient. "There's someone asking to see you downstairs, Miss Gilmore," she said. "I told the housemaid that I'd pass the message on."

Delia left the sickroom. She expected to find one of her father's friends or another of his loyal patients waiting to inquire after him. But it was an office boy from Mr. Radleigh's chambers who stood in the hall, hat in hand.

"Morning, Miss Gilmore. I've to tell you that Mr. 'Art 'as gone to Preston on Mr. Radleigh's advice. 'E said as you'd know why. 'E don't expect to be back until late tonight or perhaps tomorrow. It all depends."

"Thank you," she said, hoping desperately that Aaron had not gone on a wild-goose chase that would end in more disappointment and fresh hopes dashed. After the boy had gone she fetched her bonnet and coat and went herself to post the letters, feeling a need for a little exercise. The snow had turned gray in the streets but there was the promise of more in the sharp air which stung the color into her cheeks, invigorating her after the long hours in the sickroom. She did not turn for home again after reaching the letterbox, but continued on to the marketplace. There she searched among the stalls to find some little gifts for Roland which would help keep him amused on the long journey to Italy with his mother. She would take them to him tomorrow when she went to say good-bye to Berenice, who was planning to depart sometime in the early afternoon. Berenice would be expecting her, for she had sent a note with a servant the previous day, telling of her father's illness, and by return had come calf's-foot jelly, caudle, a beef-tea custard, and several other delicacies for the invalid.

Delia had soon collected a number of toys. There were puzzles and card-games, books of adventure stories, a monkey-on-a-stick, a box of tin soldiers, another of colored chalks, and a number of drawing-books. She bought a cheap straw bag to carry every-thing home. Melissa met her in the hall, her expression sullen.

"Why didn't you tell me you were going out? I'd have gone with you."

"I'm sorry," Delia said sincerely, putting the bag of toys down on a chair and untying her bonnet strings. "I should have asked."

"When will Aaron be coming back from seeing the lawyer?" Melissa picked the monkey-on-a-stick out of the bag and almost absently set it turning somer-saults. "He's been gone ages. I was thinking of walk-ing to meet him."

"He's left there—and journeyed out of Penghyll. Mr. Radleigh's office boy brought a message." She told Melissa what it had been. Melissa had heard at breakfast from Aaron about the railway company's causing such a turn of events, there being no secret about it, and he had discussed it with both her and Delia. She had commiserated with him on such ill fortune, showing an exceptional concern and looking quite dewy-eyed over it. Again suspicion had leapt unbidden into Delia's mind, but she had thrust it from her as being the return of an uncharitable thought that must not be allowed to rear up again.

"Shall you wait up for him?" Melissa asked, her lashes shadowing a sudden alertness in her eyes as if the monkey-on-a-stick had begun to interest her.

"No, but my bedroom is above the vestibule and I sleep so lightly that I'll hear him if he returns during the night."

"Won't his knocking wake Uncle Charles?"

"I've thought of that. I'll see that the door is left unlocked."

"That's a good idea." Melissa put down the toy, a sly look on her face that she kept to herself. It had been something of a shock at breakfast that morning to hear that Aaron had apparently lost all chance of acquiring Halewood, but after she had mulled it over she realized it was probably all for the better. He'd go back to the New World. She did not fancy living in Boston, but beggars could not be choosers and she would have to make the best of it. At least she could expect to enjoy the comforts and luxuries of life, and in the book of prints of his city which he had given Delia there was evidence to its prosperity and fine proportions. As for Aaron himself, she could never love him, although that was unimportant, for she had put love from her forever, but his physical appearance was pleasing to her recently awakened sensuality and her mind dwelt on the breadth of his powerful shoulders, the horseman-trimness of his waist, and the tautness of thigh and length of leg revealed by the slender well-cut trousers that he wore. When he behaved toward her as a husband should there would be compensations for all she had left behind, for Richard had taught her much in the brief, idyllic times they had spent in each other's arms and she had been an apt and willing pupil, delighting in sensations that had made her wonder at his power to waken such secrets from her body, which previously she had not known existed. Yes, she was resolved to wrest from life what she could to make up for all that had been taken from her. The only time she had cared for anyone more than herself had been disastrous. It would not happen again.

Later when Delia was in the sickroom Melissa went

upstairs. On the landing she looked about to make sure no servant was nearby, then quickly she slipped into Delia's bedroom. It did not take her long to discover the dispensary key, which was in a box on the dressing table. Within five minutes she had been down to the dispensary, taken the blue glass bottle from the cabinet, poured some of the liquid out into one of the clean physic vials ranged on the shelf, corked it, replaced the bottle, relocked the dispensary, and returned the key to the box upstairs. Nobody had observed her. It was done.

She was shaking in every limb when she reached the safety of her own room with the vial, which she hid safely out of sight in a bonnet box. Almost in a state of exhaustion, she lay down on the bed to recover from the nerve-racking suspense of her actions. Staring up at the ceiling, she recalled hearing it said that there was a small bridge between love and hate, and now she knew that to be true. She hated Richard for all that he had brought upon her and for his desertion. But she welcomed that feeling of icy hatred. It was the fount of the strength she needed in this battle for her very existence. Never again would she give way to weakness and tears as she had done on her first night at Sycamore House, when she had poured out the whole story to Delia. Those days were over.

It was shortly after two o'clock in the morning when Aaron's hackney cab drew up outside the gates of Sycamore House. Wearily he stepped out and dived into his pocket to find money and pay the driver. Opening the gate, he went through at a slow and dejected pace, but he did not forget the sick man who lay behind the curtains of the only lighted window in the house and kept to the grass verge in order to avoid the scrunch of gravel.

He guessed the door would be left undone for him, but even as he reached the porch there was a click of the latch. To his astonishment, the candle held

by the pale figure showed the face of Melissa framed
by the tumble of her golden hair. She put a finger to
her lips as she admitted him.

"Shh! Come into the drawing room."

Silently he removed his caped coat, hat, and gloves,
and followed her. When she had closed the double
doors of the drawing room after him, he spoke to her
with some impatience and more than a little anxiety.

"What's the matter? Is Dr. Gilmore—worse?"

"No. There's no change. I couldn't sleep, and I happened to be at the window when your cab stopped
outside. I thought you might like something to eat and
a hot drink."

Such thoughtfulness from Melissa was unexpected,
but he appreciated it, not knowing that she had removed to the kitchen the covered supper-tray that
Delia had left ready for him. "That's most obliging of
you. It is many hours since I last ate."

She put down the candle and went to poke the fire,
which had been kept stacked up for his homecoming.
The coal fell into dancing flames, flooding the room
with red gold light, and thankfully he went across to
warm his hands, for he was chilled through. It had
been a long, cold journey and his mood of near-
despair had done nothing to insulate him as optimism
and hope would have done. He saw that Melissa was
wearing only a ruffled peignoir and a nightgown, and
as she leaned towards the fire he looked down on the
soft curve of breast and shadow. A faint bouquet
came to him from her body and there was a fragrance
about her hair. When a coal crashed out of the fire
with a shower of sparks she drew back, seared by the
heat, and the glow shone through the delicate garments that she wore. One spark alighted on the gossamer folds spread out about her on the carpet and he
stepped on it swiftly with the toe of his shoe. She
looked up at him, lips slightly parted, the tip of her
tongue showing pink and moist in the corner of her
mouth, and she put her hand on his foot.

"That could have been dangerous," she said breathlessly.

"I think not," he remarked drily, and he reached for the tongs. "Move out of the way, and I'll put that piece of coal back on the fire."

She rose in a billowing cloud of soft ruffles and moved back to stand by the sofa. "You haven't told me yet how things went today. Did you get the loan?"

He replaced the coal and let the tongs fall with a little clatter back on the fender. "No," he answered, speaking more to himself than to her. "I did not."

She watched him throw himself back in the wing chair, his elbows over the padded arm and his legs stretched out before him, his gaze never leaving the leaping flames.

"I'll fetch you some supper," she said on a note of commiseration. "In the meantime a glass of wine will help to refresh you."

"Er—what was that? Wine? Oh, yes." He saw her take up one of the decanters on the wine table and he waved a hand to show he would do it, bestirring himself from the chair. "Leave that to me."

She went soundlessly from the drawing room. He removed the stopper from the decanter and poured the claret. Taking a deep gulp, he stood lost in his gloomy thoughts, paying little attention to what he was drinking, while his mind went over the disappointments of the day. He had to face the fact that he wasn't going to raise that extra money unless— by some miracle—something happened, during this last day before the auction. He glanced at the clock. It was exactly half past two. How odd. That was the time set for the commencement of the auction thirty-six hours hence. With a faint groan of despair he turned back to the decanter and refilled the glass once more. For the first time he noticed that it had left a slightly acrid taste on his tongue, which was strange, for Dr. Gilmore kept a good cellar. He was about to lift the decanter to see if he had disturbed some sediment when the door opened and Melissa returned with a tray on which was set a cold collation.

"That was quick," he said, going across with the intention of taking the load from her, and to his surprise he staggered slightly. Too much wine on an empty stomach. He had gone unvittled far too long. The sooner he ate the better.

She put down the tray and pulled a small table across to the wing chair. "Sit here," she said, patting the cushioned back. "I'll set your supper beside you."

He sat down rather heavily. She placed the tray on the table and picked up the folded linen napkin to spread it crackling across his knees. "Thank you," he said. "Now don't let me keep you from repose any longer—"

She sat down opposite him, leaning back in a green velvet chair. "I don't feel tired and it's cozy in the firelight."

He gave her a long look, but said nothing. He would have preferred to be on his own, having no need for company. Had she been Delia it would have been a different matter.

"Shall you go to the auction tomorrow?" she inquired.

"Naturally. I intend to go down fighting."

"And after that? When you've seen Halewood sold beyond recall?"

He paused in his eating, his brows snapping together in a frown. "I'm enjoying the food, but not the particular topic of conversation chosen. I'd prefer not to pursue it."

"But you must have thought about what you will do."

He controlled his impatience with a suppressed sigh, giving in to her tactless persistence. "Eventually I shall return to the States. It depends on how long it takes Dr. Gilmore to recover."

"I'm not surprised to hear you won't want to stay in

England, but why should your plans depend on Uncle Charles?"

He put down his fork, eating no more, finding he was not as hungry as he had imagined himself to be, and he sank back in the chair, putting a hand to his brow. An amazing sense of peace and tranquility had come upon him. It was the strangest kind of drunkenness he had ever experienced, for although he was not in the habit of being in his cups he could recall vividly the wilder days of his youth.

"It must be fairly obvious." He noted with satisfaction that at least his words were not slurred. "I don't intend to leave without Delia. She's more to me than a thousand Halewoods."

A silence fell in the room, which seemed to him for no reason he could define to be particularly tense and almost palpable. Melissa rose and picked up the decanter to fill up his glass again, but he shook his head and placed his palm over it. She did not return to her chair after replacing the decanter but came instead to sink down in her billowing ruffles, with a gust of her own particular potpourri of perfumes, onto her knees by his chair, and she rested hands and elbows along the arm, letting the side of her cheek lodge there as she looked up at him.

"She will marry Matthew. You'll never break the bond between them."

"I happen to think differently."

"My poor Aaron, don't you see? She's enjoying having two strings to her bow. It's never happened to Delia before. Matthew has always made sure of that. She'll never go to the New World with you. She lacks any sense of adventure. I'm not like that. I'd go anywhere—do anything."

Normally his irritation with Melissa and her ways, never far from the surface, would have erupted into anger that she should speak thus of Delia, but he seemed incapable of rousing himself from the curious mental languor that had possessed him. He knew only that he wanted to be rid of Melissa. With effort he put both hands on the arm-ends of the chair and thrust himself to his feet, where he stood reeling.

"You must have drunk an awful lot of wine." Melissa's voice seemed to come from a distance, but her body wasn't far from him. She had entwined him in her arms, pressing herself to him. In his soporific state he had the sensation of being entrapped in scented cobwebs and he thrust up an arm to free himself, but she clutched him all the tighter. "I'll help you to bed. You'll never get there on your own. You'd better take your shoes off first or you'll wake the household."

Such a simple task was beyond him. She knelt and he lifted one foot and then the other for her to slip them off.

Her arms were around him again. "Lean on me and don't make a sound. Remember Dr. Gilmore. We mustn't disturb him."

The staircase loomed high as a mountain, making him wonder if he'd ever reach the top, and the candle she held glinted on distorted picture frames and mis-shapen doors. With one arm about her shoulders and a hand on the bannister rail he made the ascent slowly and reached the landing without mishap. In his room he stood swaying while she helped him off with his coat. Like a pale golden moth she beat at him with swift fingers, unbuttoning his waistcoat, which fell from him with a swish of silk lining, and untying his cravat. He knew himself to be asleep on his feet. His body was locked in inertia while one tiny corner of his mind struggled in vain to regain mastery. A faint coolness of air on his chest and back made him realize she had ripped his shirt from him. He gave his head a shake to clear it, but felt consciousness slipping from him. Then he reeled about and fell face downward on the bed, where he became lost in sleep.

His slumber was deep and black and soft as a velvet sea and he was being wrenched from it by some power that he wanted to resist. He threshed about aware that he was naked, sweat streaming from every limb, his own gasping breath roaring in his ears. Somewhere in that abyss a sobbing, persistent and subdued, came and went, and now and again a whispered entreaty seared through his brain, but the words seemed to lack meaning and he could not comprehend them. Gradually his body seemed to become buoyant in those dark, warm waves, and he knew whatever danger he'd been in had passed. Quiet sleep drove out the nightmare and enfolded his limbs in rest.

He awoke to a cold, gray day and a sensation of nausea. Reaching out carefully, he felt for his watch on the bedside cabinet, but it was not there. Propping himself on both elbows with the thought that it must be on the dressing table, he saw the state of his room and all the events of the previous night came flooding back to him. His clothes lay where they had fallen. The state of the bedclothes bore witness to his nightmare struggles, for they were twisted and tumbled and half on the floor. Of his shoes there was no sign and he supposed them to be still downstairs in the drawing room. What a crazy fool he'd been to drink all that wine! He must have had more glasses than he'd realized while waiting for Melissa to bring in the supper. Perhaps it wasn't surprising, for his mind had been on the disappointments of the day, the shaking heads of bankers, the blunt refusal in the voices of others, and he had drunk the wine automatically, giving it no consideration.

He was thankful that no servant had come knocking for admittance and walked into the untidy room. On any other morning shaving-water and copper cans of steaming bathwater would have been brought at eight-thirty, but on this occasion Delia, having discovered his return, would have given orders that he was not to be disturbed.

He put his feet to the floor. Fortunately the nausea had subsided and he felt better than he had any right to feel after imbibing with such reckless thoughtlessness. He put on his dressing robe and looked about for his watch. It was on a chair. He picked it up, snapped it open, and saw that it was almost noon. Only a little over twenty-four hours left before Halewood came under the auctioneer's hammer. At least Delia had promised to be there with him. She was such a talisman for good that he found it difficult to accept that her love-magic would not be able to counteract the forces of greedy commerce that would be ranged against him. But hard facts had to be faced. When he staked all he possessed in the world on a last throw for Halewood, if it soared out of his grasp in the tinkling of thousands more golden guineas, he hoped he would accept defeat with dignity and without bitterness.

He began to pick up and fold away his scattered clothing. His complete nakedness on waking gave him some thought, and he realized he must have torn off the rest of his garments when he had been in the throes of that awful sweating that had been like the approach of death. He shuddered at the thought of it, doubting that he would ever be able to stomach the taste of claret again.

He crossed to the bed to pull it into some semblance of order. Out of the confusion of sheets as he jerked them there floated up into the air and down to the carpet at his feet a strip of torn pink ruffle. Slowly he bent and picked it up, frowning as he smoothed it in his fingers. How had it come to be in his bed? And when had it been torn? It must have occurred when he'd thrust Melissa from him. But surely that had been downstairs?

Still frowning, he put it in his pocket and went to jerk the bell rope for his bathwater. At the same time his attention was caught by the sound of hooves and wheels in the drive below. He went to the window in time to see Delia driving herself in her blue-painted gig out of the gates into the avenue. He guessed where she was bound. To Halewood. He watched her out of sight.

❧ 9 ❧

DELIA looped up the reins, stuck her whip in its holder, and, picking up the straw bag of toys for Roland from the seat, she alighted from the wagonette. She had chosen this day to drive through the archway into the inner courtyard and up by the grand entrance, which she had studiously avoided since that fateful day when Halewood had reached out as though to hold her to its mist-swathed, ice-cold breast, but this was probably her last visit and curiosity compelled her to discover whether the house knew it too. She had planned on the way to enter by the heart of it, and on the steps of the massive entrance she paused deliberately on each wide breadth of stone, almost with an air of challenge.

Her horse whinnied. She glanced back over her shoulder toward it and saw that it tossed its head restlessly. Slowly she scanned the great courtyard under the bleak afternoon sky. In Penghyll the snow had turned to gray slush and was fast disappearing, but here it still showed a pristine whiteness in crevices and corners. Through the archway she could see the branches of the birch trees bordering the drive weaving black, skeletal patterns in the wind, but within the courtyard it was, as always, sheltered and still.

She shivered, more from an inward chill than from the coldness of the day. The house was watching her. Holding its breath. Every window an eye. And she

171

in turn loving and fearing and pitying it. With a swirl of bonnet ribbons she went hastily through the porch and pulled the bell. She was admitted and went through into the great entrance hall, where trunks and boxes were stacked high in readiness for shipment to Italy. There was an air of bustle and departure, with servants scurrying and dootsteps echoing. Every piece of furnitue, as yet still in place, had a label tied to it, ready for packing and delivery to the London auction rooms.

It was a poignant moment for Delia. She was to say good-bye to both Berenice and the house. Nobody she knew would be the purchaser of Halewood, but should it be someone with whom she was on nodding acquaintance she would never want to cross the houses's threshold with all links severed. How would Halewood fare in strangers' hands? It would not tolerate violation of its boundaries and new vengeance would be wreaked on whomever was foolhardy enough to take up residence under its roof. Looking about her at the wonderful proportions of the hall and the rooms beyond, which she could see through open doors, she was terribly afraid that future inhabitants, driven out by the house's hostility, would leave it to collapse in ruins, a blind and empty shell against the sky, deserted and avoided by all.

"Where's Lady Hart?" she asked a passing footman.

"In t' yellow drawing room, I believe, miss."

Berenice was at the window when Delia entered, and she turned to come with hands outstretched. "How is your dear father?" she exclaimed at once, taking Delia's hands in hers in a gesture of concern and commiseration.

"He is a little better. Dr. Pomfret believes that the attack, alarming and terrible though it was, hasn't done the damage that he had at first feared. He says he considers it a grave warning that the time has come for my father to retire and live a quiet life."

"That won't suit Dr. Gilmore!"

"I agree, but I hope to console him with the thought that he'll at last have time to finish writing his book on the history of this district, which he has been researching for many years."

"You're quite sure that he's getting the best of medical attention? Should you have a second opinion as to the treatment he should be receiving?"

Delia reassured her. "I've heard my father praise Dr. Pomfret's medical skill many times. I have no doubts on that score at all."

"I'm thankful to hear it. I've had another hamper prepared with delicacies for him. Can you take it home with you?"

"Yes, indeed. That's most kind." They sat down in neighboring chairs. "I told him you had sent him the caudle, among other things, when I fed him a few spoonfuls of it."

"The poor gentleman!" Berenice raised clasped hands from her lap and let them fall again. She was in a traveling costume of brown grenadine trimmed with bands of velvet, ready for her early-evening departure. There was a pallor in her face and her cheeks seemed to have taken on a deeper hollowness. It was as though she had sunk into a state of ailing that was to know no lifting up or brief returns to better spells. At the present time she looked as if she lacked the stamina to survive the long journey to Italy, but she would be traveling with a small retinue of servants, including her lady's maid, who would take good care of her. Delia hoped the sea would be kind on the voyage from Liverpool, and then at least Berenice could rest after all the upheaval of leaving Halewood.

"It's many weeks now since I first composed that letter to Aaron telling him about the forthcoming sale of Halewood," Delia said, deciding to tell her of the railway company's interest without further delay, "but his journey to England to purchase it has been in vain on that score."

Her listener showed no surprise, but lifted a languid

173

hand. "I know. Mr. Radleigh came to see me about it. How has Mr. Hart reacted to the blow?"

"What do you expect?" Delia exclaimed. "He is quite shattered! He spent yesterday dashing from place to place trying to raise a last-minute loan. I've not seen him yet today because he arrived home in the early hours of the morning and was sleeping when I left, but Melissa heard him come in and had a few words with him. He had no success."

"How disappointing for him." Placidly. Almost uninterestedly.

Delia bit her lip. She could not expect Berenice to be moved as she was by Aaron's plight. After all, Berenice, although she probably did not need it, was to become many thousands of pounds richer by this new development. What was more, she did not care what happened to Halewood or who lived in it, but nevertheless Delia found it hard not to make some retort. Berenice must have seen this, for she said, "I have much on my own mind at this time. You must pardon me if I seem detached, but I've already talked at great lengths with my lawyer about the sale of Halewood and as far as I'm concerned there's an end to it. You think me heartless? Forgive me. Don't let it taint this time of farewell between us when we've been such good friends. I know how much I'll miss your company and all the news that you entertained me with from the town, the market, and your own circle of acquaintances."

Reminded of the market, Delia opened the straw bag to reveal that it was full of differently shaped little packets, each toy wrapped individually in brightly colored paper. "I've some surprise parcels for Roland. There's one for every day of the journey and I've marked them with the dates for opening. There's a special one for when you both arrive at the villa in Florence. I hope it will amuse him and take away any homesickness."

"What is it? May I ask?"

"It's a railway locomotive with a little spirit stove in the boiler that puffs smoke, and two carriages—an open one for passengers and another for goods."

"What a splendid gift!" Berenice peeped into the bag. "Such a collection! How thoughtful of you!"

"Has Roland become reconciled to leaving Halewood?"

Berenice let the bag's handle slip from her fingers, her expression wearied. "There have been scenes and tantrums for days. One morning he locked himself in the stable loft and refused to come out. Now that the day of leaving has arrived at last he has lapsed into a kind of quiet despair, packing together his own small treasures. I've allowed him to take a sixteenth-century ivory chess set that he's always liked, and that seems to have consoled him enormously."

"I'll find him before I leave and bid him farewell. Perhaps I can encourage him to write to me. I'll want to keep in touch."

Berenice's mouth showed a faint smile. "You know my dislike of putting pen to paper, but even if Roland cannot be persuaded to correspond you shall have word from me sometimes."

"I look forward to that. I hope to send good tidings of papa's complete recovery. After that there may be other news to confide, but it's too early to talk of it."

Berenice tilted her head more in emphasis than inquiry. "You want to break off your betrothal to Matthew."

Delia's eyes widened. "How did you know that?"

"I could tell you had fallen in love the first time you came to see me after Mr. Hart's arrival. It wasn't anything you said. It was more what you didn't say. I could tell it troubled you to talk about him, and there was a new awareness of living about you. It showed in your eyes, the tilt of your head, in your whole attitude."

"That was very observant of you," Delia admitted tremulously.

175

"Is that surprising? I spend so many hours on my own that I've become observant of all things. Until I came to Halewood I was unaware that truly to observe life one must draw back from it. That knowledge at least I take with me from this hostile house. Not much to learn from the eight years I've spent here, but it is a kernel of comfort for all the time that is left to me."

"I wish you good fortune in Italy with all my heart." Delia said, rising. "I mustn't stay any longer. As soon as I've seen Roland I must get back home. I don't like to leave papa for any length of time."

Berenice rose from her chair. "I thank you for coming. There's one last thing I want you to do for me."

"Gladly. What is it?"

Berenice went across to the escritoire and opened it. She took from an inner drawer one of the smaller notices of the sale by auction of Halewood, which had been printed for distribution.

"You will remember that I talked about getting these leaflets printed to help advertise the sale still wider and Mr. Radleigh dealt with the matter for me. He also had bigger posters with bolder lettering pasted up over those already in position."

"Yes. I think you saw I wasn't keen that it should be done. To me the more widely it was advertised, the more chance there was of Aaron having to go to a higher figure to get it, and I knew how much he wanted to restore the house throughout and the vast expense that would involve him in. But it wasn't for me to persuade you against your action. You had every right to try to get the highest price for Halewood and Aaron would have been the first to agree with me. Never did I dream then that the railway company would come upon the scene."

Berenice looked down at the leaflet which she held at opposite corners between the thumb and forefinger of each hand. "I had my reasons for wanting Mr.

Radleigh to handle the reprinting for me. I had need of his advice on it, because there was something I wanted altered, although I said nothing to you about it."

Delia was puzzled. She could not remember noticing any errors, but there must have been a mistake in the original printed description of the house somewhere.

Berenice handed the leaflet to her. "Read it. Read it well. Remember what the first posters said, and keep what you notice until the time is right—and you will know when that will be without my telling you. Only then may you inform Mr. Hart."

In complete bewilderment Delia took the leaflet. She scanned it quickly. At first she noticed nothing different. But when she read it again, dissecting every line, she came across the time of the auction. On the earlier notices it had read "2:30 p.m." Now it read "2:30 o'clock." Almost in disbelief at what it meant she raised her head and looked at Berenice.

"It's the only way it could be done," Berenice said, answering Delia's unspoken question. "As you know, Sir Harry had written in his will that the estate must be sold by public auction, no matter if it was in my lifetime or after."

"You're almost giving Halewood to Aaron," Delia exclaimed emotionally. "At two-thirty in the morning there'll be nobody else there!"

"That's why you must not let anyone else know about it. Mr. Radleigh thought it best to keep even Mr. Hart in the dark until the last moment, lest his lack of concern give rise to any questions or queries. Even the Assembly Rooms have been hired from today in order that only those directly involved in the coup be present in the building."

"I can't thank you enough! It's the most wonderful news I've ever heard! Although he's faced the loss of Halewood with fortitude, I know him well enough to comprehend that without it life could never be the same for him again."

"Not even with your love to fill the void?"

Delia shook her head dismissively. "No matter how much I demonstrated my love for him I could never have made him forget Halewood."

"Then let us be thankful that matters have been arranged as they are."

"You should have been the one to tell him," Delia declared generously, "instead of leaving that happy task to me. I could have brought him with me. Didn't you think of that?"

A look of utter desolation swept over Berenice's face and possessed it. "I thought of it. But I can't allow myself to see him again."

Delia caught in her breath sharply, understanding. Berenice was in love with Aaron. She must have known she loved him during their first meeting. From that moment forth she had decided to give him Halewood. It was an unselfish token of her love, which could never be fulfilled in any other way.

"Does he mean that much to you?" Delia inquired huskily.

Berenice answered brokenly, her eyes heavy and glistening with tears. "I glimpsed him first from the windows of my apartments. I looked down and watched him step out of his carriage. As he stood there studying the house I saw his face and knew that the only man I'd longed for all my life was about to cross my path too late. Insurmountable barriers, kinship through marriage being one of them, stood between us. Yet I contrived a way to see him again when he was in the portrait gallery, deliberately passing where I could look in on him. Had that been all I might have spared myself some of the pangs I've endured since, but fate brought him into the very room where I was sitting and it was my point of no return."

"Is that why you came to the Penghyll Ball?"

"I wanted to dance with him once. To feel his arms

about me once." Berenice made an almost girlish movement with her hands, at once both timorous and vulnerable. "Such was my passion for him that I put from my mind all caution from your father not to overtax my strength in any exercise. If that waltz shortened my life by ten years I care not."

"Have you never loved before?" It struck Delia how quiet and sad were their voices in that exquisite, sun-colored room with the gray day pressing against the windows.

Berenice gave her a glance that was worn out with despair. "I've known many men. Some have been gentler with me than others, and some have loved me, but I've never been able to love any one of them. My heart was born that day when Aaron came to Halewood."

"He'll always remember you as the donor of this house," Delia said, deeply moved. "In that way you'll have a special place in his life."

"But it is you who must insure that no disaster comes to him through my gift." Her appeal was throbbing and urgent, and she took hold of Delia by the shoulders, giving her a little shake to emphasize the importance of her entreaty. "Use your love to protect him. I thought to slip free of Halewood, but it has played its old tricks on me. I'm doomed to unhappiness like the rest of the Harts who've lived on Howling Hill. Until the end of my days I shall yearn for a man who never loved me."

"I'll do everything I can," Delia promised fervently.

"Now we must say good-bye." Berenice kissed her affectionately on the cheek. "I've kept you from your sick father far too long." She reached out and took up a sealed letter from where it lay on top of the escritoire. "I've written a note of appreciation for all the care he has bestowed on me during my time as his patient. Please read it to him when you are able. It carries all my kindest regards."

"I'll do that. May the city of Florence bring you

solace with its beauty and Roland prove a comfort to you."

Berenice inclined her head with dignity, her smile wan. "I trust so. Farewell."

Delia dipped a curtsy. In respect. In gratitude. In tribute. Quickly she left the room. Choked with pity for Aaron's benefactress, she folded the sale leaflet and letter away in her reticule and hurried in search of Roland. To have loved and lost Aaron was a particular hell she could fully comprehend and identify with. Pray God it never happened to her!

As always, after even the shortest absence, she went first to the sickroom on her return. Melissa was at the bedside reading a copy of *Lady's Magazine,* which she lowered to speak in a whisper.

"Uncle Charles is alseep. Have you been at Halewood all this time?"

Delia nodded, crossing to look down into her father's face. How much better his color was, and he breathed easily. There was no doubt he had improved since yesterday, when he had first asked her how long he had been ill and expressed concern that her wedding had been postponed. She knew he was not out of the woods yet, but the light through the trees shone bright and clear, lifting a new hope in her. Was it possible that the dark clouds that had gathered over her recently were to be dispelled one by one, advanced by her father's recovery?

"Aaron is out," Melissa remarked, still whispering. "He doesn't know when he'll be back."

The information thudded home. Delia spoke on a note of startled dismay. "Where's he gone?"

"He didn't say." Melissa's face held a curious expression that was a blend of triumph and mockery. "He wasn't very talkative at luncheon. I think he must have drunk a great deal of wine over his supper last night and was still suffering the aftereffects at midday."

"But didn't he give any hint of what time he expected to return?" Delia demanded agitatedly.

"I heard him tell Ellen that he wouldn't be in to dine, but there was no need for a supper-tray to be left. It's my guess he's gone hunting down the real old dyed-in-the-wool moneylenders. Why shouldn't he when all else has failed?"

"Oh, no!" Delia gave a soft groan. "That means he could have traveled far afield again. He might be as late—or later!—coming home as he was last night!" She gave Melissa a distracted glance. "About two o'clock, didn't you say?"

"Er—I think so. Why are you so worried about his coming home late? The auction isn't until tomorrow afternoon."

Delia was brought up sharply to the realization that she had brought upon herself the very queries and questions that Berenice had wanted avoided. She must cover up quickly and not forget again. "You're right. There's plenty of time left. Hours—and hours." She had looked at her father's watch hanging in its bedhead pocket, which she had embroidered for him while still a child in her best cross-stitch. Eight and three-quarter hours, to be precise. She was foolish to worry unnecessarily. At any moment after the evening dining hour the front door could open and Aaron walk in.

She looked towards the watch again. In her mind's eye she could see the procession of vehicles with the blink of carriage lamps through the trees that would be wending its way down the winding drive from Halewood and out through the gates. In the first carriage would be Berenice and Roland in furs and with knee-rugs. Behind would follow the other carriages bearing boxes and baggage, the two personal servants she was taking with her, and the boy's tutor. Berenice would not give the house a backward glance. Soon the glowing eyes of the lamps would be swallowed in the darkness and there would be no sound but the perpetual moaning of the wind. On the hilltop Halewood would be waiting, with a few pale, lighted windows in the servants' quarters and the rest dark, helping to shroud it in blackness against the winter sky. Its future ownership, plotted with such care by Berenice and her legal adviser, hung precariously in the balance, everything depending on Aaron's chance return in time to attend the auction.

Delia and Melissa dined alone together. Afterward they went to sit by the drawing room fire where Melissa finished reading her magazine and Delia tried to play patience, but she could give no attention to the game, her thoughts directed toward Aaron and his possible whereabouts.

"What *is* the matter with you?" Melissa demanded with an exasperated sigh when Delia went again to the window.

"I'm anxious about Aaron," Delia replied frankly, the truth on that point being impossible to hide. "Moneylenders are notorious for their high rates of interest. I hope he hasn't done anything foolish."

"I doubt it," Melissa stated casually, helping herself to another piece of Turkish delight from the round wooden box of it on her lap. She had developed an absurd craving for it. "He'd hardly be likely to commit himself to anything that would bring him to bankruptcy. Better to let the house go now than to the bailiffs later."

"I'll go back and sit with papa for a while. Nurse Baker always welcomes a little extra time to herself, I'm sure."

She was almost at the flight of stairs when she heard the crunch of gravel underfoot on the drive. Aaron had come home! With an exclamation of mingled joy and relief she grabbed up her skirts and flew back down again to charge through the vestibule and fling open the door before he had time to ring the bell.

"Aaron! Thank God—!"

But it was Matthew. His own smile at the sight of

her faded. He had seen the light go from her eyes and the expression of intense disappointment wash over her face. She had recovered herself almost at once, but he was hurt and annoyed by her reaction and he showed it.

"I had hoped to give you a pleasant surprise," he commented sarcastically, removing his hat as he entered, "but you looked as if you wished me the other side of England."

"It's not that," she explained tensely. "Aaron is late home. Melissa thinks he's gone to moneylenders. In any case, you did tell me that you expected to be away until the end of the week."

"Plans have been changed. One of the directors, knowing I live in Penghyll, called me into his office today. I'm to accompany him to the auction tomorrow. He is to put in the railway company's own bid for Halewod. I've just had dinner with him at the Red Lion Hotel where he's staying overnight."

That was situated not more than a stone's throw from the Assembly Rooms on the opposite side of the square! Delia's nervousness increased. If Matthew caught the faintest hint of what was afoot he'd get that director to the auction in no time at all!

They had gone into the drawing room and he greeted Melissa, who offered him a Turkish delight from her box. He took a pink, sugary piece and popped it in his mouth.

"Thank goodness you've come," she said touchily. "Delia has been like a cat on hot bricks all the evening, starting practically out of her skin at every tick of the clock. Perhaps she'll settle down now." Although Melissa spoke criticizingly of Delia she was far from relaxed herself, even though she had gone into Aaron's room earlier to make sure he hadn't packed his bags and left, for with all chance of Halewood gone from him she felt she had to watch him closely. There was no telling what any man would do in a fit of pique or temper. After what had happened with Richard, she put no faith in any man's word, and Aaron's declaration that he was in love with Delia she had taken with a pinch of salt. He probably was at the moment. Men were like that. But she sincerely believed that all along, had Aaron been given the choice of Halewood or Delia, he would have chosen the house every time.

Delia saw that Melissa's ill-chosen remark had made Matthew look more disgruntled than before and she sought to distract him. "I was on my way up to sit with papa when you came. Would you like to see him?"

Dr. Gilmore was awake. With the doses of laudanum cut down, he was beginning to be more alert. Matthew and Delia drew up chairs to the same side of the bed in order to spare him with the exertion of looking one way and then the other.

"It's good to know you're making progress, sir," Matthew said conventionally.

"I'm feeling much better," the doctor answered weakly. "The pain has gone."

"I'm very pleased to hear it."

"The attack was no surprise to me. It had been coming on for some time."

Delia widened her eyes. "That's the first I've heard about it."

"The surprise was that I should survive it. That's why I wanted to see you wed, my dear." He showed distress. "Now I've been the cause of your marriage being postponed."

Matthew answered him. "But not for long, sir. You'll soon be on your feet again."

To Delia's relief Matthew left the subject of their marriage and went on to tell Dr. Gilmore what he had been doing, holding his interest. Delia could see it was doing her father good to have a visitor.

"Lady Hart sent you a letter," she said when the conversation had turned to Berenice's departure after Dr. Gilmore had inqured after her.

"I'd like you to hear it," he said, pleased, "if Matthew doesn't mind."

Matthew smiled. "Not at all, sir." Then seeing Delia was about to rise, he added: "Where is it? Can I fetch it for you?'

"Would you? It's in my velvet reticule on the dressing table in my room."

He brought it to her, dropping it by its cords into her hands. She stretched the gathers to take out the letter. As she did so it became caught up with a sale leaflet, which fluttered to the floor.

"What's this?" Matthew reached down by his chair and picked it up. The black lettering stood out. His voice took on a bitter tone. "You're actually carrying one of these around with you, I see."

She held out her hand for it, but in his irritation at what he considered to be her obsession with the house he pretended not to notice, reading it slowly through. Turning to Berenice's letter, she opened it for her father, telling herself that the notice was no different in any way from those pasted about the town for all to see, and there was nothing uncommon about *"a.m."* or *"p.m."* being omitted on daytime events. There were some people who might be pedantic about it, but there was no reason for Matthew or anyone else to question the time of the auction. As far as she knew there had never been one held in the middle of the night in Penghyll or anywhere else, and it wouldn't occur to anyone—unless their suspicions were inadvertently aroused—that Halewood was to change hands in the dark hours. Provided, of course, that Aaron returned in time.

Dr. Gilmore listened to the letter and asked Delia to acknowledge it for him. He would have liked them to stay longer talking, but Nurse Baker came in to have a look at him and signaled to Delia that she thought it had been long enough.

As they went out of the room Delia pretended to have forgotten that Matthew still held the leaflet, but she could tell he had not finished with the matter and was intent on worrying her with it, being in a mood that was all too familiar to her, and her heart sank. Even in their childhood days when something she had said or done had irritated him he had refused to let the matter rest, harping on about it until eventually she had snapped into temper or dissolved into tears. The pattern still continued on a more sophisticated plane. If she showed anger he would welcome the excuse to quarrel. If she became distressed he would immediately be contrite and seek with a loving embrace to make amends. But she was wearied with such petty niggling and all patience with him had fled.

"Where did you get the leaflet?" he persisted as they stepped from the last stair to cross the hall.

"I picked it up at Halewood today," she answered in what she hoped was a casual tone. "They were all over the place." That was true. She had noticed several stacks of them.

"You can't see or read enough of the blasted place, can you!"

She turned on him, eyes flashing. "No, I can't! I'd live and die there if I could!"

"Well, there's no chance of that! I wouldn't make a home for us in that morgue if it were given to me free!"

She bit back the retort that sprang to her lips and deliberately let her anger drain from her. Bickering with Matthew was a foolish waste of time for both of them. In addition there was the danger that he might goad her into making some slip that would set his mind on the auction in such a way that there'd be no diverting him until the truth was out.

"You'd best leave, Matthew," she said calmly. "I don't want to quarrel and I can see that will happen if we continue any kind of discussion at the present time."

Unnoticed, Melissa had come to the open drawing room door, and she pouted prettily. "I don't want you to go, Matthew. If we're to sit up half the night waiting for Aaron to come back you can at least help us to pass the time in a game of cards."

Delia felt herself go pale. "I said nothing about sitting up."

"But you will, won't you?" Melissa challenged. "You'd never be able to sleep not knowing whether or not he's managed to get the loot from the moneylenders. I intend to sit up anyway. I find it all quite exciting."

"I'll play cards with you," Matthew stated heavily, seizing on the opportunity to thwart Delia's desire for him to be gone, and he strolled toward Melissa, crumpling up the leaflet in his hand at the same time. "I agree with you. It will be interesting to hear if Hart is going to put up a fight at the auction tomorrow or not. What shall we play? Cribbage? *Ecarté?*"

"I don't wish to take part," Delia said, knowing that she would not be able to concentrate on a single card.

"Then let's play piquet," Melissa suggested to Matthew.

"Very well." To Delia's relief he hurled the crumpled leaflet into the fire before starting to unfold the leaves of the card table. At least temporarily the auction had been put out of his mind.

As the two of them settled down to play Delia put a silver dish of bonbons on the table for them. "A glass of wine, Matthew?"

"Thank you," he replied with icy politeness. "If you please."

Delia opened the cabinet doors to take out the crystal decanter needed, but to her amazement it was empty and had been washed clean. At the table Melissa spoke up.

"I told you I thought Aaron had been drinking a lot last night."

Delia said nothing, but she went from the room to get her household keys and fetch a bottle and decant it. She was surprised that which ever servant it was who had cleared up Aaron's supper-tray that morning had forgotten to tell her that more claret was needed. And it was odd that the washed-out bottle should have been replaced in the cabinet. Dr. Gilmore did not allow the servants to go to it except when specially instructed. Having had experience of drunken servants in his time, he had banned them also from the cellar. On her way back with the replenished decanter in her hand, she lingered by the hall window to watch the lamps of carriages going past, hoping that each one might stop to let Aaron alight, but she was doomed to disappointment.

Melissa and Matthew enjoyed their cardplaying, both fiercely competitive. The French clock on the mantel struck each hour with a delicate chime. Delia, making a pretense of reading, heard midnight come and go, and then one o'clock rang out. She had formed a plan in her mind. At two o'clock she would announce she would sit up no longer. But instead of going to bed she would slip out of the back door and go to the auction to bid on Aaron's behalf. She had an idea what reserve price Berenice would have put on the property, but she was certain it would be within easy range of the figure that had been bandied about as the most likely sum the house would fetch. With this resolution made she became a little easier in her mind.

"Ring for more coals to be put on the fire," Melissa said, looking over her shoulder at Delia. "If we're sitting up until dawn it will get cold." She and Matthew had switched to backgammon some time earlier and the game was in full swing.

"The servants will have gone to bed long ago," Delia said, putting down her book and seeing the fire had reduced to white-gold embers, "but there's coal in the scuttle."

"I'll do it." Matthew went across to take up the tongs and lift the coal from the bucket-shaped copper scuttle. As he did so Delia saw that the crumpled leaflet had not burnt up as she had supposed, but must have lodged at the side of the grate and rolled out again when she had been attending to the decanter. Holding her breath, she watched Matthew hook it up out of a corner by the fender with the tongs and, instead of throwing it at once onto the embers, he looked at the singed paper for a fraction longer than seemed necessary. The paper had uncurled slightly with the heat; "2:30 o'clock" was the scrap of lettering revealed.

Then she relaxed, trembling, as he cast it onto the embers where it immediately burst into flame. He heaped on the coals and, returning to his chair, took up the die to shake it as if there had been no interruption in the game.

"I'm sitting here no longer," she said at last, closing her book with a snap. It was almost two o'clock. "If you like I'll make you some tea and then you must excuse me."

Melissa hid a deep yawn behind her hand. She had had almost no sleep the night before and her intense tiredness was affecting her playing. She had lost the previous game and it was obvious she was going to lose the one in progress.

"I'd like a cup of tea," she said sleepily, "and then I'll go to bed too."

"That leaves me no choice but to go home," Matthew said cheerily, very much alert and on his mettle, "but I'll enjoy that tea first."

In the kitchen Delia set the kettle on the hob. Cook had made some oven-bottom cakes and Delia popped them in the range oven to heat, ready to be split and spread thickly with butter. She was getting cups and saucers out of a cupboard when the clop of hooves came to a halt at the gate. Aaron! Swiftly she put her head into the hall to make sure the others had not heard the vehicle stop, but they were arguing noisily and with laughter, intent on the final stages of the game. Back into the kitchen she went and across to shoot the bolt of the kitchen door and dart out into the freezing night. The lawn sparkled with frost in the moonlight and she took a short cut across it, the grass crackling under her racing feet. The cabby was leaning down from the driver's seat to take the fare from Aaron when she arrived breathless at the gate.

"Aaron! Get back in the cab and go at once to the Assembly Rooms!" she gasped, giving him no time to speak. He had turned to her, surprised and startled by her sudden appearance, and she leaned over the gate to snatch at his collar and bring his ear close to her mouth, not risking the cabbie overhearing her urgent whisper. "The auction is to take place at half-past two! Berenice arranged it for you! It's been kept a secret! You'll be the only bidder!"

"Come with me!" He made a quick move to open the gate for her, but she stayed his hand.

"I can't! Not yet! But I'll follow and be there with you as soon as I can. I'll explain then!"

He kissed her warmly and swiftly. With a swish of coattails he was back in the cab. Delia was already rushing back to the house when he thumped with his cane as a signal for the cabbie to proceed with all haste to the destination given.

Swiftly she bolted the door again. The kettle was steaming and she warmed the pot and made the tea. She had buttered the cakes when Matthew came into the kitchen to carry the tray for her.

"Who won the game?" she asked, handing it to him.

"I did." His gaze was hard on her. "It went badly against me for a while. It happens that way sometimes. But, as always, I was determined to win in the end."

It was a barb directed at her, but she chose to ignore it, holding the door to enable him to walk through with the tray. In the drawing room Melissa exclaimed at the cakes and took one. She bit into it with her small, white teeth.

"Mm! Aren't you going to have one, Delia?" she asked incredulously, buttery-lipped.

Delia shook her head. "I'm going upstairs now. Good night."

Matthew followed her out to the hall and caught

her by the wrist, but she remained with her back towards him, stiff and unresponsive, impatient at the unwanted delay.

"Is there anything you should tell me, Delia?"

She froze. Did he mean that he understood she
wanted to end their betrothal or did he suspect that
something was amiss about the auction? She dared
say nothing in reply that might give the latter away.
Not turning, afraid her face would reveal her confusion, she answered him briefly.

"Nothing that can't wait until our next meeting. The
hour is too late. Good night again, Matthew."

He released her wrist. She was aware that he remained where he was, watching her go up into her
room. As soon as she had closed the door behind her
she opened it a fraction again and listened. She heard
him go back into the drawing room, but if he drank
the tea he must have downed it in a gulp, for he left
soon afterward. It was not long before Melissa came
slowly from the drawing room to mount the stairs,
dragging up one foot and then the other, yawning as
she went. By that time Delia, clad in her warmest coat
and the Spanish shawl draped over her head, had
reached the kitchen. Waiting there in the darkness, she
heard the boards creak overhead as Melissa entered
the guest room to go to bed. Swiftly Delia unbolted the
kitchen door for the second time, and once again she
sped across the lawn. Out through the gate she went
and away down the avenue in the direction of the
market square, her footsteps echoing. A canopy of stars
hung over the sleeping town and underfoot the thawing
slush had frozen with the night-fall of temperature to
form a thin and treacherous coat of ice which made
running hazardous. She was forced to slow her pace
after twice narrowly saving herself from falling by
clutching first at a wall and then at a fence, snagging
and tearing her gloves.

Several times she glanced nervously over her shoulders as she hurried along. She had never before been

out on her own late at night without male escort and never on foot. Once she stopped, her heart thumping, convinced that she had heard a footfall somewhere behind her, but there was no one to be seen. On she went again. Never had she realized from the comfort of a carriage how singularly dark and ill-lit the streets were for pedestrians. Then she did see someone, but this was a drunken man ahead of her who was reeling unsteadily from side to side and constantly missing his footing on the icy ground, tumbling down with grunts and groans. She kept to the opposite side of the street, thankful for the first time for the black shadows, and slipped past without his seeing her.

She reached the market square. It appeared deserted. A few lights shone in the hotel and others in some upper windows above the shops, but not a glimmer showed from the Assembly Rooms where the auction was to be held in the large hall at the rear of the building. Then she did hear the scrape of a sole on a cobble and knew she was being followed. It was not her imagination! Unhappily she recalled the garroter who had never been caught after strangling one of the market traders less than three months before, and there were other cases of attack and rape that until now had been reports in the newspaper to be shuddered over from a distance. But no longer! Danger stalked her!

Bunching up handfuls of her skirts to lift the hems, she leapt forward and ran full pelt in a direct line across the square towards the Assembly Rooms. The man behind her knew he had been discovered and no longer made any attempt to concealment. His footsteps came pounding after her. Her breath rasped in her chest, for she had used a fast pace since leaving home and her scarred leg, which always gave her trouble if used too violently, shivered with weakness. She had only one thought in her head and that was to reach the doors of the Assembly Rooms. Aaron would have set someone in the entrance hall to see her in. She dared not scream or shout for help, or she would bring half the inhabitants of the square prying into why she was about at such an hour.

Barely able to believe her good fortune, she reached the wide steps of the Assembly Rooms, and a sob of relief escaped her as she charged up them. But her attacker was on her. He whirled her about and she threw up her arms in defense to ward him off, knocking his hat from his head, and even as the involuntary scream rose in her throat she recognized him with a different kind of horror. It was Matthew!

"What the devil do you think you're about?" he stormed, his nostrils flaring, his whole face livid with rage. "First making out you were going to bed, and then creeping through the streets like a draggle-tail!"

"You've spied on me!" she expostulated furiously. "And frightened me! I thought—oh, I don't know what I thought I was so frightened!"

He had clamped her to him in his temper, his iron grasp crushing the flesh of her arms through the thickness of her dress- and coat-sleeves. His face jerked toward the doors of the Assembly Rooms and then back to her. "Why did you run in this direction? What brought you to this dark, shut-up place when you'd no idea who it was on your heels? Whom were you expecting to meet—or to rescue you?"

A single booming stroke from the church clock resounded hollowly over the town roofs. Half-past two! The auction would be starting! At all costs she must keep Matthew from suspecting what was afoot or he could still leap in there and ruin everything. For all she knew he might in such an unusual contingency be able to take upon himself the power to bid and be commended for it. But it was too late to say anything. Comprehension was dawning in his face.

"I believe I'm getting it! I was able to tell all the evening you weren't yourself. I've known you too many years to be deceived! You were particularly agitated when I picked up that Halewood sale pamphlet. I couldn't think why. Something lay at the back of it all that was different from any other tiff we've had about the house, but I couldn't puzzle out what it might be. I thought about it again when I picked up the pamphlet out of the fender and threw it back on the fire. It worried me. All those hours playing cards and backgammon never took my mind away from trying to guess what it was. In the end I thought to ask you outright and to clear the air between us. But oh, no! You couldn't come out with whatever it was! That's when it came to me you were sheltering Hart in some way and for some reason that you didn't want me to know about!"

"But how was it you followed me?" She had to keep him talking. With any luck he could be on a wrong tack, imagining she had planned a secret rendezvous with Aaron for a reason other than that of the auction.

"I saw your footsteps across the frosty grass when I left the house. It told me you had been out once, and I remembered thinking I'd heard a carriage stop outside when you were getting the tea, but then when Hart didn't come in I told myself I'd been mistaken. Now I knew you had stopped him coming in. I waited under the trees and watched your bedroom window. Your lamp was on only for a minute or two. As I'd expected, it wasn't long before you came out of the side door." He looked again towards the entrance doors of the Assembly Rooms and his hold on her relaxed. "I don't think that place is as shut up as it looks! You were going to meet Hart in it. The auction! Two-thirty o'clock, that pamphlet said! I was staring at the solution to the whole thing and didn't know it."

He released her and would have made for the doors, but knowing only that she had to stop him she grabbed his coat and hung on with all her strength.

"No, Matthew! No! Let Aaron have Halewood!"

His inexorable young face did not change expression. "Never!" he ground out bitterly. "If he gets

Halewood he'll get you too! I have the power to prevent that happening and I intend to use it!"

He tried to thrust her from him but she would not release her hold, dragging on him with all her weight, and when he grabbed her wrists, intending to snatch her grip away, she lurched toward him. She had not intended it, but her leg had given way at last under her, throwing her off balance, and the sudden impact of her body against his caused him to miss his footing on the icy step. As though jerked by a rope, his head thudded back against the stone column behind him with all the violence of a mighty blow and he pitched forward down the steps, taking her with him. It all happened in a matter of seconds and even as she cried out she found herself lying with him in a tangle of legs, petticoats, shawl, arms, and coattails. His tall hat, which she had knocked from his head at the first moment of onslaught, lay on the cobbles some little distance away.

He had broken the impact of the fall for her, for she had tumbled across him, and she struggled up to a sitting position, scooping her hair back out of her eyes. "Oh, Matthew," she moaned tragically, "I never wanted anything like this to happen. I do love Aaron and I had no idea you had guessed. I've been trying to find a way to tell you—"

Her voice trailed away and her eyes dilated with an awful terror. He was lying sprawled half down the steps, with his head resting on the cobbles where it had cracked at the foot of them, his eyes closed. Frantically she called his name, springing up to lean over him and cup her hands under his head. Blood seeped into her palms.

In the hall of the Assembly Rooms Aaron sat alone in the third row of over a hundred seats that had been set out in readiness for the expected bidders for the property of Halewood. On the rostrum stood the auctioneer and back by the wall his clerk waited with all the necessary papers. Mr. Radleigh, who was himself present, seated at a side table with his spectacles on his nose, had had the two men brought from London, telling them nothing until they had arrived at the hall.

The auctioneer cleared his throat after giving details of the property for sale. "Now who will start the bidding?" he questioned as though every chair held an eager buyer. "Let us open it—at one guinea."

Aaron straightened in his chair, scarcely able to believe what he had heard. A token sum of one guinea! Berenice had been munificent indeed! How he wished Delia were here! He had paced the floor waiting for her. Slowly he raised his catalogue.

"Thank you, sir! Any advance on one guinea? Going, going, gone!" The hammer crashed down. "Sold to the gentleman in the third row."

The clerk went through the formality of scribbling down his name while the auctioneer proceeded with the next part of the sale, which to Aaron was totally unexpected, and it was a nod from the lawyer that had kept him in his chair.

"Now the fine contents of Halewood Hall. Do I hear a guinea from you again, sir?" asked the auctioneer.

Aaron put up his catalogue. The hammer was lifted again while the final call was made. Down it crashed once more. Everything was his. The house, the paintings, furniture, tapestries and silver, the carriages and blood horses, the land, the livestock, and all the outlying farm property. But where was the girl who was to be his wife and the mistress of it all?

He sprang up to go in search of her, accepted Mr. Radleigh's handshake of congratulation, and was almost at the doors leading into the corridor when they swung open and Delia rushed in. Her face was drained of all color, her hair dishevelled, and frozen slush was melting on her coat. He thought she must have run to get there and taken a few falls on the way. Her distress he took for her failure to arrive before the auction was over.

"Halewood is ours, Delia, my love!"

She scarcely seemed to hear him. "It's Matthew! He's badly hurt! He's lying outside!"

He did not stop to ask questions but was ahead of her out through the door, leaving her to summon up the others' assistance as she followed him. As he rushed to help the injured man, not knowing what he would find, he knew with a despairing flash of insight that fate had cloven Delia asunder from him in some totally unexpected way. His triumph in the possession of Halewood had been shortlived. Had its curse already fallen on him?

∙⊰ *10* ⊱∙

AT first Matthew lay in a coma. When at last he recovered consciousness he was incoherent, not knowing anyone, unaware that he lay in a darkened sickroom in his grandparents' house, a delicate and dangerous operation having been performed on his head to remove a clot of blood. Christmas came and went. His fever had long since passed and the bandages about his head were no more than a protection over a healed scar when he eventually opened his eyes with recognition of his surroundings. Delia was at his bedside and she dropped the tatting she had worked on to while away the hours, leaning over him.

"What's that noise?" he whispered. It was almost as though he had been wrenched from the lost depths that had held him by yet another distant boom beyond the town, which rattled the windows and shook the ground.

She answered him in a voice shaky with joy that he had come back to the world. "It's the blasting for the new railway line. The company settled without further delay for their second choice of route for the tracks."

"I should be there." His murmur was agitated.

"No, no," she said soothingly. "Time enough when you're well again."

He looked at her, confused and puzzled and distraught. "I thought I'd lost you."

"Why should you think that?" she asked tremulously.

"I've been calling for you all the time, but you never came!"

There was no point in telling him he had only babbled her name occasionally and never once had he cried out as he imagined he had done, but with a wrenching pang she wondered what terrible anguish he had endured whilst floating up and down again on waves of near-consciousness. "I was here, Matthew. I've spent hours every day at your bedside."

"Don't leave me again." He would have attempted to raise himself up to reach an arm to her but she restrained him quickly, knowing he must not move, and sat on the edge of the bed, exerting a little pressure with her hands on both his shoulders.

"You mustn't worry about that or anything else," she said placatingly, but he was not to be distracted.

"Promise me!" He was restless and disturbed, a very real fear of retreating back into that abyss without her showing in his eyes, and he strove to lift himself towards her.

"I'll be with you as long as you want me," she cried, frantic with concern.

He relaxed, his lids drooping with exhaustion, and gave a long sigh. "That's forevermore."

She saw that he slept. There was a faint smile on his lips and she touched them with her fingertips, tenderly, but as she would have touched a frightened fawn or child or any other helpless creature that had looked to her for succor and solace, but her own face was wan and hollow-eyed. She knew to what she had committed herself.

Rising soundlessly from the bed, she went to find his grandparents and give then the glad tidings that their beloved grandson had spoken lucidly at last. Both of them were true northerners, inclined to understatement and not given to displays of emotion, but on this occasion they embraced her and each other with tears of thankfulness.

Matthew spoke again several times that afternoon, but he was content and placid and there was no further talk of his earlier fears. Delia knew she had set his mind at rest.

When she walked home in the gathering dusk, passing the street lamplighter going about his task, her thoughts dwelt on all that had happened since Matthew had first been carried from the market square and laid in that bed. Aaron had settled into Halewood, but she had not yet visited him there, having no time to spare, although they had seen each other when he had called in at Sycamore House at regular intervals. Her father had made excellent progress and was now allowed to sit out in a chair in his bedroom, where he spent most of the day reading. He could even walk slowly with a stick, but realized he must accept enforced retirement, aware that he would never be the same man again. Fortunately he was not low-spirited and was determined to make life as full as his capabilities allowed.

Melissa had used the excuse of wanting to do what she could to help during his convalescence in order to stay on at Sycamore House and avoid returning to London, where Uncle Henry had won his by-election. No objection was raised by her parents, and Delia believed them to be relieved not to have to set eyes on their daughter again for an indefinite period, forgiveness being out of the question.

Delia had been quite glad of her cousin's company, for she had made an effort to be helpful, although that helpfulness had waned considerably as soon as her continued sojourn at Penghyll had been assured. Recently she had lapsed into a state of ennui, which she declared was a delayed reaction to all she had been through, and Delia did not question it.

Having reached the market square, Delia followed the pavement past the Red Lion Hotel, not looking at the Assembly Rooms on the far side where the sight of the flight of steps evoked painful memories. There had been practically a riot when those who had hoped to purchase Halewood discovered that the auction had already taken place, but there had been nothing any of them could do about it and after more angry discussion they had dispersed. Nearly all were outsiders and no local ill feeling remained to fester against Aaron; on the contrary, it was considered only right that a Hart should be residing at Halewood, and whatever misfortunes should befall him there were only part and parcel of his birthright and he had to take the rough with the smooth, as his predecessors had before him.

It had started to rain by the time she reached the gates of Sycamore House and she was glad to get indoors. On a salver in the hall was a letter from Italy and she recognized the writing. She took it with her up to her father's room, where a cozy fire glowed and the curtains were closed against the dismal evening. Dr. Gilmore woke from dozing in his chair.

"The most wonderful thing happened today," she announced emotionally, kissing his brow. "Matthew recovered consciousness completely and spoke to me! In fact he talked quite a lot. Dr. Pomfret called shortly before I left and seemed extremely satisfied."

Her father expressed his pleasure, smiling at her thankful face. "Nobody could have been more patient and attentive at his bedside than you've been during these worrying weeks. You've probably done more to help him than you'll ever know."

She gave her head a little shake. "You're quite wrong. I've done nothing. He had no awareness of my presence there at all. He told me."

He saw how sad and thoughtful her expression had become and sought to distract her by mentioning the letter that she held. "Have you had word from Lady Hart at last?"

A smile took over her face. "Yes, she has written,"

she said, opening it. "I'll read it to you. Ah! It's no longer than the one I received from Roland."

It was a brief note, but where Roland had merely listed the reasons why he hated Italy and wished he were home in England, Berenice wrote of her delight in the villa that she had made her home. It was everything she had hoped it would be. Unfortunately Roland was being naughty and difficult. As an extreme measure she had allowed his tutor to beat him, but it had done no good at all and she wouldn't let it occur again. She sent her regards to Dr. Gilmore and would Delia be so kind as to tell Mr. Hart she had received his letter of thanks for donating Halewood to him, for she would not be acknowledging it and considered the correspondence closed. She remained, affectionately, Berenice Hart.

"Hmm." Dr. Gilmore gave a reflective nod. "Lady Hart was generous beyond all count in insuring that Halewood became the property of Mr. Har, but in my opinion she has no liking for the young man. That remark about the correspondence being at an end amounts to a very noticeable snub."

Delia, folding the letter up again, made no comment. Poor Berenice. The very reverse was the reason why she could not bear to receive any more letters from him. "I'll write tomorrow and tell her about Matthew. She'll be glad to know he's on the road to recovery."

"You must not look for a speedy return to health," he advised seriously. "I fear it may be many months yet before you stand at the altar with Matthew. Dr. Pomfret will keep Matthew lying in that darkened room for some time to come. It's too early yet to tell whether any real damage has been done to the brain, and he suffered a double blow—from the pillar and from the sharp edge of the broken cobble. That he must have continued, absolute quiet goes without saying, and no upsets of any kind."

"I realize that." Her head was bowed, her attitude grave.

He put out a hand and with his fingertips he lifted her face upward to him. "Matthew is never going to need you more than he needs you now. You must give no more time to me. Nurse Baker will stay on for as long as she's needed and after that you shall employ a suitable housekeeper. Your duty is only to the man to whom you are betrothed. Nobody else."

"I know." Her voice was barely audible. He withdrew his touch and her chin sank to her breast. She was aware that he had no real idea of the conflict of loyalty and love she was enduring, but she could not talk to him about it. With hands motionless in her lap, she sat very still, her shoulders dipped, lost in thought. When the doorbell rang in the depths of the house she did not stir, nor yet when one of the servants went to answer it. Only when Aaron's voice sounded did she sit up with a start.

"Aaron has come with those books from Halewood's library that he promised you." She sprang to her feet, putting her hands instinctively to her hair as if it might have been disarrayed by the very turmoil of her thoughts. "I'll go and meet him."

He had already reached the landing and carried three enormous vellum-bound tomes in his arms. "Look at these vast volumes on Halewood's history that I've brought for your father to peruse." He gave a laugh and lifted them slightly. "Do you think his reading table will be strong enough to hold them?"

She faced him in the lamplight, her bottle-green gown dark against the crimson wallpaper and carpet, her face ivory-pale. "Matthew knew me today for the first time."

His expression mirrored his immense exuberance at the news. "That's wonderful! Splendid! He's going to be all right again!"

She was quite motionless. "Nobody can be sure about that yet."

"But he will be." He shoved his load of books onto the bow-fronted chest of drawers that stood near at hand. "It was only a crack on the head after all. That happens to lots of people. I was out for two days myself once when I was thrown from a horse."

"There's a difference between two days and several weeks—and there are other differences, too."

He screwed up his eyes speculatively at her, black brows drawing together, and he stayed by the chest of drawers about a yard from her. He had become accustomed to her withdrawing from him since the night of the auction, her melting tenderness quickly suppressed, her mouth half-surrendering and then closing defensively, but he had been patient, understanding that Matthew had come between them in an entirely new way and knowing that until the unfortunate man was well again that was how it would be. But this evening there was something different in her whole attitude. As if the whole of her being was one despairing cry. Not in physical yearning, which made her breath sob and her flesh leap under his touch, but in a complete rejection of him.

"Yes?" he questioned, warily.

"Nobody else caused you to be thrown from a horse, but I brought about Matthew's fall."

"It was an accident! You can't hold yourself responsible!"

"But I do. I'm the one who made him lose his footing. However one looks at it, I pushed him down those steps. I alone am the reason why he's been lying sick all these weeks. Whatever ill effects he still may suffer can only be laid at my door."

"He has nobody but himself to blame! If he hadn't spied on you, followed you—"

"That's beside the point. None of that brought about his injury. It was the fall and only the fall. Had I not panicked and struggled with him it wouldn't have happened. I should have reasoned with him somehow."

"This is hindsight! Mere supposition! You took the only course that seemed open to you at the time. Why do you speak of it as though it occurred through some selfish whim of your own? You sought to stop him going into that auction for my sake."

Her cheeks went hollow. "I nearly killed Matthew for you."

He caught in his breath sharply and lifted his hands in appeal. "Don't torture yourself. Matthew didn't die and he's not going to die. He'll recover and take up his life again."

"I must help him do that."

He refused to accept the significance of her words: and made a swift, impatient gesture. "Yes. Naturally. A few more weeks—"

"Longer than that."

His mouth felt dry. "How long?"

The effort of answering seemed almost beyond her. Her lips hardly moved. "For as long as he wants me. I told him that today."

He stared at her. Shock went through him like a deadly current. She whom he loved beyond all measure, whose body he looked upon as the perfect complement of his own, whose being gave him the entire reason for his existence, had with a few words severed herself from him to a point of no return. He tried to speak, but no sound came, every muscle of his throat seemingly paralyzed.

She half-extended her arms, her hands curled upwards from the wrist in an attitude of abject sorrow and defensiveness. "Don't look at me like that," she implored in a heart-torn whisper.

He found his voice. "You can't mean that this is the end of all that lies between us."

"I do." She was barely audible. "Nothing can make me change my mind. Nothing at all. This is how it has to be."

His face was haggard. Suddenly, out of the unbearable hurt, the unendurable sense of loss, came a great gush of searing anger. It was a white-hot rage directed against the cruel capriciousness of fate, but he made her his target.

"So this is how little you loved me!" He did not shout, his low-spoken words the more devastating because of it. "You did not care! Your heart was never mine! All along Matthew has come first with you! It's he whom you've loved all the time."

He wanted her to deny it. To cry some protest. To show some sign. But she only stood as though all power to move had deserted her, an awful look of desolation on her face. Her silence was infectious. It choked into him and he hurled himself about and ran down the stairs to snatch up his hat and his cape, which he threw over his arm. As he wrenched open the vestibule door he stopped and looked up over his shoulder. His eyes blazed at her. In fury and in love and in despair. Then the vestibule door crashed after him and there followed the more resounding thud of the front door. Outside, hooves leapt and slithered on the gravel as a whip cut home, and went galloping away into the night.

She moved stiffly and went to the books he had left behind. *The History of Halewood* in three volumes. Stunned with grief she lowered her head and put her cheek against the top volume, encircling the pile with her arms.

It was the creak of a floorboard on the landing that made her raise her head. Melissa had come from the guest room in outdoor clothes. Her face showed that she had overheard all that had passed between them.

"You may not want him, but I do!" she declared, her voice vibrant and high-pitched. Seeing Delia's incredulous expression she gave a shaky little laugh which revealed her extreme nervousness. "I'm going to make myself mistress of Halewood. Even my father will approve of that!"

She darted down the stairs, her skirts swooping out as she swung around the bend of them to traverse the rest of the flight. When she reached the vestibule door she paused as Aaron had done, but her eyes had a very different look in them. Delia had seen it only once before, and that had been in the eyes of a man in the gaming room at a party. All had gathered around to watch the cardplay. He had staked far more than he could afford to lose on the hand he held.

"Be magnanimous!" Melissa cried imploringly to her on a shrill note of desperation. "You're the only friend I ever had. God alone knows what Halewood will do to me!"

She had gone. Delia, unable to comprehend why Melissa should imagine Aaron would turn to her, knew a new sense of foreboding to add to her agony, but she was given no time to remain there on her own as she would have wished. Her father was ringing the little handbell by his chair, no doubt getting impatient to see Aaron and thinking he was a long time coming to see him. Picking up the heavy volumes, she went in to him.

Dr. Gilmore exclaimed at the size of the books. "They're too heavy for you! Put them down quickly —yes, over there on the table. That's it! I declare, you've exhausted yourself! You're quite pale." Then he looked towards the door she had left open, and back to her. "Where's Mr. Hart?"

"He was in a hurry," she managed to say, running her shaking fingertips along the gilded edges of the pages. "These are splendidly bound books. I'll have to fetch the larger reading stand up from the study. The one you've been using will be top-heavy."

"Would you read the opening chapter of the first one to me, my dear?"

It was the last thing she felt like doing, but she could not refuse him. "Yes. Of course." She took her place beside him, the book heavy on her lap, and opened it at the first page. Quietly she began to read, but her eyes and tongue seemed to be acting independently of her mind, which was following Melissa, who was herself in the wake of Aaron, on a fateful journey through the rain to the distant black outline of Halewood on the hill.

The chapter seemed endless, and when she came to the last line of it she looked up and saw that her father had dropped off to sleep. Not knowing how she had been able to make sense of the words, she leaned her head back against the chair in complete exhaustion, one hand resting on the book, the other falling limply to her side. Her eyes were deep, dark pools in her white face, her gaze distant and unfocused, her heart yearning toward the man who could never be hers.

At Halewood Aaron stood silhouetted against the huge fire of blazing logs on the hearth in the long hall, feet set apart, hands clasped behind his back, head thrust slightly forward. All the old angers, sorrows, lost-love pangs, and immeasurable miseries that had permeated the walls over the centuries seemed to have seeped out and gathered into his frame. The weight was heavy on him, and when a footman announced there was a young lady to see him no hope flared, for every fiber of his being would have known and thrown off the shackles if by some miracle Delia had come to retract her rejection of him.

"Miss Barton, sir."

Aaron turned slowly and leaned an arm along the stone mantel, one foot coming to rest on the hearth, as she entered. He gave her no welcome, his cold stare designed to show his resentment at her intrusion, which increased when he saw that she had left bonnet and coat with the footman, obviously intending to make herself at home. That her outward composure hid an inner anxiety of desperate proportions he did not suspect.

"Good evening, Aaron." She walked towards him. She had a graceful walk and covering the length of the hall between them gave her a chance to show herself off to advantage, the shot-silk gown she had chosen with care to wear changing color from rose to gold with every rippling gather, its neck high and modest, the sleeves long and tight.

"I'm in no mood for social chitchat," he stated bluntly. "If there's some purpose for this visit please state it and be gone."

She seated herself in a chair where the firelight danced over her face. "I have kept my own counsel, wanting to be sure before I mentioned the matter to you, but I can't believe you haven't been somewhat prepared for the possible outcome of that night when I let you late into Sycamore House."

He threw up his hands in exasperation. "What the devil are you talking about?"

"Have the looks I've given you, the chance remarks I've let fall, meant nothing to you?"

He was completely baffled, and angry with it. "Have you come for some belated and additional apology for my drinking more than I should have done on that occasion? If you have, I think you could have chosen a better time. I recall apologizing next morning, and as I said to you then it's not my habit to imbibe inordinately and the lack of food for more than fourteen hours had had unprecedented results. I'm sorry again for any embarrassment I might have caused you. There! Does that suffice?"

"It wasn't an apology I wanted. I've come for more than that."

He dug fists into his hips, elbows jutting, strained almost beyond endurance by the unwanted interview. "What, pray?"

"I want your name for—our child, which was conceived that night."

He thought at first he had not heard correctly. But even as she had spoken her nerve had given way, her apparent composure had dissolved, and she pressed shaking fingertips against her mouth, her eyes quite terrified of him. Had she shown bravado or hostility or arrogance he might have doubted that she was

210

speaking the truth, but to him her helplessness and fright rang completely true. He was aghast and put a hand to his head, trying to remember the events of that night, but as always everything eluded him. He could see himself staggering to the foot of the stairs holding on to Melissa for support, but beyond that—nothing. Except that she had wept. Continually. And cried out to him. Had he believed himself to be holding Delia in his arms? Frantic to possess her, had the wine so clouded his senses as to create the illusion that it was not Melissa he was compelling into surrender?

He paced to and fro. "We must talk about this. Tell me everything."

Sheer fright that she would fail to convince him continued to lend a note of authenticity to all she said. Truth and lies blended together. She made it impossible for him to doubt her. No innocent girl, such as he believed her to be, strictly brought up and carefully chaperoned, could have made up the details she was divulging to him. She took care to remind him in an indirect way that she had gone nowhere without Delia in her first days at Sycamore House, and that he himself had escorted her to the Penghyll Ball. In no way could he connect her with other male company. Again she congratulated herself that inadvertently she had insured that no word of Richard's impact on her life had ever reached him.

She could tell he remembered nothing of that night she had plotted with care. Her own experience of the drug which she had added to the claret had not played her false. True, there had been a terrible couple of hours when she'd been afraid he had taken too much of it and would die, but it had worked better than she had dared hope. Now was the time to deal the last stroke.

She stood up and faced him squarely. "What's done can't be undone. You'd not see the heir to Halewood born out of wedlock!"

He looked at her with loathing. As a man of honor he accepted that there was only one course open to him. As a man in love with another girl, no matter that he had lost her, he was repelled by the sordid events in which he had become embroiled, and the prospect of a marriage precipitated by them was abhorrent to him in every way.

"You're right," he said bitterly, "but the marriage of convenience in which we'll both be unwilling partners shall be no more than a civilized and legal arrangement. Should you find it intolerable to continue living under this roof after the baby is born you'll be free to go and live elsewhere. I'll make no claims on you. You shall have the house of your choice and a settlement for life."

"And the child?"

"The heir to Halewood remains here. There'll be no further contact between the two of you ever again."

She was willing to agree to anything, enervated by the ordeal she had been through, sustained only by triumph. "Let's be married tomorrow. There's not a day to waste. I can't lace myself indefinitely. I'm not going back to Sycamore House. Send for my baggage. I left everything packed."

His face was set in hardness. "What of your parents? Should I not go to London to see your father——"

"No!" She fluttered her hands in protest. "Suppose he insisted on some delay? You must do everything to salvage my reputation!"

He sighed. "Whatever you say. Whether we can be married as quickly as tomorrow I've no idea, but I'll do all I can. Now I'll see that your boxes are sent for and summon a servant to show you to a suite of rooms."

He left her alone in the long hall. She hugged her arms in jubilation. She had done it! She had guaranteed a future for Richard's baby! She had averted disgrace and humiliation! She was free of her hateful father! In fact, when the next six months were over she would have freedom beyond her wildest dreams! She wouldn't have to stay in this cold, drafty house a moment longer than was necessary. And what a cold place it was! How eerie the moaning of the wind in the chimney!

She shivered, rubbing her arms instead of hugging them, and she drew nearer to the blazing fire. As she did so a great gust of wind blew down with a sudden roar, puffing out smoke, scattering the hot ash onto her skirt, singeing countless tiny holes and causing a small flame to flicker near the hem. She gave a shriek and extinguished it before it took any hold, but she was severely shaken and she drew back to a safe distance. How odd that gust had been, and totally without warning. Almost as if the very house had struck out at her in hatred.

She gulped. That was nonsense. She mustn't let her imagination run away with her. Many a time she'd said she didn't believe a word of the old tales about Halewood, but that had been easy to say when she'd been far from it.

On the hearth the huge logs were spitting and crackling, roused by that gust of wind into a kind of fury, leaping up high in showers of dancing sparks, but instead of the warmth radiating toward her she felt colder than ever. It was as though she stood entrapped in the eye of a circling draft.

Panic rose in her. "Aaron!" she cried frantically. He would be a shield between her and the house. He'd let no harm come to her. She sobbed his name again and broke into a run back down the length of the hall in the direction of the archway, intent on finding him. But she tripped and fell, crashing down on a vast spread of carpet, which slid into folds under her. She lay there gasping, telling herself that she must have caught her toe on the fringe, but it was as though she had been given a violent push in the back, so great was the force with which she had fallen. No! No! To think such thoughts was inviting madness!

She was getting to her feet again when Aaron returned and he rushed to help her up. "What happened?"

"I was running—and I fell over the edge of the carpet," she explained shakily.

"Running?" he echoed with a grim anger. "There'll be no more running or hurrying or any kind of stupid behavior that might harm the baby you're carrying. You'll take the greatest care at all times. Understand?"

"Yes," she said meekly, lowering her lashes to hide the malevolent satisfaction in her eyes. He had given her a weapon to use against him if need be. If his concern for the unborn child was to be so all-enbracing she'd only have to threaten some harm to it to get anything she wanted from him.

"You'll be shown to your rooms now," he said, walking with her to the archway. By the foot of the stairs a maidservant waited in a bobbing white cap and streamers. "I must write a letter to Delia explaining why you're staying and what is to take place."

"You'll not find her unprepared," she answered, turning to take the way indicated. She did not care what he wrote. Nobody suspected that she had been pregnant when she'd come to Penghyll. She hadn't known herself at first, although there had been some indication. It was hard not to laugh out loud at the way she had fooled everybody. Little did Aaron know that far from seducing her, he had not laid a finger on her except to try to thrust her from him in one last effort to be free of her company before the drug had finally overtaken him.

Following the maidservant, she noticed how the wind beat ceaselessly against the house, rattling windows as she passed them, swirling curtains in a draft, and always keeping up an endless moan that rose and fell perpetually. No wonder that the house had an icy atmosphere that the heat of fires could not banish.

Suddenly a howl, more eerie than anything she had

ever heard before, seemed to rise up against all sides of the house. She came to a standstill, a nervous hand to her throat. "What's that?"

"Nobbut t'wind, miss. It allus gives newcomers a bit of a start, but you'll get used to it."

Melissa shivered, hurrying after the maidservant again to let no distance fall between them. "Why should it do that? I've never heard such a dismal sound."

The cap-streamers flicked out as the girl glanced back over her shoulder. "They say it's summat to do with how the current of air cuts through t'fells from t'south and meets another blowing from t'sea. That's how this hilltop where Halewood stands got its name. Howling Hill. Have you never heard that?"

"Yes—but I didn't realize it was so bad."

"Oh, it's extra noisy this evening." The clicking heels came to a halt and double doors were opened into a pretty lilac drawing room. "It happens like that now and then. It's supposed to mean there's no good afoot. That's th'old tale anyroad."

Melissa looked about at the room. There was the sparkle of crystal lusters on chandelier and wall-sconces reflected in exquisite Florentine looking glasses. But she returned her attention to the maidservant, who was stooping down to add more coal to the fire. "Doesn't it frighten you?"

"No, miss. Why should it?" The girl straightened up pertly and smoothed down her apron. "I ain't a Hart. T'curse only falls on t'family, and on them that become family when they marry them."

Melissa clasped her hands together. "Do you believe that there is a curse?"

"Course I do. So does my grandma. She remembers tales of what happened to th'Harts at Halewood that her grandma told her. So it goes far back."

"Tragedies happen in all families."

"I know, but it's summat special what happens to th'Harts. It's allus to do wi' love, miss. Nowt ever goes

215

right for a Hart that weds and lives i' this house. I like weddings, but it's to be hoped as t' new master of Halewood stays a bachelor for his own heart's sake, but that's hardly to be expected wi' his fine looks." The girl's voice trailed away, something in her listener's face telling her she had let her wagging tongue run away with her. "I meant nowt disrespectful, miss."

"I hope not!" Melissa's mouth was very tight. "I'm here to marry Mr. Hart."

Crimson flooded the maidservant's face. "Beg pardon, miss. I wasn't gossiping. Only answering t'questions you asked me."

"Show me the rest of the suite," Melissa demanded irritably. The maidservant sprang with alacrity to open more doors, thankful she had said no more than she had.

It was a little over an hour later when Aaron's letter was delivered into Delia's hands. Ellen brought it to her in the drawing room where she was sitting in the firelight, the lamps unlit.

"There's two Halewood grooms come to fetch Miss Melissa's boxes out to a carriage," Ellen informed her. "One of them says she'll be staying up at the big house."

Delia's head jerked and her back straightened as if she had been pulled upright by a puppet's string. "Then show them where her baggage is and let it be carried out."

Left alone, Delia slipped from the chair and sank to her knees, where she sat back on her heels by the brass fender. With nerveless fingers she opened the letter and held it to the firelight to read it through. A numbness came upon her as the words leapt out in the fine black ink.

Delia, my beloved,

Had I harbored any doubt about the existence of the evil curse of Halewood it would have been doubly dispelled this night. After your dismissal of me a second calamity befell to snap the

*last lingering thread of hope I would have been
foolish enough to cherish yet, and it causes my
hand to tremble as I write. It pains me beyond
measure to have to tell you that Melissa is with
child by me, and we are to be married without
delay. I make no excuses for myself. The blame
is entirely mine. I fell into my cups in your father's
house when I arrived home late after a long
and fruitless journeying-out after a loan to secure the purchase of Halewood at auction. In my
drunkenness I knew nothing and forced Melissa
to submit to me. By my action I brought humiliation to an innocent girl and offended against
the gracious hospitality your father extended to
me. My sense of shame knows no bounds. Most
bitter of all is the knowledge of the irreparable
harm I have done to that sweet and tender emotion that bound us together, whether you wished
it or no. I cannot ask for forgiveness. That would
be impertinent. I only ask that you do not harden
your heart against me, but know that I have
loved you and love you still.*

A.

The letter drifted from her shaking fingers and she
dropped her face into her hands, racked by an anguish that made her moan softly over and over again.
She stayed there until the fire died down and shadows
took possession of the room. Somehow she knew that
at Halewood Aaron also sat alone, reaching out in
his despair to her as she did to him.

Another who stayed in wakefulness throughout
those long hours was Melissa. After her baggage had
arrived and been unpacked she had retired to bed, but
the noise of the wind shaking the windows and howling in the chimney of her bedroom filled her with a
gradually increasing fear that eventually turned to terror. A lamp had been left alight by her bed but it

gave her no comfort, for beyond the narrow radius of its glow the fire played strange tricks. She had the uncanny sensation that some indefinable force was flaying itself both without and within, and the creaks and groans normal to an ancient house settling itself at night seemed to her more sinister than anything she had ever heard elsewhere.

Her highly nervous state made her cold. Or was it that the temperature in the room had fallen ominously in spite of the leaping fire in the grate? She must put on a robe for extra warmth and tomorrow she would have extra bedclothes piled on her bed. Shivering, she turned back the covers and ran over to the closet, from which she took the silken garment that she sought. She was slipping it on when she noticed one of the windows shaking more than the others. As if someone—or something!—struggled with invisible hands to seek an entrance, the latch dropping slightly with each fresh gust of wind.

For a few moments she stood paralyzed, such a dread of whatever was there making it impossible to move a limb. But then, when the latch fell to within a fraction of an inch of opening, a sense of self-preservation moved her. She rushed to the window and reached to clamp it secure. She was too late. The window burst inward, catching her a blow across the face before it went crashing back against the wall with a smashing of glass, and the wind leaped on her like a physical being with icy breath, tearing at her hair, clawing at her nightgown, and sending her robe billowing out around her as if it had taken on a life of its own. And worst of all, in her ears rang a demented howl that she could not believe to be part of any natural force, for it seemed to pass upward through her bones to reach her hearing as if it had come from the depths of the earth. From a grave. From a trapped soul!

She gave a desperate cry and made for the door. Out into the corridor she ran, turning in the direction

of the head of the grand staircase, lighted lamps showing her the way. Once she glimpsed her reflection
in a pier glass and saw her face drained of all color,
the cut across her cheekbone red and bloody. She felt
sick and had to hold onto the wall for support, but
the sensation of nausea passed and she stumbled on.

Her bare feet made no sound as she descended the
great flight to the hall, where she crossed to the
arched entrance of the room where she had lied so
desperately and with such cunning to her unsuspecting
benefactor. He was seated in a wing chair half-turned
to the burning logs on the huge open hearth. She
thought at first he was asleep, but then she saw that
his dark and despair-ridden gaze was set unseeingly
on the flames that danced before him. She did not
dare to intrude on him by making her presence
known; instead she approached silently as near as she
could and sat down on the floor against the wall, leaning against the side of a carved chest, where she was
able to feel some of the warmth that radiated from
the fire. In the corner a tall clock ticked away the
night.

He discovered her there when he finally stirred from
his chair as dawn grew gray through a crack in the
curtains. "How long have you been in this room?"
he asked in a dry and tired voice.

"All night." Self-pitying tears gushed up and overflowed from her eyes.

He was unmoved. "Why?"

"I was frightened!"

"By what?" He reached down and helped her to
her feet.

She almost told him of the fiendish howl she had
heard, but stopped herself in time. He must not
suspect that Halewood was turned against her or else
he might start to ponder on the possible reasons for
it.

"The way the wind blew. It was—terrifying. One of
the windows in my bedroom blew in and the glass

smashed." She turned her face to display the cut across it. "See that happened when the frame struck me."

He frowned in puzzlement. "I see nothing."

She put up her hand quickly and felt her cheek. It was smooth and unblemished, with a slight tenderness over the bone to suggest a bruise under the skin. Dear God! What was happening to her in this hateful house! Had it been a trick of bemused eyesight or had she been shown some future injury that would be inflicted on her if she did not withdraw from Halewood. But she had no choice. She had to stay.

"I'll see you back to your room, Melissa."

"Not the bedroom! It's—it's drafty there. I don't like those apartments." She took courage. "I want a grander suite, more fitting to the mistress of Halewood."

"You shall have another in the same wing." He did not intend that she should have the apartments next to his own, which were those he had thought to have occupied by Delia. Before going to sit the night through by the fire he had locked them and pocketed the key. They would never be opened again in his lifetime. It was as if he had padlocked away love and with it the last hope of happiness.

❧ *11* ❧

DELIA stopped to look in the milliner's window. Although spring was still far away it was a joy to look upon the pretty straw bonnet that had been put on display. Yellow silk roses clustered under the brim and the ribbons were striped in the same color. When she had more time she would go in one day and try it on, but Matthew was expecting her and he did not like her to be late.

Her thoughts dwelt on him. He was a difficult invalid, but that was natural to a man who had never been ill before in his life. Some days he was plagued by terrible headaches, and then the opiate given on Dr. Pomfret's instructions caused him to sleep for hours at a time, but on other occasions he appeared to be quite well and almost recovered.

She stepped off the pavement and the crossing sweeper sprang in front of her to clear mud and dung out of her path with his broom. When she handed him a coin on the other side of the street a commotion caught her attention. A young woman coming from a draper's shop to get back into her waiting carriage had collapsed in a faint. It was Melissa!

Delia ran to her, thrusting her way through the people who were gathering, and reached her side at the same time as the groom who had leapt down from the back of the Halewood carriage.

"Lift her up!" Delia instructed. "Lay her on the carriage seat, and then drive back to Halewood."

The second groom had come to help him and Delia sprang into the vehicle ahead of them to clear a space, for the seats were covered with dress- and bonnet-boxes, showing that Melissa had been on a shopping spree. The shopkeeper had come with smelling salts, which Delia accepted, and when she spotted the shop boy standing uncertainly with a pile of packed purchases that he had been bringing out to the carriage she beckoned him forward and took them from him.

Quickly she dived into her reticule. "Here's a six-pence," she said, taking it out. "Get your master's permission to go at once to Number Twenty-three, Holly Place. Tell Mr. Matthew Shaw that Mrs. Melissa Hart is indisposed and Miss Gilmore will be accompanying her to Halewood."

Melissa was laid on the seat and a few seconds later the carriage rolled forward. Delia loosened her collar and waved the smelling salts under her nose. It took effect instantly and as soon as Melissa opened her eyes and saw Delia she burst into tears and sat up to throw her arms about her neck.

"Hush! Hush!" Delia said with concern. Melissa's storm of weeping was completely abandoned, with great snorting sobs and gushing tears and strangled cries.

"I'm so unhappy! Why haven't you been to see me?"

Delia bit her lip. "I couldn't come. You know why. You heard all that Aaron and I said to each other on the night you went to Halewood to tell him about the baby. I have to forget him. He's your husband—"

"Husband!" Melissa almost spat the word, an angry self-pity drying up her tears, leaving some still sliding down her cheeks. "He denies me nothing but his company!" It irked her that she could have clothes, trinkets, and any kind of food she fancied without a word of protest from him, foiling her original intention to use the well-being of the baby she carried as a threat to get her own way, and in truth it was not his company she wanted, being a little afraid that she might make a slip of the tongue that would give her away, but loneliness was lying heavy on her garrulous tongue and it relieved her to set all her troubles at his door. "I hardly ever see him. He never comes near me if he can help it! All he thinks about is Halewood! Do you know, the other day I found him in his shirt-sleeves helping the laborers to shift some stone in the restoration work! I eat alone! I sleep alone! I pass the endless hours with nothing to do and no one to talk to!"

"You could invite people to Halewood," Delia pointed out, "and surely invitations have been coming to you both since the announcement that your marriage had taken place was in the newspapers. I'm not your only friend in this neighborhood."

"Yes, you are! I told you that the evening I left for Halewood. The others are only acquaintances. But it's more than that." She frowned sullenly. "Aaron has forbidden me to lace myself, and I'll not have those hateful girls and their mothers staring at my waistline and working out the months behind my back!" She set her hands on her waist as she spoke and eased herself uncomfortably. "I laced myself this morning in case I met anyone I knew. I loathe looking plump."

"But when the baby is born—"

Melissa tilted her chin defiantly. "Seven months! I'll tell everyone it came at seven months!" Then she groaned in weary exasperation. "Aaron is like a madman about the baby, but only because he wants an heir for Halewood. He's made up his mind it will be a boy. I don't care either way. I detest children. I don't want this one—and don't you dare say I'll feel differently when it's born, because I shan't. I've detested it since the moment I began to realize I must be pregnant, and it's to blame for all the misery I'm going through, both physical and mental."

"The baby is innocent!" Delia protested. "You mustn't blame—"

Melissa interrupted her ferociously. "It's there! Inside me! A horrible lump that's going to get bigger and bigger! That's its crime! And I have to go through all the dreadful business of childbirth, which I find too frightening to think about." She uttered a despairing sigh. "How I wish babies came floating down on angels wings as we were taught in the nursery and the schoolroom!". .

Delia raised her eyebrows. "Actually I was never taught that. Being a doctor's daughter, I saw too much of the patients to be brought up in ignorance. The first home I remember was in the market square above the surgery."

Melissa made a fastidious little grimace. "That was the dreary time before Uncle Charles had any rich patients, wasn't it? Mama mentioned it once. A poky place by all accounts."

"We had happy times there. My mother was alive then."

"I forgot. So she was."

"At least neither your mother nor your father had anything to complain about in the size of Halewood when they visited you after you let them know you were married. Aunt Rachel was overwhelmed and Uncle Henry—even though he'd arrived in a towering rage—had nothing but praise for the house and approval of the match when they came back to Sycamore House afterwards."

Melissa's face tightened. "Halewood hates me!"

"Why do you say that?"

She clutched Delia's hands. "It's true. I'm made to feel an intruder there. Some force of resentment is working against me. Halewood despises me and wants me gone. I know it!"

"But there's no reason for that," Delia insisted placatingly.

"You don't know! I—" She clamped her lips together, keeping to herself what she had been about to say.

"Yes?" Delia prompted with a puzzled frown.

Melissa realized how nearly she had given herself away. She avoided Delia's gaze, looking aside through the carriage window where the outskirts of the town had given way to the countryside. "It's a tormented house," she said soberly. "I only wish I'd never had cause to set foot inside it, but don't let's talk about it any more."

When the carriage passed through the gates it was a deeply emotional moment for Delia. She looked toward Halewood with pain and love. The pale morning sunshine lay like a transparent veil over the old house and the window panes were molten gold. To her surprise the coach driver did not sweep towards the grand entrance through the inner courtyard, but drew up at the side door that she had usually used in the past.

"I prefer this entrance," Melissa said in explanation, preparing to get out. "I never feel able to breathe in the courtyard, and it's always so exceptionally cold there."

Delia made no attempt to get out after her. "I'll borrow the carriage to return to town if you don't mind, and I think you should take off those stays and go and lie down."

"No! You mustn't go!" Melissa grabbed at her. "I insist you come in for a cup of tea! Oh, please! You won't see Aaron. He went off riding early this morning."

She went with Melissa into the house. It seemed to breathe a welcome over her and she touched an ancient chest in passing, rested her fingers on a vase, brushed a chair, and set her hand on a door jamb. Talking to the house with her touch. Letting it know she'd missed it.

She stayed no more than half an hour. When she reached Matthew he spurned her greeting and looked at her with cold and angry eyes from where he lay on his pillows.

"How often do you go to Halewood?" he demanded testily.

"This was the first time since Berenice left."

"I don't believe you."

Knowing that the last thing she must do was to get annoyed or argue with him, she answered him with her usual calm mien. "I've no time to go visiting—and I don't want to. I only went today because Melissa fainted and I didn't think she should go home on her own. Have you forgotten that Aaron and Melissa are married?"

He did not always recall what he had been told, but in this case he did remember. "That's not to say you and Aaron don't want to go on seeing each other."

She sighed inwardly. He was in one of his old goading moods and she would have to put up with it. "I don't want to see him," she said truthfully, for it was a special anguish she had so far avoided and hoped to continue to avoid, "and I'm sure he doesn't want to see me. Melissa is going to have a baby. She told me that Aaron thinks of nothing else but Halewood and his future heir."

Matthew's too-brilliant gaze did not leave her. "If you were having my child," he said carefully, "I'd think of you first and the house and baby afterward. Why did he marry her when he doesn't love her?"

She turned her stricken face from him and unhappily rubbed her palms together in her lap. "Circumstances brought their marriage about. That's all I can tell you."

He caught his breath incredulously. "Don't tell me he got her in the family way!"

The euphemism made Delia shudder. She clapped her hands over her ears to shut out the sound of his laughter. It was the first time he had laughed since the accident, and she had never dreamed that the sound she had longed to hear again would be the cause of gouging anew her very deep and personal agony.

Matthew continued to make good progress as the weeks went by. Gradually the force of his headaches grew less, and as time went on there were longer spells between them. His forgetfulness ebbed and he began to look forward to when he could return to work. His colleagues in the railway company called often to see him, reporting on the progress of the new line, which he was impatient to see and chatted about to Delia. His first walk of any distance was with her to view the new terminus that was being built in the town, a grand edifice of pillared gateways, elaborate brickwork and chimneys, and pie-edged platform roofs supported by iron columns ornamented with pineapples, oak leaves, lilies, strawberries, and chestnuts. The coming of the railway to the area had brought a new population to flood the town. The railway navigators, or navvies, as everyone called them, were everywhere in their distinctive dress of square-tailed coats of velveteen, canvas shirts, waistcoats that were often of rainbow colors, and moleskin trousers. On their heads they sported at rakish angles white felt hats or sealskin caps. Wild and rough and illiterate, some had moved into lodging houses in the poorer parts of town, but most of them were housed in huts erected out in the working area where the land was being gouged by spade and shovel, accompanied by the constant rumble of wagons, barrows, and tip-trucks, the clang of hammer, clink of chisel, and thud of pickaxe. A motley collection of women, whom the navvies had brought with them or had attracted from local sources, cooked for them in the open air, washed their clothes, suffered their battering, and joined them in their drunkenness. Fights and brawls in the town inns had become daily and nightly affairs, although vast quantities of cheap beer formed part of the men's remuneration for their labors, and they frequently

worked in a drunken state. Delia had glimpsed some of
the huts from a distance, but they were best avoided
and fortunately as yet she had had no cause to follow
any of the routes out of town that would take her into
the vicinity. In all the weeks that had made up the
passing months she had done little more than walk
or ride between Matthew's home and her own.

It sometimes seemed to her that he no longer talked
of anything but the railway. He never discussed when
they should set a wedding date, although he did once
express concern over the house at Fellfoot, hoping
that it was not getting damp. She had been able to reassure him, having given a key to a local woman who
lit fires and looked after it, and after that he did not
mention it again. She realized he wanted to take up
the threads of his life fully before their marriage took
place, making sure that he would be the competent
breadwinner and once more in the peak of health,
and she was thankful that he should feel that way,
being in need herself of a chance to recuperate after
looking after invalids, first her father and then Matthew, although she had a new responsibility in Melissa, who made continuous demands on her time and
patience.

Melissa had become a frequent visitor at Sycamore
House. At times she arrived in tears, wallowing in
self-pity, at others in an ill temper, and she was always gloomy. She was ailing in her pregnancy and her
earlier nervousness had developed into an almost
hysterical fear that she would die in childbirth, if
not before.

"The house wants me dead," she moaned on the
day she arrived with a bunch of daffodils that she
had picked for Delia in the gardens of Halewood. "It
plays its awful tricks on me all the time. I trip on
stairs. My bedroom windows fly open at night and
the wind sweeps in cold enough to give me pneumonia.
I've never dared to go through the portrait gallery

since the day one of those heavy pictures fell from the wall and missed me by inches."

There was no questioning Melissa's genuine fear, but Delia refused to accept that the house would deal out physical harm. She knew through her own experience, as well as Berenice's sensitivity toward its atmosphere, that it was able to communicate through a receptive mind, which could drive a nervous or frightened person toward some perilous action, such as when she herself rushed straight into a half-hidden man-trap, but that was the limit of its powers.

"You must take more care on the stairs," she advised, "and hold on to the bannister rail. Then you won't trip. Tell the housekeeper that you want new catches fitted on your windows—I expect the old ones are worn. You can also give orders for a handyman to check all the hangings of the paintings and looking glasses throughout the house, because I don't suppose they've been seen to for years."

"You think I'm letting my imagination run away with me!" Melissa cried, clutching at Delia's hand. "But I'm not! You must be with me when the baby is born, otherwise I'll be at Halewood's mercy! The baby and I will have little chance of survival!"

"Now that is nonsense," Delia said firmly. "Halewood has done no harm to any brought-to-bed mother or newly born child in all its history. I know, because I've read right through three huge volumes about the house that Aaron lent to papa. Be sensible! The house will welcome an heir."

"But this baby isn't—" Melissa bit deep into her lower lip until it showed white, her eyes enormous and tragic and brimming with her easy tears.

Delia's color faded, some sixth sense telling her what Melissa had been about to blurt out, and she grabbed her by the shoulders. "Go on! Finish what you were about to say!"

Melissa swallowed, and she spoke faintly. "It isn't a true Hart. Aaron isn't the father."

Delia shook her wildly. "Then who is?

"Richard Dibley."

"How can you be sure?"

"For the simple reason that Aaron never touched me. I only pretended he had. You see, Richard never knew I was pregnant. I'd discovered my condition by the time of our planned elopement. That was why it was a double shock when he jilted me. Oh, Delia! I had to save my skin somehow! Please understand! Aaron was an obvious choice."

Anger blazed within Delia, searing, white-hot anger such as she had never known before. She struck Melissa hard across the face and sprang to her feet from the sofa where they had been sitting. "You despicable little cheat!"

"Don't turn from me!" Melissa became frantic, falling to her knees at Delia's feet and clutching at her skirts in the same childish way as once before, when she had appealed to her out of misery. "I had to do it! Papa would have turned me out! I was desperate!"

The whole story came tumbling from her. When she disclosed how she had stolen the drug Delia stared down at her in horror. "You could have killed him!"

"I know that now! I really thought he was going to die. I cried 'Don't die! Don't die!' to him over and over again!"

Delia took a step back from her, dragging her skirts free. "Yet you didn't summon help!"

"I was panic-stricken! I couldn't think!" Melissa shuffled forward on her knees. "I'm not like you! You're practical and level-headed and capable. I'm none of those things! For mercy's sake don't desert me now or Halewood will murder me for my deceit! Please! Oh, please!"

She collapsed in a sniveling huddle. Pity and anger and contempt blended together in Delia as she looked down at her, but also came the thought that Melissa could well harm herself and her baby through terror of Halewood if no helping hand was held out to her.

"What of Aaron?" she asked coldly. "Do you intend to confess to him as you have to me?"

Melissa raised a startled, piteous face. "I can't! I daren't! I never meant to tell you, but somehow it slipped out and I'm not sorry it did, because you can't repeat anything I've told you to anybody. It's all part of the secret about Richard, which you promised to keep silent about. But now you know why I need you to protect me from Halewood."

Delia stooped to help the girl to her feet. "Why do you imagine I have special powers?" she inquired uncompromisingly.

"Because you love the house! We all know that. I've said many times I want you to be there when the baby is born. Now I've told you the reason you won't desert me, will you? Say you won't!"

"I won't desert you," Delia said in the same cool tones. She remained straight-backed and unbending while Melissa hugged her gratefully, for she was thinking with compassion of Aaron, her heart aching for him.

She had seen him only twice since it had all ended between them, but neither time had he seen her. Once he had been engaged in conversation with two other gentlemen on the steps of the Red Lion Hotel and she had been quick to lose herself among the shoppers in the crowded market, and the second time had been shortly after Matthew had returned to work in an advisory capacity, giving her time to herself again, and Aaron had ridden by on a glossy black mare, not knowing she had spotted him through the lace curtains of the dressmaker's establishment, and she had scattered pins from her half-fitted gown to dart across and watch him out of sight.

He had called on her father any number of times, but always during the day when she had been with Matthew, and recently he must have heard that Matthew was back at work for he never came without sending a messenger to ask if it would be convenient, which gave her the chance to be out of his way if she wished it. And she did. From the start she had known, as he had, that it was best that they avoid each other's company. People she met, assuming she was in continued close communication with him since he had stayed in her home, questioned her inquisitively, much as they had done about Berenice in the past, wanting to know why the new master of Halewood and his wife had not only done no entertaining yet but had politely declined all invitations except those he accepted on his own to entirely male gatherings for dinner, cards, or billiards. All knew that Melissa was expecting a baby, for no secret had been made of that, and those among the girls with whom Melissa was acquainted, married or single, who had looked forward to gossipy sessions over the Halewood teacups, were huffy when she was not at home to them when they called. Servants' gossip had leaked out and they were curious to know if the haughty Melissa, whom few had really liked, was further gone in her time than she should be, for it opened up the most intriguing speculation about what had been going on beforehand. Delia parried their probing questions as adroitly as she had parried all others in the past, not caring when they became disgruntled and at times almost rude.

The final stages in the completion of the railway branch line coincided with the remaining weeks of Melissa's pregnancy. The last balustrades and green-painted seats and marble-topped refreshment counters were being set in place in the Penghyll terminus. There was to be a grand opening, and Matthew and Delia were to be among the special guests invited to enjoy a train ride to the first halt and back in the company of railway directors, local dignitaries and their wives, and other people of importance.

Matthew drove Delia along part of the route when he went to check on some final work being carried out at a certain point. He was in high good humor. Gradually he had reinstated himself with the railway company, and that morning he had been informed of another much more important line that was to be laid down, for which he was to be entirely responsible.

"It's more than I'd dared hope for," he confided cheerfully. "One of my chief worries during that long convalescence was that I'd be forgotten by the people who matter and stepped over by fellows with less qualified experience than myself. My! Isn't it a grand day!" He grinned appreciatively up at the sun.

It was indeed a grand day. The soft May sunshine was warm in their faces and was held as though reflected in the golden tip of celandine, cowslip, and dandelion which showed amid the meadow-grass. The earth about the track itself lay raw and open, a running scar that vanished through a tunnel in the distance and was lost amid the hills beyond. The lane they were following led on to Fellfoot, and he had suggested they go on there and take a look at Wisteria Lodge.

"It's time now to forget all that has happened over the past months," he had said. "We must settle our wedding plans."

It was near the tunnel that Matthew drew up. Saying he would not be long, he went clambering down the embankment to where a gang of navvies was at work. Waiting for him in the gig, she wondered how she would feel re-entering the house with him where once she had looked to a contented future as his wife, never dreaming that a passionate love such as she had never imagined possible was to twist and turn her life about, leaving her bereft and with a loneliness of spirit that nothing could ever abate.

The screeching of quarreling made her turn her head. Away on the opposite side of the track were some of the mud and brick shanties that housed the navvies, and she could see a couple of women almost coming to blows over a clothesline strung between two of the ramshackle buildings. The shanties presented a sorry sight, the litter of the past months strewn about, and one was a burnt-out shell where a drunken brawl among the men sharing the hut had led to a fire in which several of them had lost their lives. Not only had the navvies made a nuisance of themselves on drinking randies in Penghyll, but their fighting with each other had led to the infliction of terrible injuries and even to murder. Matthew had told her that the men had taken a dislike to the Penghyll line, for it had taken its toll in a record number of accidents, and once there had been a near-riot when a part of the tunnel being excavated had caved in and buried three men.

"Now we can go on." Matthew had returned, and he sprang back up into the seat beside her and took the reins. "It's a good thing the line is almost ready. I'm not sorry I've had nothing much to do with it."

"More trouble?" she inquired.

"It's the mood of the navvies. They've put in a claim for a compensation bonus and they'll never get it. They must stick to their original contracts and there's an end to it."

They came at a spanking pace to the village of Fellfoot and followed the main cobbled street, which was flanked by seventeenth- and eighteenth-century houses, some of them quite large, which were interspersed with several little shops and rows of thatched cottages. Passing the Norman church and a copse, they came to Wisteria Lodge. He helped her alight, and together they went up the path. Like most of the other dwellingplaces in the district, it was built of graystone. The wisteria that had given the house its name spread gnarled branches over the porch and bay windows, the foliage hanging like a green lace.

"How neat the garden looks," Matthew remarked approvingly, pausing to gaze at the colorful flowerbeds and well-trimmed lawn. "The gardener you employed from the village has done his work well."

She made no answer, looking at the house itself, her heart hollow. Where was the joy with which she had first sighted it? The garden and the orchard, overgrown then, had echoed with her laughter and his when together they had explored every inch of their land, which stretched down to the river. With dull eyes she watched him set the key in the door, and when it was unlocked she stepped ahead of him into the light and sunny hall with a feeling akin to despair.

The furniture, which they had chosen with such interest and pleasure during the days of their betrothal before Aaron's shadow had fallen across her life, was covered with dust-sheets, but the local woman in charge of keeping the place clean had been as conscientious as the gardener and there was a freshness in the air that told of frequently opened windows. Matthew, not noticing how subdued she had become, took her with him on a tour of inspection, holding her hand affectionately in his. On the landing he decided to examine the attic and make sure that certain roof repairs had been carried out to his satisfaction, and he left her for a few minutes to fetch a ladder from the coach house and set it up.

"I think we should have a narrow staircase built up to the attic," he said, checking the ladder to make sure it would not slip. "It's pointless not to have easy access to storage space." He smiled at her. "Would you like to take a look at the very top of the house? You haven't seen it yet. I'll open the trap door and then come down the ladder again to help you up."

She managed her full skirts as best she could and was able to step without too much difficulty into the attic. It was large and roomy, but unlike the rest of the house, it smelled dusty and airless. A single window gave light, but had no catch to open it. She stood looking about her as Matthew clambered into the attic after her and went straight to the patch of roof he wished to examine. Almost aimlessly she crossed to the window and cleared away some cobwebs to peer through one of the dirt-grimed panes. Then she drew in her breath sharply, able to see from her vantage point across to distant Howling Hill. On its summit, its windows blinking at her in the sunlight, was Halewood. Such love for it moved her, such passion for the man who lived in it stirred her, that she pressed her face and hands against the glass, heedless of the dust. She knew that no matter how long she lived at Wisteria Lodge or what happened there, she would often steal away to this quiet place and look out at Halewood as once she had viewed it from her childhood room in the house in Penghyll's market square.

A sudden creak in the floorboard nearby made her start. Turning her head quickly, she saw that Matthew stood there watching her. How long his eyes had been on her she did not know, but they glittered brightly with suspicion, as if he had guessed at what she had been gazing with such yearning on her features. Yet he chose to pretend otherwise.

"What are you looking at with such rooted attention?" he demanded harshly.

She drew back in an unconscious attitude of defense. "Halewood. I hadn't realized it would be possible to see it from here."

"You had an expression on your face that you've never had for me!"

"I don't understand you!"

"You were looking at Halewood as if it were your lover!"

"That's absurd! You know how drawn I've always been to it. You can't give it flesh and bones!"

"What of its owner then?"

"He's my cousin's husband!" There was anguish in her cry. "You are to be mine!"

He was unappeased by the bare presentation of facts, jealousy tearing at him. "Halewood and everything to do with it has long stood between us! But *this* house, Wisteria Lodge, our future home, must come first with you from now on!" He threw out an arm and pointed in savage fury at the window. "Those panes shall be boarded up! There'll be no staircase built up to this attic! You'll never gaze out at Halewood from here again!"

The retort burst from her before she could stop it. "Do what you like! Deny me what you will! Your possessive nature demands it, but tell me—is this to be the pattern of our lives under this roof? Am I to be smothered out of existence as a person in my own right by your endless tyranny!"

She had never spoken to him on such a note of bitter wrath before. It was all he could do not to strike her. She had held a mirror to the truth and he recognized it. Her lively will, her strength of character, her determined independence had always represented a challenge to him, and his ego had fed on her everlasting submission to him whenever there had been a clash between them. Only over Halewood had she ever defied him. And she would go on defying him if he failed to drive it from her. He knew that not until he had her truly meek and obedient in all things would he be satisfied, the conquest of her mind as important to him as the possession of her body. Only thus would she be wholly his.

"A wife complements her husband," he retaliated fiercely. "Nature has prepared her for her role."

"Oh, Matthew!" she exclaimed in despair. "Don't be so pompous!"

His control snapped. The sound of the stinging blow that the back of his hand made across the side of her face seemed to hang in the air seconds after his arm had fallen to his side again. Neither of them moved, he as stunned and horrified by what he had done as she was to have received the blow. Then abruptly she came alive, darting toward the trap door to descend, and he sprang forward to catch her about the waist.

"Dearest! I'm sorry!"

She was not listening. Wrenching herself free with a strength that surprised him, her face averted as if she could not bear to look at him, she swept her skirts round and put her foot on a rung of the ladder. He dropped to one knee to hold it steady for her, fearful that she might fall, but when he reached down a hand to give her some support under her arm she flung it from her. As soon as she reached the landing floor safely he swung himself onto the ladder and dropped the last few rungs to pursue her at full speed down the stairs. Near the door he caught her and swung her back from it to twist her with a thud against the wall. Holding her body pinioned with the pressure of his own, he took her face between both his hands and forced her to look at him.

"Forgive me, Delia!" he implored desperately. "I don't know what came over me. I wouldn't hurt you for the world. You know that. I'll never strike you again. Never! I'd die first!"

She answered him in a whisper. "Say no more. I'm as much at fault for what happened. I was tormenting you. I know you didn't mean to hurt me."

"Oh, sweetheart!" He kissed the cheek he had struck and then his lips touched her eyes, her brow, and her temples, such desire for her rising in him that he knew she could be left in no doubt of his feelings. Since their betrothal he had been entirely faithful to her, and with his return to health and vigor after the accident his hunger for her, which by rights should have been assuaged in their long-delayed marriage bed, had put a tremendous strain on him. Now he could not keep his hands from her softness, and with a little moan he fastened his mouth on hers, kissing her with a passion that he had never dared before, lost to all else but a determination to wait no longer to make her his own. Then he felt her shudder in aversion.

His mouth lifted from hers and briefly their eyes met in a look of sudden, mutual distress. His hands slid innocuously to her waist and he drew back, his face bleak. She broke the terrible silence between them.

"We had better be getting back to Penghyll."

He nodded, shattered by disappointment, his ardor drained from him. To know his unspoken yearning for intimacy had repelled her to such an extent was a blow to cause him much disquiet, for he had thought to meet a warm and loving response born mostly out of remorse for her part in their quarrel, but instead she, whom he thought he knew better than anyone, had become a stranger in his arms.

"I'll lock up," he said. Picking up his hat from the dust-sheet covered chair where he had left it, he glanced about him with none of his former enthusiasm for the house. "I wonder if we shouldn't reconsider living in this place. We could sell it easily enough—and at a handsome profit, too—and buy something else in Manchester. It would suit me to be nearer the center of things."

She hoped he would make such a decision. For her part she would not care if she never saw Wisteria Lodge again. Going out ahead of him, she went to take her seat in the carriage and from it watched him locking the door after him. She noticed that he left the house without a backward glance.

When he drove her home the day had clouded over and she thought it suited their mood, both of them trying to converse in a normal manner, but the quarrel and its aftermath lay darkly over them. At Sycamore House he left her with the reminder that he would call for her later, for they were to dine together with mutual friends.

Indoors she found Dr. Gilmore reading in the drawing room. He was now allowed to master the stairs twice a day and was no longer confined to the upper floor. He looked up when she entered, untying her bonnet strings, and putting a marker in his book, he closed it. "Well, my dear, have you had a pleasant outing?"

She sat down opposite him, managing a smile. "It was interesting to see the new railway line." Knowing he would enjoy hearing about it, she described what she had seen and recounted the information Matthew had given her about it. "Then we drove on to Fellfoot and visited Wisteria Lodge." Her voice faded away and she looked down at the bonnet she held on her lap, twisting the ribbons over her fingers. "What am I to do, papa?"

He observed her wisely, fully aware of the conflict in her mind. "If I had not been taken ill you would have been married to Matthew long since, and by this time your thoughts could have been concentrated on the coming of a firstborn, not on these unhappy doubts which have been undermining your relationship with him for many months. I feel inclined to offer the same advice that I gave you once before, but it could be that your feelings have changed drastically toward Matthew. Is this the case?"

She shook her head. "That's what I can't reason out. Matthew is as dear to me as ever he was. There is a special bond between us. I should be content with that, but the thought of our marriage has become abhorrent to me. Since I can never have the man I truly love I would welcome spinsterhood."

There! She had said it. For the first time she had spoken out of her love for Aaron and the relief was enormous. Her father's expression was intensely serious and he looked disturbed, leaving no doubt that there was little that he had not noticed or guessed.

"Not spinsterhood. No, no, my dear. Not for you. You were born to be a wife and mother. Be sensible. Don't yearn after someone who can never be yours. I want to see you safe and secure and protected. Whatever Mr. Hart may have felt for you in the past, he has put those sentiments from him."

It was a blow for which she had not been prepared. Her lips felt stiff and wooden. "Why do you say that?"

"When he first visited me after his marriage to Melissa he would bring your name into the conversation as often as he could. But not any more. Now the briefest inquiry as to your health and well-being is all that ever comes from him." He sought to drive home the point he had made. "To be honest, he is much concerned with his wife, and for his sake I hope some good will come of their union as the years go by."

"It's the child she is carrying that matters to him," she argued doggedly.

"Yes, but as well as Melissa. As well. Remember that. Only last week when he was here the main purpose of his visit was to make a request on her behalf. The foolish young woman finds it difficult to sleep at night on that windy hill and wanted the name of a potion I once prescribed for her in order that she could ask for the same from Dr. Pomfret next time he attends her. Mr. Hart imagined it to be some harmless draft of sugar-water, which was what she had led him to believe, but I explained it was far more than that and there is every reason to suppose that its effect on a woman in such an advanced state of pregnancy could be akin to the unpleasant consequences of an overdose. Nature will not be interfered with. There can be no dictating to nature."

Nor to the heart, she thought. It goes its own way with a sweet stubbornness and will take no heed of reason, no matter what it suffers, no matter how torn with pain and anguish it might be. She suppressed a sigh, gathering up her bonnet and rising from the chair. Her father had given her no help, no advice that could prove useful in solving the problems that beset her—only additional agony in his suggestion that Aaron no longer looked back at what was past, but was concentrating his thought on a future in which she had no part.

"I'll write to Melissa," she said. "She is past making the journey to us now, and I can't go there until I'm needed." Without another word she went from the room and closed the door after her.

That evening Matthew made a determined attempt to act toward her as if the quarrel between them had never been and she responded as best she could, both of them being sociable company at the dinner party,

241

for neither was ever short of conversation and they were among old friends. But later, after coffee had been served and Delia was accompanying a song from their hostess at the piano, she happened to glance across at him where he stood. There was such angry desolation in his eyes that her fingers faltered and she struck a wrong note. When the evening ended he did not kiss her on the mouth when they reached her home, but took her hand in both of his and pressed his lips to her palm. He did not dare to touch her yet in any other way for fear she might again reveal involuntarily that physical aversion to him which had instantly unmanned him, a humiliating and devastating experience. If she shuddered thus in his arms once they were wed he doubted his ability to husband her, and the nightmare possibility was haunting him.

The day of the grand opening of the Penghyll branch line dawned bright and fair. From miles around people came crowding into town from the early hours. Extra stalls were set up in the market square and trade was brisk from the first light. Hundreds of navvies, many of whom had been on an all-night randy, roistered drunkenly among the ordinary sightseers, many having returned from new working sites to join in the celebrations and to lend support to a fiery show of shouted compensation demands, which caused scuffles to break out here and there. But Delia, driving with Matthew to the terminus as his guest on the train's maiden run, saw nothing of the trouble, beguiled by the banners and bunting and the holiday mood of the crowds.

Amid cheers and with whistle and steam the high-funneled, red-painted locomotive chuffed slowly out of the canopied terminus, its first-class carriages with the plump upholstered seats full of the invited passengers. One third-class carriage had been coupled up next to the guard's van, more to display the new comfort provided for the humbler traveler in the wider bench seats and the adequate roofing to keep out rain and engine sparks than to give a ride to the minor railway officials and town clerks who had taken their places in it.

It was the first time Delia had been on a train, and she thrilled to the sensation of being carried along at more than twenty miles an hour, although the pleasure was dulled for her by the strained atmosphere that existed between Matthew and her. It struck her that they were like two puppets, smiling and talking and going through the actions of commonplace social behavior, but inwardly each was suffering as much as the other, and they both knew it. He had secured a seat for her with her back to the engine to avoid the danger of any soot or cinders flying into her eyes, and he leaned forward from his seat opposite her to mark points of interest and answer the questions she put to him.

At the halt everyone got out as if they had been in the train all day instead of covering a distance of no more than ten miles, and refreshment awaited them in glasses of lemonade served under festoons of multicolored streamers, where they were watched by more spectators who had come from neighboring farms to stare both at the hissing locomotive and the fortunate passengers.

That evening there was a civil banquet attended by all those who had been on the train and other local personages. To Delia's delight, Dr. Gilmore felt able to attend the banquet, but she thought it best to take him home when the speeches were over and before the entertainment began. Matthew had collected them and he escorted them home again in his own carriage, being anxious for their safety, for there had been disturbances of gathering seriousness from the navvies all day and in spite of the extra police on duty they were still surging about the town, singing and shouting, smashing windows and picking fights with innocent passersby and with each other.

243

At Sycamore House Matthew went indoors with them, having given his arm to Dr. Gilmore for support, and was thanked for his assistance. "Have a glass of wine with Delia before you leave, Matthew," he said. "I'll not join you, if you will excuse me. I find I'm extremely tired and more than ready for bed."

"Yes, of course. Good night, sir."

Waiting on the stairs with a tray of potions, pills, and a nightcap of hot milk for Dr. Gilmore was Mrs. Wallace, the housekeeper appointed to relieve Delia of domestic duties, Nurse Baker having left long since. She was a sensible and capable woman who watched over Dr. Gilmore unobtrusively, enabling him to feel quite independent. Although she made no attempt to assist him as he progressed slowly up the flight, she was there to make sure he did not totter or fall.

Matthew went into the drawing room where Delia awaited him, but he refused the wine she would have poured. Neither would he sit down, but instead he paced the floor slowly, running a hand through his hair. "We must talk," he said determinedly. "We can't go on like this."

"I do agree."

"If you've no objection I'll get rid of the Fellfoot house. We'll make a fresh start elsewhere as I suggested—"

"Do you really think it would make any difference?" she challenged gently, knowing that he was making a final effort to convince himself and her that a new beginning amid new surroundings with nothing of the past tagging on to them would enable them to pick up the threads again as if all that had happened in between had never been.

He came to a standstill and looked across at her. "I know it wouldn't," he conceded on a note of complete dejection. "You stopped loving me long ago."

He slumped down on the sofa and she went and

sat beside him. "I never stopped loving you in the way I've always loved you, but it was never enough for marriage. I was wrong to imagine it could be. The fault is entirely mine."

"No, I should have known. Then I did know when I saw the expression on your face at the steps of the Assembly Rooms when you implored me not to go to the auction. All you felt for Aaron Hart was in your eyes. Afterward I told myself I had imagined it and that it had been due to the heat of the moment. When I heard he had married Melissa I believed sincerely for a while that I'd been mistaken about the whole thing. But it's no good. It's all a sham. No matter whether you still care for Aaron Hart or not, you've resigned yourself to a life without him, I know that, but what's left isn't enough for either of us. We can't build a marriage on ruins. Other people might be able to, but we can't." He put an arm about her shoulder and hugged her to him, bringing her head to rest against his neck. "We've meant too much to each other."

They sat in silence there together, not moving, drawing comfort from each other's companionable nearness as they had done so often in the past. When at last they stirred he put a hand against her cheek.

"If ever you should have a change of heart—" he began.

She shook her head, wanting no pretense. "It's over. We have friendship left. That will be just as it's always been. Let's be thankful that without any bitterness or animosity we have salvaged that which has brought so much that was good into our lives."

"Dear Delie," he said, using his first childhood name for her.

She looked down and drew the pearl and ruby ring from her finger to place it in the palm of his hand. It was done. Their betrothal was at an end.

They talked quietly for a little while and in a curiously matter-of-fact way, which helped them both to get through it. He said he would be leaving for Manchester in a few days' time, but first he would locate an agent for the sale of Wisteria Lodge. It was decided that she should dispose of the furniture. It all seemed very simple and straightforward. Only when he was departing from her did the full impact of it seem to hit him. At the door he looked completely stricken and turned away from her abruptly, to throw himself into the waiting carriage and drive away into the night.

In a whisper of taffeta she went slowly upstairs to her room. There she removed her necklace and earrings and was about to unhook the back of her gown when there came the sound of wheels and hooves in the drive. Seconds later a thunderous knocking came on the door below, combined with a wild jingling of the bell. Thinking that Matthew must have returned after having second thoughts, she swept out onto the landing in dismay and distress, but as she reached the balustrade and looked down into the hall Ellen opened the door and admitted Aaron, who came rushing into the house. He saw her at once.

"Please come! Just as you are! Melissa is crying out for you!"

She guessed immediately the reason why she was needed. "Is anyone with her?" she asked quickly.

"Yes! By good luck the nurse moved in yesterday, Melissa wanting to be cosseted throughout the final weeks of waiting, but now her time has come far too early upon her. She is desperately afraid. Dr. Pomfret should be on his way, but it's been the devil's own task to get a message through to anyone. Those crazy navvies are everywhere, turning over vehicles and blocking the roads! I sent transport for you three hours ago, but the coachman and groom were pulled from it and beaten up, the horses cut loose, and the carriage upturned into the river. I came for you myself as soon as a farmhand brought word to Halewood of what had taken place!"

"I'll get my cloak!"

She snatched it up from where it still lay on a bedroom chair and hurried downstairs, telling Ellen to let her father and Mrs. Wallace know where she had gone. Then she was out into the night with Aaron, who had brought a phaeton with four horses, which stood steaming in the moonlight.

"Did you meet any of the navvies on the road?" she asked as they went bowling down the drive and out into the avenue.

"Only a few stragglers, because I came into Penghyll near the old church, avoiding the market square and the center of town. We'll leave by the same route." He dived into his pocket and put a hard metal object into her hands. "Here. Take this. Just in case there's any real trouble and I have my work cut out handling the horses."

It was a gentleman's pocket pistol such as her father had carried in the days he had attended the poor and destitute in the Liverpool slums, where it was not safe for any reasonably dressed person to walk alone, and which he had still carried when he had gone far afield on his own. She had never fired a pistol, but she knew the feel of holding a weapon through handling a pair of antique dueling pistols which were kept in the study.

"I hope I don't have to use it," she said unhappily.

"Showing it should be enough," he assured her cheerfully, "and if worse comes to worst fire into the air."

The phaeton went rattling down the narrow side streets, the wheels bouncing on the cobbles, but when the church loomed dark against the starry sky and the lane they were making for was no more than two hundred yards from them, a mob of navvies with flaring torches came swarming around the corner. At the sight of the approaching carriage a great roar went up and they began to run to meet it, waving staffs and pieces of fencing. A bottle came rippling through the air with an opal gleam and it struck one of the leading horses, which shied and wheeled, frightening and confusing the other three.

"Hold on!" Aaron instructed grimly. "We're going through!"

The whip cracked over the horses' heads and they thundered forward. Ahead the navvies scattered out of their direct path, but the boldest hurled themselves at the bridles and the shafts, the dragging of their burly weight having an immediate effect on the nervous animals, and other willing hands came forward to help. Aaron half-rose in his seat and turned his whip on the navvies, causing two or three to drop away with howls of pain. Delia felt a jerking hold on her skirt and screamed, a red-bearded navvy having grabbed at her as he clung to the side of the phaeton. The whip flashed out across her and there was the rip of taffeta as the man fell back with a yell, but another brutal-faced navvy had taken his place, his huge ham fist locked about her ankle. With a powerful jerk he would have brought her crashing down from the seat if she had not been clinging to the back of it, and she screamed again.

"Fire!" Aaron roared at her.

Even as she made a move to obey him she was snatched at again, and this time her grasp on the seat's back was weakened, for she had removed the hook of her elbow to prepare to fire. Down to the floor of the phaeton she tumbled in a sea of taffeta and hoops and petticoats, the pistol jerking out of her grasp as her wrist suffered a painful blow. Again the whip lashed for her protection, striking away those tearing at her skirts, and she sobbed as she saw the pistol sliding toward Aaron's foot. He must have realized what it was, for instinctively he raised his heel and clamped it down again on the weapon to hold it fast. With a sob she reached for it, giving his ankle a little thrust as a signal for him to release it, and with a trembling hand she aimed for the stars.

The deafening report had the desired effect. Scared

and unnerved, the navvies dropped their hold on the phaeton, released their dragging grasp on the harnesses of the wild-eyed horses, and gave vent with the foulest curses while they hurled the bludgeons that they carried. Pieces of fencing, blocks of wood, broken flagons, rocks and stones and lumps of dung all crashed and thumped and thudded against the hood and back of the phaeton, but pursuit was impossible and the road ahead was open to escape. The noisy clatter of the horses' racing hooves on the cobbles changed to a rhythmic thud on the hard mud of the lane, and the outskirts of the town soon began to fall away behind.

"Did the wretches do you any harm?" Aaron inquired anxiously, helping her regain the seat beside him.

"No," she answered breathlessly, giving a shaky little laugh. "I've suffered a bruise or two and my gown is torn, but nothing more. What of you?"

"I'm all right. What a mob! Had the thick-headed authorities listened to the genuine grievance that some of the unfortunate injured presented to them—and done something about it—all this rioting in the town tonight would never have happened. Instead the troublemakers and all those ready enough to fight have taken up the cause with drink and violence and intimidation, and no good can come of that either."

They reached the open countryside and he eased the pressure on the horses, although he kept them at the fastest pace possible for safety along the rutted lane.

"What a way to bring you to Halewood," he remarked wryly. "After months of not catching as much as a glimpse of you, I snatch you from your home and bundle you through mob-infested streets to enable you to carry out an enforced promise to Melissa, who swears she'll not survive the malevolence of Halewood without your protection."

"I'm glad you fetched me. If my being with her

gives her peace of mind, that isn't much for me to do
for my own kin. She is my cousin, after all. Unfortunately she is sadly afraid of childbirth and she has
added her own terror of Halewood to it. Are you
harboring some objection to me being there?"

He shrugged. "None at all. Indeed, if you're to be
the talisman that Melissa confidently expects you to
be I can look forward to the arrival of a strong and
healthy son."

She glanced out of the corner of her eye at him.
His profile was illuminated by the glow of the phaeton's lamps. "Why have you made up your mind that it
will be a boy?"

He turned his face towards her, and she saw clearly
the sad and bitter look in his eyes. "It has to be. It's
my only chance of a legitimate heir."

When they arrived at Halewood she was surprised
that he did not take her to Berenice's former apartments, which by tradition were always occupied by
the mistresses of Halewood. Instead he took her to
the lilac suite and escorted her into the bedroom,
where Melissa lay tossing on the draped four-poster
bed, alternately sobbing and shrieking. Dr. Pomfret
had not arrived and the midwife looked annoyed
and harassed. When Melissa sighted Delia she struggled up against the pillows and gave a long, appealing
cry.

"I thought you'd never get here! Oh, Delia! Don't
let me die! Don't let me die!"

Delia went to her and smoothed her tumbled hair
back from her pain-shadowed eyes. "You're not going to die," she said calmly. "Everything will be fine.
Dr. Pomfret will soon arrive, and if he should be delayed we have the most capable midwife with us who
knows exactly what to do."

The bedroom door closed. Aaron had gone, Delia
thought, to find out if the doctor's carriage could be
seen coming up the drive.

But Dr. Pomfret did not come that night, being

kept busy with casualties in the town, several of them cases of life and death. After a hard and difficult labor, Melissa gave birth to a puny little girl with pale yellow hair.

"I don't want to see it!" she cried with distaste, turning her face away when the midwife would have shown her the baby wrapped in a shawl and ready to place in her arms. "Take it away! Put it in the nursery! Get a wet-nurse! Never bring the wretched creature near me again!"

The midwife clamped her lips together in shock and disapproval. Holding the baby to her, she stalked from the room in the direction of the nursery, which was at the far end of the wing.

Melissa lifted her head from the pillows and glared at Delia, who stood at the foot of the bed. "You make sure the wretched woman doesn't disobey me, or I won't be responsible for my actions toward that baby!" Her head fell back again. "Oh, God! What I suffered! Never again! No, never again!" Delia's silence acted like a barb to her and once more she raised her head, keeping a need to sleep at bay a little longer, her lips parting in a vindictive grimace. "What are you standing there for? Go and tell your beloved Aaron that he has a daughter!"

In the corridor Delia met him coming from the nursery, his face dark and brooding. They faced each other in the early sun's rays that poured through the embrasured windows.

"I've seen the child," he said heavily. "She isn't mine."

It was pointless to make any comment. Wearied to the point of exhaustion by the night's events, she sank down on one of the window seats. A few untidy wisps of hair hung down by her cheeks and the torn folds of her wide skirt draped on the floor. He did not sit down with her but set a foot against the edge of the seat, leaned an arm across his knee, and let his unfocused gaze drift down to the courtyard below the window.

"The baby is perfectly formed—eyelashes, finger-nails—and her weight, so the nurse informed me, well over seven pounds. Nothing premature there, would you say? Yet the night I'm purported to have seduced Melissa falls short of a woman's full time by quite a number of weeks. I realize now that I've had doubts at the back of my mind for some time, but I suppose my pride wouldn't let me face up to have been tricked, and I can't deny that a child of my own would have meant much to me. A future. Some joy again. A reason for living." He paused before adding bitterly, "For a Hart to fly with hope in the face of the Halewood curse is an Icarian folly, doomed to disaster. I'll not forget again."

Still she did not speak, not knowing how to comfort him.

"I can recall many other points that should have awakened me to the truth before now. Melissa forgets herself when she is in a temper or in fear, and Halewood has not been easy on her. Then there's that fateful night when the claret took such ill effect. The symptoms I experienced were exactly like those which your father described to me as the effect of an over-dose of a certain opiate that he has in his dispensary. Melissa had knowledge of it. Did she administer it to me in the food or in the claret?"

He had not directed the question at her, but Delia answered it unthinkingly in her tiredness. "She put it in the decanter."

He shot her a hard, sharp glance. "How did you discover that?"

"She confessed to me after you'd married her and it was too late to change anything. I couldn't tell you then."

He gave her a half-smile. "Don't worry. I understand. You were in an intolerable position. I'll not ask you who fathered the child. Melissa herself shall tell me." He set his foot to the floor again and stood looking down at her, a wry twist to his mouth. "When I heard her cry out to you last night not to let her die it struck a chord in my memory, but I wasn't able to place what it was. Now it's suddenly come back to me. I can remember her calling to me in a similar way when I was deep in that soporific state on the night I was drugged. 'Don't die!' she begged over and over again like a monotonous prayer. I did believe I was about to die, never having felt more ill in my life. Melissa caught me in a web of lies and deceit, but I share the blame. If I'd had my mind less on the possibility of losing Halewood and more on the suspicious nature of the uncharacteristic kindness she was showing me it might never have ended this way."

"You'd had a long and exhausting day," she reminded him.

He reached out a hand and touched her hair. "Do you remember me telling you once that I didn't look for happiness in the possession of Halewood? At the time I'd thought to find a rich compensation in a loving union. I'd even hoped that such a special love as ours would have been strong enough to break the curse. What a vain hope that was! The curse is as old and dark as time. There's no breaking it. I know that now."

She listened in love and sorrow. She believed, as he had, that if she had come to Halewood as his bride their passion for each other would have been strong enough to at least abate the ancient curse and perhaps even destroy it. But it had laid its hold on him as soon as he became earmarked as the house's next master. They had been defeated from the start.

Yet she could not hate Halewood for parting them, because never once had she felt there was anything evil or malevolent in the stones and mortar of the beautiful old house itself. It was held as firmly in the grip of the curse as all the unfortunate Harts who had ever lived in it. Then from whence came the tainting? Wherein lay the source if not in the house itself? Could it be from the land on which Halewood stood? But that was surely an entirely fanciful idea? Nevertheless it was one to give some thought to later on.

She stood up. "I'd like to go home now. I'll come back later in the day and see Melissa. She's in good hands. There's nothing more I can do."

"I thank you for coming." He walked with her down to the entrance hall. A manservant brought her cloak, which Aaron put about her shoulders. His attention was caught by her left hand as she fastened the clasp, and he looked gravely and questioningly from her bare third finger to her strained and tired face. "Is it ended then?"

"Yes," she said quietly. "It's over."

He had sent the manservant to summon a carriage for her and they were alone in the hall. "I'll not be here when you return later. I've made up my mind to go away for a while. I've seen nothing of the rest of Europe and this seems the right time to take a vacation."

She nodded wordlessly. It was as well. Perhaps when he returned he would find himself able to forgive Melissa. The carriage was drawing up outside, but although he put his hand on the great door to open it for her he paused before turning the handle. "There's a certain favor I'd like to ask of you."

"What is it?"

"I've no idea yet what Melissa will decide to do. It was agreed between us that if she wished to leave me after the baby was born she was free to go, but I was to keep the child. It's possible she will still want me to hold to this arrangement. I have nothing against the unfortunate infant. It is a Hart by name if not by lineage. If Melissa leaves her here and I'm still abroad, will you visit Halewood sometimes and make sure that the nurse is fulfilling her duties and the little girl is being well treated?"

"I'll do that gladly," she said, touched by his generosity of spirit. He opened the door for her. "Farewell, Aaron."

He did not answer her, all the pain of parting in his face. It echoed her own torment. She hurried from him. The morning sun shone on her bedraggled evening finery as the groom assisted her into the carriage. Then it was bowling her away, back to Penghyll.

Melissa stayed exactly a month at Halewood after the birth of her baby. Not knowing when Aaron would return, his travel plans having been fluid, she wanted to be gone and not meet him again. She had made up her mind to reside in Paris. With her untouched inheritance and the adequate allowance she was to receive from Aaron, who had kept his word in their bargain in spite of discovering the truth, she would be able to live comfortably. It also put the Channel between herself and her parents, whom she had not invited to the christening, a private affair with Delia and Dr. Gilmore standing as godparents, and she had composed a tale to relate in her new surroundings of Aaron's unspeakable cruelty that had forced her to leave him and her child, which she considered would give her a highly romantic aura in the eyes of any of her London acquaintances who chose to visit her in Paris, as well as to all the new people she would meet.

She came down the great staircase of Halewood for the last time, wearing a striped traveling costume, violets trimming her bonnet. Delia, waiting to say good-bye, wondered how she could leave so blithely, not even going along to the nursery to take a final look at the child whom she would probably never see again. Emma was the infant's name. It had been Delia's choice, for Melissa would come to no decision, proclaiming a complete lack of interest right to the door of the church on the day of the baptism.

"Well, I don't think I've forgotten anything." Melissa gave a cursory glance toward the trunks and hatboxes being carried out to the waiting transport by a small army of servants. "I've taken nothing that belongs to Halewood, needless to say. I want no reminders of this hateful house! If ever you're in Paris, come and visit me. I'd like to hear from you if you feel like writing to me, but never mention Halewood or anyone in it. I've shaken its dust from my skirt-hems forever."

She went sweeping out through the great porch. She was leaving defiantly by the grand entrance, and a traveling chariot waited to transport her to the Penghyll railway terminus where she was to set off by train on the long journey to her destination in France. Before getting into the chariot she looked about her for the last time at the inner courtyard and gave a merry little laugh that rang with triumph. She had used the house for her own ends and won through. Its curse had failed to touch her after all. She was free!

Her gray-gloved hand showed at the chariot window as she gave a final flick of a wave to Delia, who was standing in the shadow of the porch. With a jingle of harness and clop of hooves she was carried away from Halewood and down the winding drive to the gates.

At the Penghyll terminus the train was waiting. Porters unloaded her baggage from the chariot, and with an entourage of them bearing the many trunks and boxes, she paraded up the platform, aware of heads turning and other passengers staring at her from the train. The stationmaster, who happened to sight her, hurried forward to open the door of a first-class compartment for her and handed her in himself. She thanked him graciously, well pleased with the little sensation she had caused, and settled herself in a corner seat. One of the two grooms from the Halewood chariot, having been instructed to buy magazines and newspapers for her, came with them while the other placed on the seat opposite her a hamper from the house with a picnic luncheon for the journey. The door was shut. Both grooms bowed to her and departed. A whistle blew. The locomotive hissed like an angry giant and then slowly and almost imperceptibly the train began to move.

She giggled with excitement. She was off! Away! It had all been worthwhile. Taking a final look at the departing town of Penghyll, she pulled the brocade blind halfway down the window by its tasseled cord to shade her eyes from the sun, and then opened her magazine. The train gathered speed. The wheels rattled merrily on the shining rails.

She had not been reading long when a tremendous feeling of unease touched her. It had nothing to do with the light romance she was reading and she lifted her head, looking first to the left out of the far window to get her bearings and then to the right, raising the blind as she did so. And regretted it. Far on the distant hilltop Halewood stood sharp and clear against the azure sky, seeming to mock her with the sight of itself, almost as if it was showing her she had not escaped it yet. Then the train swept into a tunnel and blackness shut out that last vivid view of Halewood and the daylight—and even life itself, for at the precise moment the driver of the locomotive slammed on his brakes in a vain attempt to avoid disaster, having seen too late the buckled, distorted section of rails lying ahead, prized up to cause the maximum damage by half a dozen disgruntled navvies with an unappeased compensation grudge against the railway company. Melissa was catapulted from her seat at the moment the locomotive was derailed, the carriages concertinaing into each other within the confines of the tunnel walls, and she knew no more. She did not hear the terrible crash and the echoing thunder, the splintering of wood, the shrieking of twisting metal, the screams, the cries, and the dying groans.

Delia was among those who waited long hours into the evening dusk on the embankment. By the light of flaring torches Melissa's body was finally extracted from the wreckage and placed on a stretcher. With a sob Delia stumbled down the grassy slope to her. Begrimed by dust and dirt, Melissa lay as though asleep, unmarked except for a deep gash across her cheek. Then someone threw a sheet over her face and she was carried away.

12

IN the garden of Sycamore House Delia sat having tea with Dr. Gilmore in the shade of an apple tree. She wore a black and gray muslin gown in deference to her cousin's death. The deep shock of it was with her still, even though almost a month had elapsed since the funeral, which had been held in London where Melissa had been laid to rest in the Barton mausoleum. By rights she should have taken her place in the Hart vault, but Delia knew that her cousin would never have wished to lie there, and it was at her suggestion that Melissa was taken home. Aaron had had no say in the matter, for the funeral was over by the time he was contacted in Milan and Delia had written that it was pointless for him to cut short his travels and return. He was grateful for her handling of everything for him, but she had had Mr. Radleigh to turn to for advice and felt she had done little enough.

"I went to see little Emma at Halewood today," she said, offering her father a plate of paper-thin cucumber sandwiches. The bright spot in her life was Emma, whom she had come to love dearly. The baby was a plain little thing with none of her mother's pretty features, but she had an engaging smile and a gurgling laugh.

Dr. Gilmore took a sandwich. "How was she?"

"Thriving and bonny," she answered. Then her

face clouded and she frowned. "The nurse is a most competent woman, but the nursery is run by the clock, and the only cuddling and loving the babe gets is from me." She gave a sigh. "I pray she won't grow up associating Halewood with loneliness or become frightened of it as her mother was. Poor Melissa. Surely no other mistress of Halewood ever met a more tragic or unexpected end."

"There was the wife of Raoul Hart, who built the house," Dr. Gilmore reminded her. "She was killed by falling stonework before Halewood was even completed." He picked up his cup of tea and stirred it reflectively. "I often think it's no wonder that sorrow and tragedy haunt that house. It should never have been built on the summit of Howling Hill in the first place."

"Why not?" she inquired curiously.

"For the simple reason that heaven alone knows what violence was done in earlier centuries for possession of the most strategic spot in the whole of this district. From it the view is open as far as the eye can see. Whoever held Howling Hill could claim mastery over all the surrounding countryside, which must have grown good crops with the right husbandry even in primitive times."

She leaned forward eagerly in her basket-chair. "That surely means you share my belief that it's not the house itself that is responsible for all the misery that has befallen the Hart family there! I've considered the possibility that in some strange way the curse may be centered in the very ground on which Halewood stands. That's your opinion, too, is it?"

He held up a hand, smiling. "Now don't jump to conclusions. I'm not saying I believe anything. But I have a healthy respect for the effect of the power of suggestion on the mind. If generations of Harts and their nameless ancestors before them have passed down the superstitious fear that whoever owns the house—or in earlier times whatever primitive dwelling-

places, fortified and later unfortified, which stood on
that site in the past—is cursed by it, it is bound to
have created a tendency toward depression, anxiety,
and other dark moods of the mind, which in turn will
affect the lives of all concerned. Inevitably, in many
cases, with tragic or disastrous results."

"Do you mean it was the precarious position of the
chieftain or leader—first one and then another slain
in succession as rival bands fought for possession of the
hilltop—that gave rise to the original superstition that
ill luck always ruled the one who held Howling Hill?"

He nodded. "In all the reading I have done on
folklore in Lancashire and other parts of Britain I have
always tried to sift out the possible source of any
legend that has particularly interested me. The Halewood curse is one of them for which I have given you
a perfectly logical explanation. Had the house been
built on any other site there would have been no
old, dark tales lingering on from the past to throw a
shadow over all who lived in it. It only needed that
unfortunate, fatal accident to Raoul Hart's wife, which
was doubtless caused by some workman's carelessness
on the scaffolding, to stir up local memories of the ill-
fated hill and give rise to talk of other tragedies remembered from the dwelling that was replaced by
Halewood. The seal would be set on the curse. Those
old beliefs linger yet."

The discussion continued. By the time Ellen came
to clear away the tea things Delia had reached a decision, which she disclosed to her father as soon as
they had been left alone again.

"I'm going to delve into the origins of the curse,
papa! Will you help me by giving me the benefit of
your time and knowledge?"

He spread his hands wide. "My time is entirely at
your disposal, but my knowledge is not extensive
enough to answer all the questions that you'll come up
against. You'll have to do a great deal of research
yourself, going through whatever old records are stored

at Halewood and thumbing through every page of any
book remotely connected with the subject that you can
get your hands on. I know Halewood's library is extensive, and I'm sure you would find books there to
aid you. But tell me, for what purpose are you launch-
ing youself into this mammoth task?"

She moved from her chair to crouch beside him,
looking up into his face. "It's for Aaron's sake! And
for Emma's! If I could just untangle and unwind the
deadly heritage that afflicts all the Harts and bring
it out into the light of day, I may be able to find
some way to lay the Halewood curse once and for
all!"

"An admirable motive." He cupped a palm against
her cheek and looked at her searchingly. "In the end
it could be for your own sake, too. I have been awaiting an opportunity to put a certain question to you.
Have you given consideration to the fact that there are
no longer any barriers between you and Mr. Hart?"

She lowered her lashes. "I dare not let myself think
on it. I once severed our relationship forever, and although he cared deeply for me in the past I've no no-
tion of what his feelings for me are after this long
time."

"What of yours for him?"

"Unchanged," she replied in a whisper. "I'll love
him until the day I die."

"Hush. Let us have no more mention of death.
Let me hear instead when you intend to start your research?"

She looked up at him again with renewed eagerness.
"Tomorrow! I'll not delay a day longer."

The staff at Halewood was used to Delia's visits to
see the baby, and when she informed the housekeeper
upon her arrival at the house next morning that in future she would be doing bibliographical work daily
in the library it was accepted without question, the
only query being about the hour at which she would
require luncheon.

In the days and weeks that followed, Emma became as well used to the library as Delia. When not in her nursery or her perambulator she would lie on a plaid woollen rug spread out on the library floor, her contented cooing and the tinkle of her ivory-handled silver rattle doing nothing to disturb, or find herself being cozily cuddled as Delia cradled her in one arm while she read yet another ancient, yellow-paged volume that had not been opened for years, or scanned one of the many sets of vellum-bound documents and other Hart family records which occupied a whole section of the shelves. In between there were periods of play, games of rock-a-bye-baby and peep-bo, when happy chortling and laughter mingled, causing the nurse some annoyance when she came to collect Emma and was met with a noisy protest of tears that lasted all the way to the nursery.

Yet the very nature of the baby's routine meant that Delia had more time on her own in the library than with company, and she steeped herself in Lancashire's early history in order to gain a good foundation on which to work. The Viking invasions of England from the eighth century to the last great battle at Stamford Bridge in the eleventh century were of particular interest to her, because those that took place in the northwest had a direct bearing on Halewood and she could well imagine how the swords had clashed for possession of the strategic Howling Hill. In the evenings over dinner at Sycamore House she would discuss all she had read that day at Halewood with Dr. Gilmore, and afterward they would go over her copious notes and try to sift out any small fact that could be of vital importance.

She did not find the research at all arduous, for she was fired by her interest and the goal for which she was aiming. During her reading she discovered that she was not the first to make an investigation into Halewood's past, although the previous probing had been conducted in an entirely different way. It came to light in an old book on witchcraft in Lancashire, where she read that Alice Hart, who had gone to the stake as a witch, had *"by wicked and divers means summoned up a she-devil out of Howleing Hill and did converse with the same, which name was Gyda and deade these many years."* But that had been only one of the numerous crimes listed against Alice Hart by the witch-finder who had brought her to justice and although Delia read a full account of her trial, there was no further mention of the unknown Gyda. Delia made careful notes, but was forced to leave that section of Halewood's chronicles for lack of more information. Nevertheless there remained at the back of her mind the conviction that when Alice Hart had been casting spells over cattle and decocting magic potions and behaving in an unseemly manner with a local coven, she had been just as interested in the old curse and had sought to find out about it through weird, primeval methods of her own.

Several days later Delia was on the library stepladder looking for a certain book on an upper shelf when she heard the clatter of hooves and the arrival of a carriage in the courtyard, but she paid no attention, for it did happen occasionally that people would call to see Aaron, not knowing he was still absent. Locating the volume she had been seeking she descended and carried it across to the table where there was a clutter of her notes and writing materials, but even as she was about to sit down again she heard voices in the hall and lifted her head sharply. Among them was a voice more dear and familiar to her than any other she had ever known. Her heart leapt with a delirious rapture. He was home! Aaron was home!

She left the book on the table and rushed for the double doors, which she threw wide to run through. There he was! But he was not alone. With his back toward her, he was saying something about the grand staircase to the young lady and two gentlemen of about his own age who were with him. By their accents she could tell they were fellow countrymen of his, and by the amount of travel-labeled baggage being brought into the house by the servants it looked as though they had come to stay for a while. The young lady, whom Aaron addressed as Isobel, noticed Delia first and cast an inquiring gaze in her direction. She was a tall, slim girl with a bright, intelligent face, her hair abundant and dark beneath a becoming leghorn hat.

Aaron must have guessed immediately at whom she was looking. Delia saw his shoulders straighten and after a second or two of apparent hesitation he turned around slowly to look toward her. He had deliberately composed his face against any revelation of expression, for it gave nothing away, and his eyes had narrowed to bring the thick, black lashes mingling together.

"Welcome home," she said faintly. Disappointment hacked at her. She had expected him to be subdued by returning a widower to Halewood. No man of compassion such as she knew him to be could have remained indifferent to the tragic end of Melissa, no matter that she had played him false. But she had thought when they met again to see her own deep and quiet joy in their reunion reflected in his face. Instead there was nothing to be fathomed in those features that she loved, nothing to embrace her in that mere glint of guarded eye.

"Thank you, Delia." He spoke quite formally. "I've brought three compatriots of mine home to show them the beauty of the Lancashire countryside. They were under the impression that it was all mills and coal mines. I'd like you to meet Miss Isobel Mitchell, and allow me to present her brother, Mr. Theodore Mitchell, and an old school-friend from my boyhood days, Mr. Oscar Wasilewski."

With the introductions over, Aaron led them all into one of the drawing rooms, Isobel admiring all she saw. Delia soon learned that Aaron had run into Oscar in Venice and through him had met the Mitchells, after which the four of them had traveled on together. It did not take Delia long to see that Isobel was much attracted to Aaron and sought to hold his attention, which was given willingly enough.

"Halewood is everything you promised me it would be," she said to him in her warm, attractive voice, green eyes sparkling.

"I'm gratified to know I've not disappointed you," he replied easily.

Refreshment was served. Afterward the guests were shown to their rooms and Delia and Aaron were left alone together. He opened and glanced through some of the letters that had been stacked up for his return while she informed him on various matters which he questioned her about at the same time. It was while she was talking fondly of Emma that he pushed aside the letters impatiently, shoved his hands into his pockets, and strode across to the window, where he stood looking out at the spread of lawn and garden, the distant woods, and the fair hills beyond.

"How often have you been coming to Halewood to see the child?" he questioned, his back to her.

"Every day, but also I—"

"I'm afraid it can't continue."

She thought she had not heard aright. "What do you mean?"

He continued to stare out at the view. "It's not that I don't want you to take an interest in Melissa's daughter. It's natural and right that you should, being related through the mother to the child, and I appreciate all you've done. But it's more than that." Now he did turn to face her, clearly and directly, his features steeled into a mask she could not read. "I wouldn't willingly hurt your feelings in any way. I'd give my life first before letting that happen if there were any choice, but I have to tell you. I reached a decision whilst I was away. We must no longer see each other except—considering that we live in the same district—when circumstances make it impossible to avoid a meeting."

Stunned by what he had said, it seemed to take her several seconds to find her voice. "You no longer care anything at all for me. Is that what you're saying?"

"I prefer not to answer on that point."

"You don't have to!" she gasped, pale-lipped, not knowing how to endure the blow he had dealt her. Too late she realized how deeply she had cherished the unacknowledged conviction that nothing would have changed between them. "There's someone else, isn't there?"

His eyes did not falter or leave hers. "There's no one else."

"You're lying to me!" she cried accusingly. An unbearable agony of spirit consumed her and found an outlet in anger. "It must be Isobel! That's why you've brought her home to Halewood, but you don't dare to tell me! You're taking the coward's way! Pretending! Shamming. Making me a fool. I saw how she looked at you! She's ready to fall at your feet! But perhaps she has already done so! Venice is a romantic place for lovers, I'm told."

"Delia!" He thundered her name at her, but there was no stopping her tirade. She knew she had lost him. It had been there in the inexorable tone of his voice. There was no going back. All the longing and loving, the yearning and the adoring and the endless heartache, broke through in an undammed flood, her helpless fury a raft to which she clung for survival.

"You care nothing for me! You don't know what it is to love anything but Halewood! I feel sorry for Isobel or anyone else you marry! She'll take second place all her life! And as for myself, I agree with you! We must no longer see each other! My only regret is that we ever met!"

She spun about and ran blindly from him back to the library. There she shot all her things from the table into the woven bag she had brought with her. Throwing her shawl about her shoulders, she darted from the house. In the driver's seat of her wagonette she whipped up the horse. A great gust of wind swept up the hillside as if to beat her back into the house, tearing at her hair and snatching her shawl from her shoulders to send it flying away. She did not as much as glance in its direction. She was going and never coming back. She set her chin into the blustery wind and drove at top speed down the hill and out through the gates.

In the drawing room Aaron stood with his hands clenched as if it were taking all his willpower not to follow after her and bring her back.

Many weeks passed before Delia opened the woven bag to take out a pen she needed, and she saw with dismay that she had brought away with her the book she had taken from the shelf as Aaron had arrived home. She pressed a distressed hand over her mouth. Her lonely pining had done nothing to lessen her love for him. She was committed to loving him for the rest of her life and there was no way out of it.

The book must be returned to him. He'd had her shawl sent back to her. She had come face to face with him the day after she had received it. At her father's side she had been riding in an open carriage on one of Dr. Gilmore's fine-weather drives to take the air, when Aaron with Isobel Mitchell beside him came alongside in his curricle, driving in the opposite direction. Isobel had inclined her head in friendly recognition and Aaron had raised his hat, his face as taut and strained as Delia had felt her own to be.

Since then she had not seen him, but she had had news in plenty, for he was a topic of conversation at tea parties, musical evenings, and other social gatherings. The three American visitors had stayed a month. He had taken them to all the historic places of interest in the county. Rumor had it that Miss Mitchell would be returning to Halewood in the spring. Other wagging tongues declared he was to visit her, taking a vacation in his own land. Delia had listened and said nothing, but her heart had answered them. This is his land now! He *is* Halewood! He belongs nowhere else! And in love he belongs to no one else but me!

With a heavy sigh she opened the book, seeking in idleness to refresh her memory as to why she had taken it down from a shelf at that time when Aaron's return to Halewood had interrupted her. It was a book of Lancashire folklore and included a chapter of sagas from Viking times, which she glanced through, flicking the pages. A name leaped out of the page at her. *Gyda!* The she-devil from the past with whom Alice Hart was said to have conversed! Suddenly alert, Delia started on the ancient tale. It was not very long or detailed, and the name of the site where the events had taken place was not mentioned, but as she read it was easy to picture the summit of Howling Hill and a cluster of primitive buildings built in a square there. It was an account of battle with an attacker and his berserks killing the defending warlord, and then the saga took a particularly interesting turn. The widow, Gyda, described as being exceedingly fair of face with hair the color of the sun, had been taken to wife by the victor, but she had cursed him and his house, being an unwilling partner to the match, for he had failed to give honorable burial to her late husband, whose valor had been prodigious and whose skill with a sword renowned far and wide.

That was all. Delia closed the book and sat deep in thought. Nothing much to go on. No proof that it had ever taken place on Howling Hill. And there was a strange reference to the victor treating the slaughtered loser as straw underfoot. Suppose Alice Hart, being an eccentric person, had heard the tale and imagined the whining and wailing of the chimneys of Halewood to be the voice of the still-mourning Gyda wanting honor done to her long-dead love. If Alice had gone about the house talking back to that imagined voice it was no wonder that the witch-finder had seen that odd behavior as further evidence to stack against her.

Delia drummed her fingers on the cover of the closed book. If only she could revisit Halewood armed with this new knowledge to continue her original investigation. And why not? She would return the book herself instead of sending it with a servant, and she would see Emma at the same time, for it was a long period since the baby had last been brought by the nurse to Sycamore House, Aaron having arranged this way of allowing her to see the little one. She stood up quickly. She would go now! Without any delay.

"Mr. Hart's away, Miss Gilmore," said the footman who opened the door of Halewood to her.

"That is of no account," she replied, entering. "I've come to see Emma and return a book to the library."

"T'bairn's proper poorly, miss."

Fear struck. "Not well? What is the matter?"

"Measles, miss."

Measles! Children died of measles! It happened frequently! Forgetting everything else, she rushed to the nursery suite. The nursery maid was folding baby clothes and nodded toward the bedroom door.

"Little Emma's real bad, miss." There was a tense concern in the girl's voice.

Delia went into the night nursery, where additional dark curtains had been hung up to keep out the light. The nurse sat at the cotside where Emma lay on the pillows whimpering, her little face scarlet-spotted and feverish. Delia conversed with the nurse in whispers.

"How long has she been like this?"

"Two days. It's most unfortunate that Mr. Hart should be abroad."

"Abroad? Where is he?"

"Gone back to Florence."

"I never knew he had visisted Florence before. I

remember that he went to Rome, Venice, and Milan."

"He saw Lady Hart on that tour of Italy. She sent Emma a little wooden doll in Italian costume, which she can have to play with when she's more of an age to appreciate it."

Delia was completely taken aback. So Berenice's longing to see Aaron had overcome her scruples and now he had returned to visit her again. Why should he do that unless—? Comprehension dawned as she threw her mind back to the day when he had first met Berenice at Halewood and later when he had danced with her at the Penghyll Ball. The attraction between them had not been as one-sided as she had so innocently supposed. There had been no love in his heart for Berenice then, of that she could be sure, but who was to say that it had not come to him during that reunion for them in Florence, the most romantic of all settings. He, bound to Melissa, believing that she herself could never be his, must have welcomed the revelation of Berenice's passionate love with its promise of temporary oblivion to all his cares, for there was surely no true man alive who could resist such temptress beauty when it was offered to him at such a time. Fascinating, dazzling Berenice, who had thrown aside all those grand, self-sacrificing resolutions and set out to enchant him, so that even after he had returned to Halewood he had been unable to forget her, and now she had recalled him to her with all her siren lure.

A cry from the cot distracted Delia from her tormented thoughts. She leaned over Emma and smoothed the sweat-soaked curls back from the burning forehead. "I'll stay and help you look after her," she whispered to the nurse. "A servant shall go with a message to Mrs. Wallace, our housekeeper. She will pack the few things I need and send them over."

Three days later Emma died. With her hands over her face, Delia sat in the still-darkened nursery and rocked in her grief, the tears dripping from between her fingers. In vain Dr. Pomfret assured her that everything possible had been done to save the child and commended her on her tireless cotside vigil, but she would not be consoled. Once again it fell to her to write of a bereavement to Aaron, and her tears blotched the paper. After Emma had been laid in the Hart vault, Delia returned home to Sycamore House, and although she went about her daily tasks her mind and her movements were listless and she avoided all outside company. She was far too peaked and pale for Dr. Gilmore's peace of mind and he was anxious about her. She had been home with him for two weeks when a reply to her letter came from Aaron. She felt a deep pang at the sight of his handwriting and opened it with trembling fingers. Being totally unprepared for the news it contained, she let out a desolate cry which made her father lower the newspaper he was reading in alarm.

"My dear! What is the matter?"

Her eyes glistened with tears and her voice was choked. "Aaron has written the saddest news of Berenice, which he says will come as no surprise to you."

"Ah." Dr. Gilmore looked grave. "I'm more than prepared." She began to re-read the letter aloud to him as best she could.

Dear Delia,

Your letter giving me the sorrowful tidings of Emma's death reached me yesterday. I am deeply grieved that so young a life should be thus taken, but the Halewood curse takes no heed of age or innocence, a lesson that all the Harts who have ever lived on Howling Hill have learned to their cost, and—as my father discovered— even to leave it and seek a new life elsewhere is no guarantee of escape, for there is none. I thank you most sincerely for all you have done in watching over Emma in my absences and I know that if it had been humanly possible to save her you alone could have done it. I realize how hard it must have been for you to write to me of Emma's demise, and regretfully I can write nothing to cheer you from this beautiful city of Florence, but instead must be the sender of ill news. During my first visit to Italy I called on Lady Hart, hoping to talk over Halewood with someone who had lived in it longer than I, but she would not see me, although she sent the gift of a doll for Emma to my hotel. Then—is it only a matter of weeks ago?—I received a letter from her saying it was vital to her that I come to Florence without delay. I left for Italy the same day, well pleased that there appeared to be some mission I could undertake for her as a token of appreciation for all the generosity she showed toward me at the time of the auction. But again I did not see her. An Italian lawyer acted as her spokesman. She is very ill with an inflammatory condition of her lungs, for which your father treated her at Halewood. It was he who approved her decision to move to a warmer climate in the hope that it would extend her years. In vain. Her illness has taken a rapid turn for the worse. She is dying and knows it. Her request, relayed by the lawyer to me, was that I should take on the guardianship of Roland and secure a good home for him as far as possible from Halewood. She had no one else to whom she could turn, and I accepted the responsibility gladly. The legal arrangements have taken time, but meanwhile I have talked to the boy, who is unaware that when he leaves Italy he will never see his mother again, which is her wish, for she wants their parting to be a happy one for him. He has such a loathing of tutors that when I offered him the chance to go to a school in Boston where he can mix with boys of his own age he

*wanted to leave Italy that very day, his life in
Florence having been excessively dull and lacking in young company. He talks of nothing else
but going to America. Halewood is forgotten in
the excitement, and seeing that he lacks the Hart
name the curse cannot touch him. By the time
this letter reaches you Roland and I should be
within sight of the land of my birth, for I intend
to deliver him safely into the home of kind
friends who will welcome him and make him one
of their family, and to see him established in his
school before I leave again. Once more I thank
you for all you have done. My compliments to
Dr. Gilmore. I remain forever in your debt.*

Your servant, AARON.

Delia folded the letter, racked by fresh sorrow and
filled with remorse. How she had misjudged Berenice
who had kept to her resolution at a time when she
must have longed to look upon Aaron's face again,
knowing it was her last chance. Slowly Delia became
conscious of her father's worried gaze fixed on her and
realized how stricken her expression must have become.

"This has been yet another heavy blow for you to
bear," he said sympathetically. "Why not take a short
vacation? Some sea air would do you good. You could
visit those old friends of yours at Southport. Mrs. Wallace will take care of me. Be advised and do what I
say."

She allowed herself to be persuaded and went to
the coast, where she was entertained warmly by a
family of whom she was very fond, but all the time
she was remembering Aaron's letter and his terrible
fatalism toward the Halewood curse, seeing that
through his belief in it he was destined to suffer as
much from it in the future as he had done in the
past. There surged back to her such a renewed longing

to lift its evil yoke from him that she became increasingly restless with every passing day, wanting to return to Halewood and take up her investigations where she had left off. In the end she could stand it no longer. She thanked her friends for their hospitality and traveled home again.

"I'm not unpacking my baggage," she said to Dr. Gilmore after she had greeted him. "I'm going on to Halewood to stay there for a while." She explained why.

"As an uninvited guest?" he queried drily, not displeased by the decision she had made. She seemed more her old self, with a freshness in her cheeks that had been lacking for a long time, and her eyes held a determined glint.

"I'm more at home at Halewood than anyone else," she answered with a ghost of a smile. "Aaron would never begrudge me bed and board."

"I wish you good luck in your quest, my dear. Report any success to me."

"I will."

She settled in at Halewood as if she had never been away from it, occupying a guest room near her former office in the east wing, but the restlessness that had been with her on her vacation was with her still and she recognized it as a physical expression of her impatience to solve the riddle of Halewood. No longer was she able to read quietly for hours in the library, sorting and sifting endless facts. Instead she took to wandering from room to room and out in the grounds, seeking from the atmosphere of Halewood some tiny clue that could awaken an understanding and lead her in the right direction. Cool common sense and logical reasoning no longer had any part to play. She saw the curse as the great barrier between Aaron and herself that it had always been. To destroy it had become her sole motive for living.

It was during these wanderings that she came one day into the portrait gallery. It was the first time she had been in it since Aaron had had the glass roof cleaned, allowing it to sparkle in all its original glory and give back to the gallery the brilliance of light that Halewood's architect had planned for it. How vividly the faces of the Harts gazed out at her, for now it was possible to see the tracery of wrinkles, the bloom of cheek, and the pox-pits and battle scars and warts and moles which had not been omitted through any false flattery. In front of the portrait of Alice Hart she came to a standstill and gazed long on the visage of the woman who had gone to the stake. There was no doubt she had an odd, demented look about her piercing blue eyes, which had never been noticeable in the gloom that had previously prevailed in the gallery. The poor mad creature should have been cared for and protected instead of falling victim to a witch-hunter, her own kin too afraid of her themselves to lift a finger to save her. How had she summoned up that she-devil out of Howling Hill? And where? The courtyard of Halewood was the exact center of the summit of the hill—could it have been from there?

Delia knew a quickening of excitement. Gathering up her skirts, she ran from the gallery to the nearest window that overlooked the courtyard. Below her lay the green sward where she had had that eerie experience on her very first visit to the house, and as she gazed down through the opened window she wondered keenly if the secret key to all Halewood's suffering lay therein. The grassy sward was virtually the same since those ancient days when the Viking settlers had built their buildings to form four sides of a square as a better protection for themselves and their animals against attack, much in the shape of the present house, which itself formed a quadrangle. Was it on the green sward that Gyda's warrior had fallen in battle?

In deep thought Delia sat down on the window seat and recalled the section in the book she had read of he victor treating the dead hero like straw underfoot. Had he——? Was it possible that——? Such a simple explanation had presented itself that she scarcely dared to believe she had stumbled on it. Suppose the dead hero had been laid in a grave in the heart of the conquered settlement, where every day the victor would stride across the place where he lay. To Gyda the brutal revenge would be beyond measure. Without an honorable burial her love could never take his rightful place in Valhalla. To others it would be a grim tale to tell and pass down from one generation to another, word spreading that the hill was an ill place on which to live, but the site had continued to attract men to it by its very magnificence of view and lushness of setting until at last Raoul Hart had built his fine mansion on the foundations of a humbler abode owned by his forefathers and caught an echoing note of doom when his wife had been crushed by falling masonry.

Delia closed the window and left the cushioned seat. She knew what she must do. There was a burial rite she had to perform, but she must be certain that she had every detail correct, and she would have to choose the right moment for it. All she could hope for was that by going through with the ritual she would remove Aaron's deep-rooted belief in the curse once and for all, and thus lift it from the house itself.

She surprised those servants who saw her by going at a run down to the library. There she skimmed up one of the spiral staircases and within seconds had located a certain volume dealing with the Vikings, an edition she had become familiar with in the early days of her research. She turned immediately to the chapter dealing with the burial rites of those great Norsemen, whose desire was always to die in battle and not in their beds. The details were all there. Fire and funeral pyres figured largely in the descriptive accounts, many chieftains being laid in their own longships and launched out to sea after a torch had been put to the vessel. A rising wind to fan the flame was welcomed as a good omen, for the higher an swifter the smoke rose the greater the speed wit which the dead Norseman would reach Valhalla, th hall of the fallen warriors, where he would feast wit the great god Odin through all eternity, waited on b beautiful maidens. These burial rites were carried ou with much dignity and ceremony in tribute to th dead man's brave deeds and mighty courage, an the Norseman did not go empty-handed or unarme into the other world, for he could not arrive like pauper at those celestial doors. It was known tha he would be required to do battle for Odin with th other warriors, but with death banished all the slai would rise up again after the contest of arms and tak their places at the banquet table once more, eatin roast boar and quaffing mead and ale. For that reaso shields and swords, axes and knives and chain mai were put alongside the body, as well as goblets an plates and drinking horns, chests of fine clothes an jewels for his adornment, sleighs for his transport and harnesses for the horses that were slaughtered fo his use together with his favorite dogs and falcons Nothing else that he could possibly need was forgot ten, even servants being put to death in order that h not go unattended. Frequently the woman who love him best among his wives and concubines would sur render her life and her body would burn with his.

Delia finished reading and shut the book slowly convinced that Gyda would have shared her husband' funeral pyre if the chance had been hers, for such passion, which had survived the centuries to beat i helpless fury against the walls of Halewood, woul never have let him go alone into the unknown. Sh shivered, knowing fear, but there was no going bacl now—nor did she want to. The task she had set hersel had to be done.

As the days went by she made careful preparations She had decided not to tell her father what she wa about to do, for he would most certainly forbid her to seek such a final confrontation with the source of the curse, knowing that it involved danger to both body and mind, but for Aaron's sake it was a chance she was willing to take. Finally everything was ready. She had only to wait for a misty night when she would be unobserved.

It came at last. All day the midst had been settling on the hill and tension rose in her as she watched the hours tick away. She had to wait until midnight to make sure all the servants were abed in their quarters, which were situated at the back of the house out of sight of the courtyard. Then, warmly wrapped against the cold night in a thick shawl, she slipped out of the house with a lantern and a basket in her hands.

She put down the basket where she would find it again easily and commenced the heavy work. With a hook she dragged many bales of straw from the stable and made a long, boat-shaped stack of them in the center of the sward. On them she piled twigs and sticks and branches which she had gathered from the woods during the past week and hidden in a convenient place. Then, with the aid of a wheelbarrow, she trundled into the courtyard load after load of huge logs which had been destined for the hearths of Halewood, and added them to the pile. Her back and arms ached with her labors and every muscle pained her, but she paid no heed to any of it, intent on her task.

Standing back, she viewed the pyre with satisfaction, brushing her disheveled hair back from her forehead with a grimy hand. There was one thing left to do. Fetching the basket, she took from it a loaf of bread, some fruit, a bottle of wine, a coat of Aaron's, a flintlock pistol, a pewter tankard, and some silver threepenny bits in a purse, all of which she laid on the pile, adding afterwards an old saddle and a harness that she had brought from the stable. The soul of the long-dead warrior should have had much more to take with it on its last journey, but he had been given the essentials in the symbolic trappings of clothing, food, drink, weaponry, transport, and wealth, and she had stacked the pyre into the shape of a long-boat.

She thrust a light into it. Flames grasped at the straw and swept high in a matter of seconds. A noise of crackling, snapping, and spitting broke the silence of the mist-gray night, and the heat soon forced her to stand back, the fire burning fiercely, sparks drifting on the dancing smoke like thousands of firework stars. She and the whole of the inner courtyard were bathed in a red-gold glow, the mullioned windowpanes reflecting the brilliance like watching eyes.

An enormous sense of exhilaration filled her. The thunderous roar of the blazing pyre was deafening, akin to the beating of hundreds of sword blades against the surface of studded shields. Above, the smoke was swirling swiftly higher and higher, a sight that would have gladdened Gyda's heart. She could even see the mist clearing above it, showing a glimpse of the dawn-fading stars. It was then that she realized the wind was rising with a pent-up force, and the fire was threatening to get out of hand. If the flames swept across the grass and bridged the flagged drive that bordered the sward Halewood itself would be consumed!

Yet she could not bring herself to raise the alarm and douse the cleansing fire, for unless this deed was fully done, carried through to the end, a sickness of mind would continue to haunt all generations of Harts to come. Better to let Halewood go as the ultimate sacrifice than that the curse should continue to shatter and destroy their lives.

A curious, almost unreal, sensation of bliss settled on her. It was as if Gyda were making her ecstatic triumph known that at long last the release of her husband's soul had been achieved. Yet somehow it was more than that. She felt at one with Gyda. Almost as though she were Gyda. The hollow din of Viking horns seemed to resound in her ears. The heat beat into her face and she welcomed it, moving as though in a trance through time and space to embrace the fire, which flicked out its flames toward her like waiting arms.

Below the hill a carriage was approaching along the lane. Aaron, newly come from a steam packet that had docked some hours before at Liverpool, sighted the golden flaring of fire from the window, which he let down with a slap of its leather strap to lean out and yell to the coachman that Halewood was on fire and to whip up the horses. The rough wind blew into his face, tumbling his hair as he strained his eyes impatiently in the direction of his home, and he thumped an exasperated fist against the frame whenever a copse of trees or tall bushes temporarily blocked his view. There was a short delay at the gates, but the old lodgekeeper had been retired with his wife to a cottage on the estate and it was only a matter of half a minute before the new man came running in his nightshirt to swing the huge gates wide. With a crack of the whip the horses and carriage went racing through.

The carriage came to a hoof-slithering halt by the archway of the courtyard as the first stablehands appeared, pulling on fustian jackets as they came, roused not by the fire but by the sound of their master's returning carriage, and their faces mirrored their alarm at the flickering glow. Aaron, hurling himself out of the carriage, saw in astonishment and horror that Delia stood teetering on the edge of a great, elongated bonfire, her arms outflung to the flames as if about to throw herself into them.

"Delia! Stop! Dear God! Don't! Don't!"

He reached her and snatched her away from danger even as the fire reached its peak and with a vibrating roar the whole pyre collapsed, scattering burning straw and white-hot ash, but reduced to a point that removed all threat to the house. He kissed her frantically and held her hard to him and could not let her go. Shaking and trembling, she emerged from shock, the dreamlike spell that the flaming pyre had cast over her quite dispelled by the reality of his presence and the loving strength of his arms. She jerked her head around, hearing some shouting, and saw servants coming at a run through the archway with buckets of water and others bringing a hand pump.

"The fire mustn't be put out!" she cried on the edge of panic. "It's the end of the curse that has plagued this house since its foundations were laid! I'll tell you everything if you will give me time, Aaron, but let the flames die naturally! Then it will be over! Forever!"

He did not question her but issued a sharp instruction over his shoulder to the servants. "Take those buckets and the pump away! They'll not be needed. Concern yourselves with the horses and my baggage."

She clung to him in relief, her arms about his neck, and her thankfulness that the deed was done and he was home again made her forget all the doubts and fears she had harbored about his feelings for her. She met his renewed kissing with her own, her long-dormant passion unleashed, and he was powerless to resist her, devouring her mouth with all the yearning desire for her that had long possessed him.

She drew breath, pressing her cheek against his, and crushed in his embrace she recounted all she had done to banish the Halewood curse and explained the symbolism of the burning pyre. When she had finished all she had to say neither of them moved, but remained alone in the courtyard, wrapped in each other's arms, she suddenly afraid that he, not having shared in the traumatic experience of the ritual, would be untouched by her words. But in that she was mistaken. Never had he known such a devastating moment as when he saw her at the point of death. Something primeval had stirred deep within him, giv

ig him a kind of inborn comprehension as to why
he was there and what she was doing, almost as
hough he were viewing the scene through the eyes of
is ancestors, and yet he could not have voiced it or
xpressed what he felt, so removed was it from his
rue consciousness. But now everything she had said
ad slotted into place. She had banished centuries of
arkness from his mind.

Still making no move, he raised his gaze toward
he great house that enclosed them. No black heritage
emained to taint Halewood, wherein he had thought
o live out a lifetime of lonely days, never to marry
he girl he loved, the apartments destined for her in
he west wing ever to remain sealed. After Melissa's
eath, which had given him final proof—had he
eeded it!—of the curse's evil force, he had resolved
ever to let Delia fall victim to its power by giving
er his ill-fated name, and for that reason alone he
ad forced himself to reject her. The company he
ad brought home from Italy on that occasion had
een no more than the balm of friendship to his
oneliness and his longing for her, she whom he had
oved and wanted for his own since the evening when
he had first opened the door of her home to him
pon his arrival in England.

Her tremulous voice broke in on his thoughts.
Have I failed, Aaron? Please tell me I haven't failed!"

He held her back from him with such a glowing
ook of love in his eyes and with such exultation
ighting up his face that she had her answer even
efore he spoke. "You have triumphed, my love! Oh,
ow you have triumphed! I've much to tell you, much
o explain, but that can come later. Say you'll marry
ne, my darling. Say you'll be my wife. It seems to me
hat I've waited a thousand years for this time of asking
ou."

She tilted her head back, her lashes drooping in
er happiness. "Yes! I feel I've loved you for the same
ength of time."

With his arm close about her waist, they move towards the steps of the house, kissing as they wen. The first rays of the sun were touching the tall chin ney pots and in the courtyard the air was soft an balmy, the wind having dropped as suddenly as it ha risen.

In the porch he stooped to sweep her up into h arms and hold her effortlessly. "I'm carrying you ove the threshold. It's not usual before the wedding cer mony, but I'll do it after we're married, too." His voic was tender and loving and jubilant. "Today I war Halewood to know I've brought you home to it a last!"

They smiled at each other, locked in a look of dee and intimate joy, and he carried her into the grea house.